Pel is Provoked

PEL IS PROVOKED

Juliet Hebden

Constable · London

First published in Great Britain 1999
by Constable & Company Limited
3 The Lanchesters, 162 Fulham Palace Road
London W6 9ER
Copyright © Juliet Hebden 1999
The right of Juliet Hebden to be
identified as the author of this work
has been asserted by her in accordance
with the Copyright, Designs and Patents Act 1988
ISBN 0 09 479230 5
Set in Palatino 10 pt by
SetSystems Ltd, Saffron Walden, Essex
Printed and bound in Great Britain
by MPG Books Ltd, Bodmin, Cornwall

A CIP catalogue record for this book
is available from the British Library

The city in these pages is
the capital of Burgundy in
the *département* of the Côte d'Or.
It is, however, intended to be fictitious,
as indeed are the characters.
Any resemblance to any actual living
person is purely coincidental.

Vous noterez que par le monde
il y a beaucoup plus de couillons que d'hommes.
De ce que nous souvienne . . .

François Rabelais

For my best friends:

Charlie
Cass
Harry
Billy

And new friends:

Max
Roxanne

1

'Roux wants to talk.' Pel reread the message, timed at 0834, as the car came to a halt. Beside him, Cheriff, a tall, black-haired *inspecteur* who looked more like a young African prince than a policeman, pulled on the handbrake and the two men climbed out into an empty farmyard. Lighting a Gauloise, Pel cast his eyes round the shabby property. Nothing out of the ordinary: the brown paint on the lop-sided shutters was peeling, tufts of grass grew through the cracked concrete underfoot, and two new tractors, one as big as a bus for ploughing cornfields, the other tiny for chugging between the rows of vines, were parked side by side in the hangar. Like most peasants, Roux had got his priorities right; while the house he lived in was falling down round his ears, his farming equipment was cared for and clean. To one side, a dozen or so chickens scratched in the dirt hoping to find a handful of spilled grain, and up against the dilapidated house, a tabby cat stretched in a pool of sun to feed six hungry kittens.

Pel shuffled inside his clothes, enjoying his cigarette while taking in the calm countryside. He was content to spend a few hours away from his drab office in the centre of a large city. Instead of the grey-painted walls and a glaring light bulb, he was surrounded by the bright greens of a new spring and overhead the sun shone valiantly from a forget-me-not sky. Instead of the monotonous buzz of non-stop traffic under his window, he could hear a handful of crows cawing from the trees in the undulating valley below.

A gurgling scream shattered the peaceful scene, high-pitched, horrible enough to turn a man's blood cold. Pel and Cheriff swivelled on their heels, their eyes wide, looking for the cause. Raised voices were heard, their words merciless, cruel, muffled but not far away, and still the shrieking continued.

Abruptly it stopped. The silence was worse.

'Holy Mother of God!' Pel said to his colleague, setting off in the direction of an old stone barn. He hesitated by its crumbling walls, listening for movement inside. There were at least three men in there; he could hear them clearly now. Taking a long final suck on his Gauloise, he flicked it away in a smouldering arc and put his hand on the heavy wooden door to drag it open.

As he blinked into the musty stable, the smell of last year's straw, of dust and sweat seeped into his nostrils, then a stronger odour caught in his throat, the curiously sweet smell of blood.

The only light inside came through the holes in the roof where the clay tiles had slipped out of place. Slim rays of sun, like shards of glass, pierced the darkness, picking out particles of dust, making them shine, and falling in a mosiac of startling brightness on to the casually swept floor.

Pel blinked several times, his eyes adjusting to the gloomy interior until he could make out the shapes opposite: the peasant and his two burly sons, busy disembowelling their victim.

Cheriff's shadow joined Pel's in the doorway as the intestines were pulled from the gaping abdominal cavity; there seemed to be miles of them, curling and slipping into a steaming bloody heap. Pel gulped hard. It wasn't quite what he'd expected – the stench was incredible. The man facing him, shoulders hunched aggressively against the intrusion, held a huge knife in his strong stubby fingers. He had a weatherbeaten face, like ancient leather, the nests of wrinkles round his eyes and mouth made deeper as he squinted at the oblong of sudden sunlight, trying to identify the black silhouettes standing in front of the open door. He limped forward on a twisted foot, swiping beads of perspiration from his forehead with his free arm and blowing through cracked lips at the recent exertion. His scruffy T-shirt was spattered red, and behind him hung the dead body, attached by a metal cord to the winch above, pink and limp, its life still dripping into a big crimson puddle on the pale floor.

The carving knife advanced, a dribble of blood glinting scarlet on the metal, running on to the man's muscular hands. Pel stepped back a pace, back towards the yard outside. As the peasant became accustomed to the penetrating light, he realised he was looking at Evariste Clovis Désiré Pel, Monsieur le

Commissaire Principal, the famous chief inspector, famous in the Côte d'Or anyway.

'*Eé, bé*, don't just stood there standing!' Roux shouted with delight. 'Give me the fright of me life!' He bellowed over his shoulder to his sons, 'Go on then, get along and singe the bugger, Mother'll be along for jointing any minute, you know she don't like hanging about.' He carefully cleaned the blade of his cutlass on a fistful of hay, propped it against the wall and, tripping over the doorstep, stumbled outside.

'Killing pigs don't appeal much to policemen, do it?' he said and, wiping his stained hands on a rag, led Pel and Cheriff into the clear spring morning where the sky was still cloudless and the fresh air delicious after the stuffy barn.

'Sorry 'bout that,' he went on, considering Cheriff's colouring. 'You Arabs don' eat pork, something to do with man being reincarnated in pig, innit?' He chuckled at the idea. 'If y'ask me, most men is pigs anyway.'

The two policemen followed the bandy-legged peasant towards his battered front door. He looked like an odd bird strutting awkwardly on a foot and a claw, having accidently shot off three toes in his haste to bag an escaping hare. His legs were long, thin and permanently bent, his body round and solid, shaped like a barrel, with heavy shoulders into which his neck disappeared unseen; his head was the shape of a cannon-ball, topped by a crest of dirty curling hair that jerked in rhythm with his lolloping stride.

'No need to apologise,' Cheriff reassured him. 'I'm French.'

'He wouldn't be a member of the Police Judiciaire de la République de France if he wasn't,' Pel pointed out, glad for once that his thatch was going grey, what was left of it, and that his face had a rosy tinge to it, except when he was in the middle of a coughing fit from too many cigarettes, when it turned purple – at least no one mistook him for a foreigner. Cheriff must be sick of always having to explain. He knew, however, that his colleague with a deeper than average tan was the son of an Harki, an extremely proud race of men; he'd been taught how to behave. His father's origins were Algerian. He'd acquired a number of medals and finally French nationality for his loyalty during the war of independence, choosing Burgundy for his new home. Cheriff hadn't had the choice, he'd been brought up there, like Pel. You couldn't get much Frencher than Burgundian. Bourgogne was the heart of France, where Grand Dukes had built palaces; the land of Vauban, Lamartine and Colette, where men like de Bussy-Rabutin poked fun at kings and took amused refuge from the royal court in the magnificent château at Cluny. Burgundy was the only place to live. Pel was proud of his birthplace, as was Cheriff.

It has taken a while for Pel to accept him as a fellow Burgundian, because, well, after all, he did look like an Arab, but his credentials had been faultless, and having finally capitulated, Pel was prepared to defend his countryman, a local. He was a damn good policeman too, it helped a bit.

The chattering women in the kitchen were finishing scrubbing the copper pots for making pâté, *jambonneau* and *rillettes* from the mounds of pork left over after taking the best pieces for roasting. 'Go on 'op it, got business to do.' Roux hurried his wife and daughters out into the yard. 'Women!' he said to Pel, grinning. 'Always in your bloomin' feet. Now then, I'll fetch us a bottle an' I'll tell us all about them naked ladies.'

'What do you reckon?' Pel asked, gasping at a Gauloise. He was trying as always to give up smoking, and as always it was impossible; the stress of his job drove him to seeking solace in the tobacco of La Régie Française, and the sight of blood, even pig's blood, sent his fingers swiftly seeking the small blue packet always present – for emergencies, you understand – in one or several of his pockets.

Cheriff negotiated a roundabout before replying. 'Religious sects are often a good excuse for sexual high jinks,' he said.

'Hmm, sects and sex,' Pel pondered, 'but if what he says is true, there are girls caught up in this mucky little business who are under age. We'd better take it seriously.' He inhaled deeply, asking himself if he'd ever kick the habit. 'I wonder what Roux was doing so far from home? Poaching, no doubt. Anyway, do a bit of poking around, see what you come up with. Once we know more about this Sunshine and Light lot, we'll pay them a visit. Sects of this sort give me the heebie-jeebies. There have been a few horrific mass suicides – mostly in America, of course, but it happened in France last year. I don't want it to spread to my patch, so make it snappy.'

'It'll be on your desk yesterday,' Cheriff confirmed.

The Hôtel de Police, an imposing rectangular building with its high façade and its many barred windows, sat well back from a wide tree-lined street housing mostly small modern shops with bright, winking neon signs, and old uncomfortable flats above. Very few vehicles stopped or slowed in front of the police station; their business was elsewhere, and anyway there were large 'No Parking, Police Only' signs sprouting from the pavements in both directions. As Pel started up the steps, he was almost knocked off his feet by Darcy, his infuriatingly handsome second-in-command, who was galloping out of the open double doors and grinning from ear to ear. '*Ça y est!*' he called leaping on to the pavement, making Pel spin as he rushed past. 'Kate's in hospital!' and he cantered off towards his car.

'Glad someone's happy,' Pel grumbled, pushing his way into the newly decorated beige entrance hall with its floor of dull brown tiles; the general opinion was that if it hadn't been for the dozens of posters and official notices, it would have looked like a public lavatory, such was the expertise of the City Council's architects.

The usual group of anguished faces met him from the row of metal chairs lined up against one wall. He glanced round quickly, wondering what they all wanted; reports of lost loved ones, theft, drunken husbands, kids stealing apples, noisy neighbours, kittens that hadn't come home, it was all in a day's work.

An elderly woman was sobbing at the counter; the duty sergeant was looking patient but bored as Pel approached. '*Oui, madame*,' he was saying. 'I understand your fears, however, I don't honestly think we can do a great deal to help.' Seeing the chief inspector, he straightened up abruptly and saluted.

The woman stopped crying to study Pel, the expression on her face implying, 'I was here first, so just wait your turn!' She lost interest in him quickly and, turning back to the counter, started shouting. 'I'm a law-abiding, tax-paying citizen, it's your duty to do something!'

The sergeant sighed. '*D'accord*, madame, we'd better make a note of your complaint then I'll call for someone to take a proper statement.'

'What good will that do?' she cried, suspicious of being fobbed off.

'With a detailed description, we can issue an *avis de recherche* throughout the area, throughout France if necessary.'

Pel raised an eyebrow in his direction. 'An escaped canary,' came the reply. 'I thought Misset should handle it?'

'Just the man,' Pel agreed, nodding at the distressed woman. 'Our bird expert,' and he headed smartly for the stairs before he became embroiled in the time-wasters of the city. He smiled at the thought of their fading James Bond, complete with dark glasses and his brain in neutral, having to spend an hour or so with an hysterical old dear who'd lost her budgie. Bird expert! The only birds he knew anything about were the ones he chased twenty-five hours a day, the ones in mini-skirts. Although Pel had to admit he'd been less trouble recently, since his mother-in-law had come to live with them. Instead of bleating about the extra hours all of them had to work, he often arrived early and spent a large part of the day trying to be invisible behind a report he was supposedly writing. Poor Misset, now one of his sons had returned from a spell in the army, with a girlfriend, and they didn't look like leaving – not only that, she'd brought a cat and the two idiot poodles belonging to mother-in-law didn't appreciate it. Poor Misset.

Poor Misset be damned, it was his own silly fault for having too many children!

Annie Saxe, the only female member of his team, was waiting for him at the top of the stairs; her bright red curls, cut shorter now in a failed attempt to keep them under control, made her head look as if it was on fire. 'Morning, *patron*,' she said brightly. 'Saw you arrive through the window, thought you'd like to know that the replacement is here.' Her green eyes smiled mischievously at him. It wasn't supposed to be general knowledge but most people in the Plain Clothes Department knew she'd hooked the stately Arab, Cheriff. Pel for one wasn't surprised, she got more gorgeous every year.

He allowed himself a brief twitch of the lips, which in his case passed as a smile. 'And?' he asked suspiciously.

'Would you like to do your usual Dracula act?'

'Wheel him in,' he replied surprisingly cheerfully. Annie had that effect on everyone. 'I'll give him the once-over.' But the day had other things lined up for the Commissaire.

The moment he slammed his office door shut, making the glass rattle in its casing, it opened again. Pujol, still considered the new boy of the team and always wary of his boss, stood there looking terrified, licking his lips and polishing his glasses which were as thick as the bottoms of bottles. 'Murder,' he whispered, expecting to be yelled at.

Pel glared, letting the information sink in for a second. 'You know the form!' he bellowed as he began collecting up the contents of his pockets that he'd just dumped on his desk.

Five minutes later, with Charles de Troquereau at the wheel, the three policemen sped out of the city to the scene of the crime.

'Tell me,' Pel commanded.

Pujol studied the open notebook. 'Monsieur Aynard, at Nurse Fabres's early morning surgery for dialysis. He's dead, she's badly wounded. A second patient arrived for his appointment at nine, found them.' Pujol hadn't been with them long but he'd proved to be brighter than his appearance suggested, in fact he reminded Pel of himself a couple of hundred light years ago, and he had an economical way of delivering information.

Pel nodded. 'And it took him until now to report it?'

'Said he fainted, he came round once and fainted again. Doesn't like the sight of blood.'

'And . . .'

'When he came to his senses, decided he'd better ring the police, went to phone box in centre of village.'

'Medics and scientists?'

'Alerted and on their way.'

As if in answer, a siren was heard in the distance and, as the thick morning traffic pulled over to let it cross the congested

15

junction, two SAMU ambulances shot past. The lights turned red, leaving them hemmed in all round. De Troquereau put his hand under the dashboard to retrieve the magnetic *girophare* and, clamping it to the roof, switched on its rotating blue light. Almost at once an electronic whooping announced who they were. The surrounding motorists began shunting their cars back and forth out of their path and in a few seconds they were away.

The village they were headed for was thirty minutes outside the city limits and, as the suburbs turned rapidly into rolling fields and neatly clipped vineyards, Pel stared at the map Pujol had passed him. Compared with the sprawling mass of the capital, Fontaine les Lacs was a mere dot amongst many other dots littering the countryside with hamlets and small communities.

It certainly wasn't large but it looked prosperous. The sixteenth-century buildings were well renovated and clean; the recently paved square was hemmed in by high half-timbered buildings, with a few shops on the ground floor discreetly peeping out through the old arcades, plus the inevitable bar/café. De Troquereau drove the car across the *place* into a long narrow street between tall houses. In the distance they could see the easily recognisable bright red van of the Sapeurs Pompiers and a blue break of the Gendarmerie Nationale. They parked on the edge of a smaller open square by the war memorial, behind which red and white plastic tape was looped between the stout trunks of a row of leafless poplars, effectively cordoning off a low white-washed surgery. Spectators were already gathering.

Ducking under the tape, the detectives walked through the shade of the trees towards the group of emergency vehicles parked on the tarmac outside the building. Boudot, one of the city's doctors assigned to the police, was coming out through the door as they approached. He was a big man but today his massive shoulders drooped. He glanced up at Pel. 'It's not a pretty sight,' he said grimly. 'I'll be finished shortly.'

Standing to one side they let a stretcher pass. Strapped to it was a woman covered in blood; tubes and drips were plugged into various veins and were held aloft by members of the Service d'Aide Médicale Urgence.

16

'Nurse Fabres,' Boudet said. 'Nice woman, always laughing, cheered her patients up no end, extremely popular.'

'Will she live?' Pel asked, watching her inert body being manoeuvred carefully into one of the ambulances.

'I'd like to think she has a chance but it's touch and go,' Boudet replied sadly and went back inside.

As the ambulance moved off, its siren blaring, Pel pulled a packet of Gauloises from his pocket. 'De Troq',' he said, 'send someone to the hospital. We may only have a matter of minutes before she dies – if by any chance she says something I want her listened to. And while you're at it, make sure the road blocks have been set up. We don't know who we're looking for but someone might give the game away by panicking when confronted with the police. And confirm reinforcements, the whole village'll be here in a minute, followed no doubt by the press.'

For the second time that day Pel was faced with what looked like a scene from an abattoir. There was blood everywhere, splashed on the walls and across the furniture, and lying in ghastly puddles on the floor. A male corpse was spread-eagled across the high surgery bed, partially covered by a red-stained sheet; a large part of his face and head were missing. There were unpleasant pink spots on the ceiling. Pel waved an impatient hand at Pujol who was shuffling behind him; no one liked this sort of thing.

Against the far wall there was a relatively bare patch, smudged round the edges, where Boudet had worked on the wounded nurse. A number of scarlet footprints led to and from the area.

'Jesus,' Pel said quietly, swallowing hard. De Troq' joined him and silently took in the scene of destruction.

'Where's the witness who found them?' Pel asked. 'I'd better see him first while the scientific boys do their job. Stay here and observe, hands in pockets, mouth shut, you know the routine. And where's Pujol disappeared to?'

'Bolted,' de Troq' told him. 'Can't say I blame him.' An aristocrat by birth, policeman by profession, he rarely allowed his well-bred face to show emotion but he was frowning, troubled by the scene. However often he saw the carnage human beings reaped on other human beings it was nonetheless always harrowing. It was easier to cope with it after years of practice, never less shocking.

Pel found Pujol outside, wiping his pale green face with a damp handkerchief and perspiring freely. 'Sorry, *patron*,' he said. 'Couldn't help it, had to throw up.'

'I know the feeling. Where's the witness?'

'Being looked after by the fire brigade.' Pujol's voice croaked. 'He'd passed out again, they've given him something to calm his nerves.'

By now most of the inhabitants of Fontaines les Lacs had heard of the massacre and had gathered, jostling for position, anxious to see what was going on. Pel beckoned to a young gendarme hovering on the edge of the crowd, trying to keep it under control. As he made his way across to Pel, he too was very pale.

'Threaten them with arrest, threaten them with a flogging,' Pel suggested, 'anything you like but no one's to get near the surgery.'

The man in uniform nodded. 'I've asked for more men from the *caserne* here, should be arriving any minute. Hope that's all right – they're getting rowdy.'

'Are you on your own?'

'No, sir, there's two of us but I took the call. The bloke was incoherent, said there'd been an accident, a shooting, so I assumed it was a hunting accident, we get plenty of them round here, you know, a gun goes off by mistake when it's owner's climbing over a fence or something, often happens.' His words came fast, punctuated by short intakes of breath. He sounded slightly wild, very distressed. 'So I called the local firemen out, well, they usually deal with that sort of thing, don't they? Trouble is when we got here, it wasn't, so I radioed for the emergency services.'

Pel glanced at the red van. Close to it were four firemen, some sitting, some standing, all smoking, all pale. 'Where is your colleague?' he asked. 'The gendarme who accompanied you.'

'Eh? Oh, he's round the back, sir, regurgitating his breakfast.'

'Pujol! Get round there and tell him to pull himself together! And mark every flipping footprint he's made, silly ass!' Pel studied the youngster in front of him. 'When your mates get here,' he said more calmly, 'take a breather, but don't leave your post. I want to talk to both of you later.'

A white car screeched to a halt by the war memorial; a large black and white sticker on its windscreen announced that the press had arrived. Sarrazin stepped out and hurried across the square. Although Pel loathed all newspapermen – they had a habit of jumping to conclusions, insinuating they knew everything while the police hadn't got a clue, and dramatising even the smallest event – Sarrazin had proved truthworthy in the past. They still didn't like each other much but a mutual respect had been established, which surprised them both.

'Sarrazin.' Pel acknowledged his presence, shaking the journalist's hand. 'You can take any picture you like out here but don't even ask to go inside.'

Sarrazin tilted his head to one side. 'That bad?' he said, his fingers busy with a camera. 'What happened?'

While Pel explained as rapidly as possible, the *juge d'instruction*'s car pulled up quietly behind them. Fortunately it was Ghislaine Castéou, an attractive woman, who didn't believe in interfering, unlike the other examining magistrate, Brisard, who always insisted on making it known that it was his right to meddle, even to conduct his own investigation if he saw fit.

Maître Castéou listened to the description of the scene of the crime, went in to see it for herself, coming out almost immediately, and after a short conversation first with the doctor and then with Leguyder from Forensics, accompanied Pel to interview the man who'd stumbled on the crime.

He was crouched under a blanket staring into space, nursing a half-empty glass of medicine. What he'd already swallowed wasn't having much effect: he was shaking like a leaf.

They climbed into the firemen's van and sat opposite him but he didn't seem to notice.

'Monsieur,' Pel said gently, 'I'm Chief Inspector Pel, this is Madame le Juge. I'd like you to answer one or two questions.'

The man rolled his eyes towards them and with a nod

indicated that he was listening. For a moment they looked at each other, then without warning huge tears overflowed on to his cheeks and he began howling like a schoolboy.

2

When Pel arrived home he was weary. They'd been interviewing the occupants of Fontaine les Lacs all day. As usual no one had seen a thing, no one ever did. He'd also had the grisly task of informing Aynard's wife that she was now a widow. She'd opened the door with a smile; a pretty woman, late twenties he guessed, her shoulder-length hair gathered into a flowery ribbon at the back of her head, her skin fresh, untouched by make-up and glowing clean. He'd shown her the necessary identification and asked to speak to her in private but she'd taken Pel and Pujol into the kitchen where two small children sat at the table, waiting noisily for lunch.

'I'd prefer to speak to you alone,' he'd repeated but she'd shrugged and grinned at her little girls.

'Can't leave these two terrors,' she'd replied cheerfully. 'Look at them, their tongues hanging out!'

He'd formally notified her of the death of her husband while her friendly expression clouded with disbelief. By then the children were squabbling over who was going to have the glass with a drawing of Tintin on it. She'd snapped at one and slapped the other, reducing them to shocked silence. 'I'm sorry,' she'd said shakily, 'I don't think I heard you correctly. Please would you say all that again.'

He had and, although her eyes filled with tears, she shook her head, still unable to accept the tragedy. It was never much fun announcing a death to the nearest of kin, particularly as he had to follow it with the inevitable tasteless questions as to their whereabouts at the time of the murder, leaving them in no doubt that they were the number one suspect. It was a charming job.

He'd also been to see the dying nurse's husband at his place of work in the city. He'd received the news of his wife's critical state angrily, leaping out of his executive's chair and pacing round the office demanding to know what was being done about catching the bastard: a frequent reaction to violence. He'd been incensed at being asked about his movements that morning, spluttering at the police's lack of tact, but he had eventually answered. In Pel's experience, that was normal too.

Soon afterwards, he'd crossed the city to the hospital where Angelface Aimedieu was on duty outside the operating theatre, looking glum. 'They're still fighting to keep her alive,' he said. 'I'll let you know if there's any change.'

It had been a depressing day. The road blocks had been quickly set up and would remain in position throughout the night. So far they'd produced nothing but long queues of irritable motorists complaining about the delay; however, it had to be done in case their killer decided to hop it after dark. The scene of the crime had imprinted itself on Pel's brain. He was never one to enjoy blood and guts, and this time the amount that had flowed in that one small room had been staggering.

As he opened his front door, the sound of crashing pots and pans echoed from the kitchen: his housekeeper, Madame Routy, was preparing supper. He was convinced she was a witch in disguise, or a fire-breathing dragon, or both. He'd never forgiven her for the bullying and burnt offerings he'd had to suffer before his marriage and, although it was a long time ago, this evening he wanted revenge.

Flinging open the kitchen door he shouted, 'You're sacked, you evil woman! And look slippy about my whisky, with ice cubes, not your usual snowflakes,' he added as he stormed into the sitting-room to his favourite armchair.

'Oui, mon capitaine!' she shrieked, saluting the door as it crashed shut, making the walls tremble, then 'Quel tyrant,' she muttered to herself and went on humming as she stirred a béchamel sauce that was just reaching the crucial moment of thickening on the stove.

When she banged the stout glass down in front of him, Pel was staring at her feet. Her habitual stout lace-ups had been replaced by whispering slippers. 'No hobnailed boots tonight?' he asked acidly, reaching for his drink.

'Corns,' she replied doing an about-turn and marching out.

21

'How delightful! I hope they hurt,' and he took a gulp at the glass. She'd filled it so full of enormous ice cubes that they hit his front teeth like a sledge-hammer, making him jump, and his precious Chivas Regal slopped on to his shirt front. He'd never win. Sighing, he fumbled in his pockets to find he'd forgotten his last packet of Gauloises at the office.

'Bloody woman, it's her fault,' he muttered, wondering if it was enough of an emergency to call headquarters and have someone rush them over in a marked car with bells clanging – after all, he was allowed to smoke in the evenings, he had to make up for lost time during the day.

Fortunately for those still on duty, his wife arrived five minutes later with a beautiful blue oblong under her arm. She kissed him tenderly, making him wonder how someone so elegant, so attractive, so sweet-smelling, kind and intelligent could put up with a grouchy old slob like himself.

'I bought these on my way home,' she said softly, 'in case,' and Pel fell on the *cartouche* of cigarettes as if it would save his life.

'You're an angel,' he said, ripping it open, extracting a packet and lighting up, blissfully inhaling the rich taste of dark tobacco down to his woollen socks.

'Have you sacked Madame Routy yet?' she asked, smiling lovingly at him.

'Naturally!'

'Fine. I'll go and see how supper's coming along.'

Pel finished his cigarette in peace, sipping occasionally at the whisky, and as he stubbed it out he noticed the Gameboy, a hand-held computer game Yves Pasquier, the teenager next door, had given him, sitting on the small table. He eyed it with contempt. Although he was getting the hang of the game Tetris, he hadn't yet succeeded in acquiring the little box's congratulations, but Yves had told him of the fireworks and rocket ship launching on the little screen, if only he could win. If only he could see them, just once. Cautiously, he picked the game up and switched it on, watching the screen come to life; he set it for 'high speed', level 9, and prepared to do battle. Almost immediately the phone started ringing, piercing Pel's paradise. He tried to ignore it. After the third ring it stopped and he concentrated again on the electronic puzzle.

'It's Darcy,' his wife told him, coming back into the room.

'I'm not in,' but she put the portable phone against his ear.

'Infernal instrument,' he grumbled. The Gameboy sneered – he'd lost. 'Yes, what now?'

'Two boys, just over an hour ago!'

'Two boys what?' Pel asked, expecting the worst.

'My two boys! Kate gave birth just over an hour ago. I thought you should be one of the first to be informed.'

'I'm ecstatic,' Pel replied, staring dully at the plastic box in his hand, regretting the interruption, then, as his brain absorbed the information, a hideous grin spread across his face. All Pel's grins were hideous, he'd been practising for years. '*Merde, alors! Félicitations!* Give Kate a smacking kiss. Well done, Darcy!'

'Good news, *n'est ce pas?*' his wife said happily as she retrieved the phone and disconnected the call. She'd always been fond of Darcy, he'd persuaded her to give Pel a second chance when he'd blundered badly on one of their first evenings together. It hadn't been an easy courtship but she was very pleased with the result – they'd been married eleven years.

Pel sank back in his chair, comfortable again, feeling fatherly towards the Prince Charming of his team. It had surprised everyone, particularly all his thousands of ex-girlfriends, to see him settle down with Kate, but he'd finally met his match. She had a good strong character, strong enough to handle lover-boy Darcy. He'd had to do the chasing for once, and she was, not surprisingly, lovely to look at. Divorced and already mother of two. Two and two, that made four! Four children, poor devil . . . Darcy's smooth black hair would shortly be turning grey.

As Pel pushed his way into the Hôtel de Police early the following morning, he noticed the desk sergeant looking sullenly at his pages of logged complaints. He glanced at the chief inspector with doleful eyes, then jumped to attention. 'Morning, *patron!*'

Pel scowled. 'Bet you haven't found the budgie yet!' he bellowed and headed for the stairs, leaving the sergeant to sulk.

The morning meeting was already assembled when Pel slammed open the door. Nobody reacted, they were used to him, and sorting themselves out, they settled down for the latest explosion of furious demands. They'd all heard about the murder, they knew what it meant: leaves cancelled, twenty-four-hour tours of duty, no slouching, top gear, fast efficient investigation, find the trail and follow it before it goes cold, the first few days are the most important. They'd be out on the streets until it was solved, their wives irritable at their absence, their children wondering who the stranger was who ate with them occasionally.

The door flew open again to reveal Darcy doing a good impersonation of a Disney hero, tall and handsome, not a hair out of place, his sparkling white feeth flashing with uncontrollable pride. He was met with a round of applause accompanied by hearty whistling as he sidled over to where Pel was standing.

'What are you doing here?' Pel hissed.

'On duty,' Darcy replied, bowing to the congregation.

'What about Kate, and the babies, and the other two?'

'Kate's radiant, babies healthy, and the other two are being looked after by her parents, they arrived last night to hold the fort.'

'Clever little bugger aren't you?'

'Thank you, *patron*,' he grinned, 'and thank you for the champagne you sent, Kate asked me to give you a kiss.'

Pel shied like a startled fawn. 'I'll wait, she can give it to me in person.'

The applause died down as Pel looked round the room at the expectant faces. 'Okay, let's have it, what's on the agenda?'

Methodically, they went through the million cases they were juggling. Progress was for the most part being made, two steps forward one step back, accumulating and sifting evidence, adding and subtracting suspects. It was a long and complicated process, often hampered by the fact that the general public went around with its eyes closed and its ears plugged, either that or they made it up as they went along to attract attention and add a dash of excitement into their dull little lives.

Pel listened patiently, a satisfied scowl in place, knowing they were doing everything they could. The final report was on a series of interviews concerning a sixteen-year-old girl called Patti Fauré who'd disappeared in January. An *avis de recherche* with a photo of a smiling, intelligent-looking girl with long wavy hair had been posted in the 4250 gendarmeries throughout France; every Hôtel de Police had it too, together with the investigating officer's number. Twenty-three days later she was found at Alesia, the site of a Roman dig. She was dead. On the file marked 'Patti Fauré', Pel had put a line through 'Missing Person' and written in thick red letters underneath, 'Murder'. After the inevitable autopsy, the path lab had informed the police that Patti had been knocked unconscious but had actually died of hypothermia during the night of her disappearance, when after a surprisingly mild and sunny winter, temperatures had suddenly plummeted to minus ten degrees. The case was proving a difficult one; it was two months old and they were losing hope of ever catching her killer.

'I don't think it could have been someone she knew,' Nosjean finished. 'Her friends, teachers and family can be accounted for, we've checked them all again. No one understands what she was doing out at the Roman site, she wasn't interested in that sort of thing. The archaeologists who found her when they went back to work in February don't know her. We've covered every one of them now, they all have solid alibis. We've been at it virtually non-stop and it's still a mystery.'

Pel agreed. They'd gone round and round in circles; it was an isolated death unlike any other they had on record and the man who'd knocked her silly and left her to die had vanished – all that remained of him was a microscopic specimen of saliva frozen into a love bite on the girl's neck. The forensic scientist and odontolgist had confidently confirmed it would be enough for an arrest followed by a watertight court case – once the police had found him.

'Keep at it,' Pel told him. 'Could she have had a lover no one knew about, a married man? Use your imagination even if you think your ideas are impossible, check and recheck, we can't give up.'

Nosjean sighed and sat down. He and Annie had exhausted all their ideas, where else could they go, who else could they ask?

Pel pushed himself to his feet. 'However,' he went on, 'for the next couple of days I'm going to need the two of you. Go back to it afterwards. Now, Fontaine les Lacs . . .' The team braced itself for the day's schedule. 'You all know what happened there yesterday and although we were there within minutes of it being reported, it wasn't within minutes of it happening. The road blocks produced nothing. Preliminary statements were taken throughout yesterday afternoon in the village: they must be followed up, memories jogged. The victim, Hugo Aynard, was shot and died between seven and eight yesterday morning, the time most people set off for work, someone must have seen something. Ask in the post office, they'd have been sorting at first light, the grocery store, the butcher's, the bread shop, he's got a van that goes out just after dawn, speak to the driver, the paper shop, the two bars, they open for *petit déjeuner*, the petrol station, they recognise cars that aren't local, those who work here in the city and leave early, the old dears who've got nothing better to do than watch from behind their net curtains, the local tramp if there is one, anyone who was likely to be awake when it happened. Aynard's wife said he left home at six forty-five, as he did every other day for his dialysis – he was a punctual man and liked to get the painful procedure over as promptly as possible. She left her house just before nine to take their two children to the local primary school, then went into town to shop and to keep an appointment with the bank manager – make sure she did. The nurse, Adrianne Fabres, left her husband in bed, after taking coffee up to him, at six thirty. He got up slowly, took a shower and was coming downstairs when their cleaner arrived around eight as usual, he says. The nurse collected a bag of *chocolatines* for her patients, the *pâtissier* told us she always did, it wasn't yet seven o'clock, and she must have arrived, judging by the distance she travelled, just before Aynard. There are certain preparations to be made before dialysis begins but usually it was established shortly after seven. Follow it up, be sure they were where they say they were, find out who they are, how they live their lives, if they were unfaithful, check the lot and go back and cross-check with what other people say.'

The team sighed, cigarettes were lit. It was no more than was to be expected: a sordid series of questions, digging up the worms of gossip and letting them wriggle. Unfortunately they knew it was essential, they were used to it, what they never got

26

used to was the smug way busybodies often squirmed with delight when telling it.

'Aimedieu,' Pel went on, 'what news from the hospital?'

His angelic face was serious. 'No change, she's still alive but hasn't regained consciousness. Bardolle took over the surveillance last night, I'm going to relieve him any minute now.'

'The moment I have an autopsy report on the dead man, you'll be informed. Now, get going the lot of you!'

As they collected their belongings together for a long day, Pel waited for Cheriff by the door and walked with him towards the stairs. 'As you've got the interview with the Sunshine Sect,' he said, 'go ahead, but play it down, imply we're doing a police census of people newly arrived in the area, whatever you do don't alarm them. These quasi-religious groups are safer when they're not excited. If there's any doubt about children being involved, let me know immediately – there are volumes of legislation to protect minors and armies of social workers who know how to apply it.'

Before he'd left the sergeants' room, Annie had handed him a newspaper; as Cheriff left, he unfolded it to glance at the front page. It was half filled with Sarrazin's photo of Aynard's bagged body being removed from the surgery, and the headline read, 'Bloodbath at Dawn!' Pel sighed, he'd been expecting it. However, reading what the newspaperman had written, which was succinct and to the point, he suspected the headline had been added by his editor to catch the public eye. Pel was quite surprised by the conservative presentation of the drama – Sarrazin had stuck to the facts – and he was still frowning at the print when Doc Cham, coming along the corridor from the stairs, tapped on the front of the newspaper. Pel jumped a foot in the air. 'Don't do that!' Dropping pages like leaves falling in autumn, he shook the pathologist's hand. Dr Boudet, who was allowed to assist in his laboratory, scooped up the debris grinning. Pel lit a cigarette, forgetting he was supposed to be giving up, and headed for his own office followed by the doctors and Darcy.

De Troq' slipped through the door before it was firmly closed on the outside world. By the look of the medical men, there was something odd lurking in the shadows.

Pel threw up the windows, called through on the interphone for a supply of fresh water and finally took a long puff at the smouldering tobacco before perching on the edge of his desk.

'You two always make me feel ill,' he explained, 'so I'm taking precautions before we start.' Annie came in with the requested bottle of water and paper cups, added a sachet of Citrate de Bétaine to the desktop in case of indigestion and discreetly left.

'Proceed,' Pel said.

Ten minutes later he was standing at the window gulping down lungfuls of fresh air and the doctors were looking guilty – they had a way of putting things that always churned Pel's stomach.

'. . . there was evidence of brain tissue and blood behind the remains of the head, spread across the inclined upper third of the examination table, plus multiple bloodstains on the wall and the floor. Further brain tissue and blood were found on the ceiling above.' Pel lit a fresh Gauloise and felt better hauling the nicotine deep into his lungs. 'More bloodstains and fragments of bone and brain were found on the sheet partially covering the body.' Pel exhaled noisily. 'On the left-hand side of the sheet we found a portion of brain and a number of grey metal pellets.' Cham glanced round the room at the attentive faces.

'Go on,' Pel gasped, reaching for the water.

'Now we come to the nurse,' Cham said. 'Boudet accompanied her to the hospital. Late last night he went back again to speak with the surgeon who operated.'

'She was hit in the arm and chest, left-hand side, at very close range, approximately three metres,' Boudet told them. 'It's a massive wound and contained many metal pellets. From the angle of the wound, the passage of the pellets to be more precise, it was pretty clear on the X-rays I saw, and the distance at which the shot was fired, we estimate that the gun was held at waist level.'

'Not the usual stance of a murderer,' Cham commented.

'And what is the usual stance of a murderer?' Pel asked coldly. He liked Cham and Boudet, and appreciated their attention to detail; unfortunately it often upset him. He reached for the sachet of Citrate de Bétaine.

'You tell me,' Cham replied.

Pel stirred the yellow granules into his water thoughtfully. 'I must confess a person intending to kill is more likely to raise a shotgun to his shoulder to get his eyeball behind the sights, in an attempt to aim straight. It's usually an accident when a gun is fired at waist level, but not always,' he added. 'I suppose it does indicate our murderer wasn't an habitual killer. Which is hardly surprising, Fontaine les Lacs isn't exactly known for its gangsters.'

'But there are plenty of hunters,' Darcy pointed out, 'who take pot shots at rabbits, pheasants, deer, anything that's edible – we can't rule them out because the gun wasn't apparently held correctly. There were a hell of a lot of game permits issued in that village when the season opened in October. I stopped at the Mairie yesterday to find out.'

For a moment the five men remained silent while Pel scribbled. 'We can't rule anyone out.' He swallowed his medicine and banged the glass down. 'But now the lecture on how to splatter brains and internal organs all over the shop is finished, perhaps you would kindly leave the room.'

'There's something else,' Cham said, his Adam's apple bobbing in his scrawny neck. He was folding and unfolding his long thin legs almost in embarrassment. 'The deceased, Hugo Aynard, was in a state of well-developed sexual excitement when he died.'

'I beg your pardon?'

'You know he was undergoing dialysis,' Boudet said, leaning forward. He was an impressive-looking man, six foot tall and built like a carthorse. He enjoyed the puzzles pathology set them, and the grim work they did on their cadavers never seemed to upset him, though seeing his living patients damaged or mutilated sickened him. It wasn't unknown for him to chew on a handful of his own nerve pills. 'I've checked his medical records. One of his kidneys was removed, the second one stopped functioning two years ago. Dialysis does the work of the non-operating kidney, cleansing the blood. It has to be carried out frequently, every couple of days, and the operation lasts approximately two hours. Patients are encouraged to rest, read or sleep – or, in the case of Nurse Fabres's surgery, nibble at a *chocolatine*. Aynard had not yet eaten anything that

29

morning, nor was he reading or sleeping. He was however ejaculating.'

'Good grief!'

'It's one way to pass the time.' Boudet smiled but there was no humour in his voice.

'But what about the dialysis?'

'Only one arm is needed for that.'

'Good grief,' Pel said again, 'but the nurse was in the room!'

'Yes.'

The policemen stared at the doctors. 'What are you trying to say?' Pel asked.

'The sheet covered the lower part of his legs, but he was naked from his upper thighs to his waist. His groin was exposed when I went in,' Boudet said.

'For the dialysis?'

'No, that was done through a massive vein in his right arm,' Cham exlained. 'Two veins had been joined to make one noticeably thicker. It's normal procedure.'

'Is it normal procedure,' Pel asked slowly, 'to become sexually excited during treatment?'

Boudet pulled a face. 'Well, put it this way,' he said, 'I think it's pretty bloody unusual.'

3

Cheriff and Misset were shown into a comfortable sitting-room with large sofas and a number of armchairs gathered round a fireplace wide enough to play football in. Although the spring sun was shining, the air still had a nip to it and the crackling log fire was pleasant; the Sunshine Sect certainly knew how to live. They'd taken up residence in a rambling old farm well away from the stresses of big city life; empty green fields surrounded the property, inhabited only by groups of trees and the occasional ruin. Behind the newly renovated house it was obvious restoration was about to start on the adjoining buildings; a cement mixer, lengths of newly cut beams and scaffolding had been neatly stacked to one side.

While they waited, Cheriff wondered how they did it. His eyes drifted round the room in which he sat, taking in the old but good quality furnishings. Misset was to one side of him looking as if someone had switched his brain off.

After a few minutes the oak door opened again to allow the Main Ray and his minion, Michel Moiré, presumably nothing more than a sunbeam, to join them. The Main Ray, Monsieur Viguier, was a tall, handsome man, although Cheriff noticed a small bald patch showing through his thick dark hair and wondered whether he was perhaps older than he looked. He wore open-toed sandals on his feet, on to which his loose trousers folded their extra inch; his cream-coloured smock was gathered by a belt round his hips and was open to reveal a considerable area of hairy chest, into which disappeared a heavy gold chain hanging from his neck. His face was remarkably unlined and partly hidden under a neatly clipped beard. He looked down his nose at the two seated policemen. It didn't last long, the six-foot Arab stood to shake his hand and they were eye to eye.

As Viguier sat, he grasped the arms of his chair with long supple fingers. His nails were immaculately clean and smoothly rounded; Cheriff decided he'd never done a day's work in his life. He took it all in carefully, knowing Misset wouldn't remember a damn thing.

The Main Ray waved them back into their seats while his minion, a tiny man beside his superior, hovered behind doing a good impersonation of a lap dog. Viguier had chosen a straight-backed wooden chair, higher than the others and ornately carved; he looked pleased with himself as he studied his visitors from his throne. Allowing himself a hint of a smile, his beady brown eyes glinting from hooded eyes, he declared, 'Officers, welcome!'

'Thank you, monsieur,' Cheriff said, shifting his weight back into the sofa and spreading his arms out along the top of its cushions. He too had learned about body language and wasn't going to be intimidated by a self-appointed guru. 'It was generous of you to agree to see us.'

Viguier bowed his head graciously and while Cheriff decided he was a detestable bloke, Misset blinked, impressed by his elegance, rather like Scarabee, he thought, in his favourite

31

James Bond film. A question and answer routine was established to find out how many members were present on the farm, how many were expected for the summer, how old they were and so on and so forth. As Viguier revealed all, proudly and without hesitation, Cheriff listened apparently casually, picking through the information and storing away what was relevant.

Misset was in obvious admiration of Viguier, sitting forward, his elbows on his knees, supporting his chin on his fists. When Viguier finished his little speech, Misset tilted his head. 'Can anyone join?' he asked enthusiastically. 'I mean,' trying to gather himself into his policeman stance, 'what are the rules? Is there an entrance fee? Do you accept all nationalities? What about an age limit?' For a bloke with a disconnected brain, he was doing quite well.

'There is no charge, we are not a club, we are a commune and you, and your colleague,' Viguier nodded towards Cheriff, suggesting there was no discrimination against immigrants either, 'would be allowed to accompany us in our celebrations.' He gave them a smug smile. 'No race is excluded. As to age, I have found that beyond thirty one is already tarnished, the innocence has gone, one is less receptive to our teaching, and therefore people over that age are discouraged. However, exceptions can be made.'

Cheriff resisted raising an eyebrow; the Main Ray was well over his own age limit. 'What about the other way?' he asked. 'Do you accept children, for instance?'

'All our members must be of the age of consent. I have photocopies of the *carte d'identité* of all participants – indeed, I've turned away a number of disappointed youngsters and couples wanting to bring their offspring. They would complicate the organisation of our activities.'

Cheriff asked if they could have a copy of the membership list, expecting an immediate refusal, and was surprised when Viguier agreed to provide it. 'I'll get the office to compile it for you. But these things take time – as soon as it's completed I'll send it on.'

As they left, Viguier remained in his chair extending a limp hand to be shaken. 'Farewell,' he said. 'Do not hesitate, my brothers, to return if you wish.' It was the minion, Moiré, who saw them to the door, silently crossing the wide entrance hall on slippered feet. Misset asked him if he was happy there.

'Happier than I have ever been,' he replied. 'I've found the Light, it's shown me my destiny.'

Cheriff started the car, nodded to Moiré, who was busy rearranging his long hair into a rubber band, and set off down the drive.

'Nice set-up,' Misset commented.

Cheriff gave a hollow laugh. 'Phoney, if you ask me. I looked up the deeds of this place. His dear old uncle left Viguier the farm. If you read between the lines of what he said, he's sitting pretty letting his disciples run it for him. However, he's clever, you've only to look at him to see that, he set up a home for Le Peuple de Soleil et Lumière, and bingo! A tatty inheritance becomes a paradise, his members work the farmland, tending the fields and restoring the buildings, and he pays no wages. I wonder how many have signed over their worldly goods to the cause? The radiators in the hall were working – central heating must cost a bomb.'

Pel stared at the numerous files on his desk. He pushed a pile to one corner and added 'Patti Fauré – Murder (deceased 27th January, Caesar's encampment, Alesia)'. He wasn't happy discarding the enquiry of the kid found at the Roman dig, even temporarily, but with recent events he was forced to. Lighting a Gauloise he inhaled deeply, caught himself smoking and ticked himself off. It was the new 'big push' to give up – stop gradually had been suggested, the morning first, the afternoon next and eventually the evening as well. He should crush the cigarette out immediately! What a waste ... No good Burgundian could be wasteful, he'd just have to smoke it and remember not to light another before midday. Easy really, he told himself, enjoying the smoke filling his lungs luxuriously. He pulled the Aynard/Fabres file towards him, already frighteningly thick, filled with thousands of statements taken from the inhabitants of Fontaine les Lacs and of course the experts' reports: fingerprints, forensic, pathology. He was grateful not to have to wade through the technical medical terms, all of which meant very little to him. His vocabulary on the subject was limited to femur, fibula and tibia; mandible, sternum and clavicle; pubis, coccyx and cranium – and he was pretty pleased with remembering those. Autopsy reports were written as far as he was concerned in double Dutch, if not triple or quadruple Dutch. Cham and Boudet, repulsive though they were when they put their minds to it – and he suspected they enjoyed seeing him suffer – were at least intelligent enough to tell him of their findings in words he could understand. Not like Leguyder, head of Forensics; he enjoyed blinding everyone with science and sitting simpering while the poor idiot policemen scratched their heads and were forced to ask him to explain, like ten-year-olds in a maths class. Leguyder was a bore but, Pel had to admit, extremely good at his job. He never missed a trick, and for that the chief inspector was prepared to put up with his infuriating superiority and stifle yawns for hours on end until he finally got to the point. He was surprised the scientist hadn't been in touch.

Darcy and de Troq' were deep in discussion on the other side of his desk. They too had realised that Aynard's sexual arousal had implications, it could change the enquiry completely.

'*Crime passionnel?*'

'It's a possibility,' Darcy agreed. 'We're going to have to find out. What does the nurse's husband do for a living?'

'Estate agent,' de Troq' said.

'And wife of Aynard, the dead man?'

'Typist for a wine exporter. She's been there nearly two years, since her husband fell ill and was only able to work short hours. His partner in the dental practice has taken on another dentist now, he was growing too weak to stand for more than ten minutes at a time. They said he was a brave man who never complained, but they'd watched him grow thinner every day. Apparently his diet was very limited with the kidney problem – he'd lost almost half his body weight. He spent most of his time reading and sleeping.'

'And being dialysed.'

'Every other day.'

'Can a man, in that state of health?'

'Cham and Boudet were suggesting it, and they should know.'

Pel came back to life. 'Facts!' he bellowed. 'Hypotheses lead to confusion. Aynard was on the surgery bed, and from the position of her wound we know the nurse was standing facing him, her left side turned towards the door. Aynard died where he was, still connected to the dialysis machine which means . . .'

'. . . that she was probably shot first,' Darcy carried on. 'The second blast, immediately afterwards, was for him, before he had time to move.'

'Two shots,' Pel ruminated. 'Metal pellets, that means cartridges, a shotgun has two barrels, the killer wouldn't have had to reload, so no cartridges dropped on the floor, our killer walked away with them still in the gun. Darcy, get on to Leguyder, it's time he told us something.'

Annie crashed through the door, making Pel jump, 'Ooh, sorry, *patron*, I tripped.' She grinned sheepishly under her mop of red hair.

'Perfectly normal,' Pel replied, looking at her over the top of his spectacles. 'You haven't broken anything for at least a week. We're all waiting with bated breath – no one's safe until it's happened.'

Annie smiled apologetically. 'I've brought you the replacement, Officer Jourdain.'

'Oh God!' Pel sighed, 'I'd forgotten, didn't have time yesterday. All right, hand him over for inspection.'

Pel put on his best scowl; he felt first impressions were important, and if he looked bad-tempered the new man would have reservations about asking silly questions. However, it slipped the moment she came in. The new member of his team wore running shoes, tight jeans patched at the knees, a crisp white shirt and ear-rings. She was tall with spiky blonde hair making her look as if she'd stuck her fingers in a faulty plug, she had bright blue eyes and pink cheeks, and she looked about sixteen.

'Good morning, sir,' she said, advancing, her hand outstretched ready for the official handshake.

'Not very,' Pel managed. 'How old are you?'

'Old enough,' she replied, standing to attention. Darcy and de Troq' nudged each other, winking at Annie who was trying not to laugh.

Pel rose slowly from his desk to take a closer look. 'What the hell are you doing in the police force?' he growled, stalking round her.

'I applied, trained and passed with flying colours.'

'You don't look French to me,' he said, noticing the creamy complexion under naturally pale hair and eyebrows.

'Father's family spent many generations in England – it was Huguenot originally, from Montauban. Mother's French, Burgundian. I am privileged with double nationality. I was educated here until the age of seventeen when I won a scholarship to the Lycée Charles de Gaulle in London. From there I went on to university where I got a first. I chose to return to my birthplace to work. Burgundy is the only place to be, sir!'

Pel gave her a last looking over. 'She'll do,' he said and turned back to his desk. 'Welcome to the team.'

'Thank you, sir,' and Officer Jourdain with smiling Annie disappeared back into the corridor.

'The child has been briefed,' Pel muttered as Darcy followed them out.

'A Huguenot, nonetheless,' de Troq' pointed out.

'Get it over with,' Pel sighed. 'Let's have the history lesson.'

'Huguenot comes from the name used for citizens of Geneva, *eigenot*. They were Protestants, and although they were persecuted and put to death, they accumulated in large numbers in Paris, south-west France and Navarre, the other side of the Pyrenees.'

'I know Navarre's in Spain,' Pel said through a cloud of newly lit cigarette smoke.

'Spain and France weren't quite so clear-cut in those days, *patron*.'

Pel waved a hand impatiently. 'In spite of the Prince of Condé's support and leadership,' de Troq' continued, 'hundreds of thousands fled to Switzerland, Holland, America, South Africa and, of course, England.'

'Ah, there we have it,' Pel puffed, hoping it was the end of the story.

'Their persecution, however, went on until 1787 when things started looking up and finally during the revolution, not much more than a hundred years ago, Protestants gained equality thanks to the Napoleonic Code.'

De Troquereau knew is history inside out, spoke French like a member of the Académie Française and could converse happily in half a dozen other languages. Sometimes his aristocratic upbringing was useful, sometimes it was a pain in the arse. 'Bully for Napoleon,' Pel whimpered, 'and if you don't get out now,' he raised his voice, 'and get on with a bit of revolution against this city's criminals, I'll bloody persecute you!'

De Troq' made a rapid exit and, collecting Nosjean on his way, left to see the wounded nurse's husband, Alain Fabres.

Darcy rang the forensic laboratory to speak to Leguyder but received a negative reply. 'No, we haven't finished, did you see the number of samples for analysis? There were enough from the waiting area to keep us busy for a fortnight never mind the treatment room. The entrance porch was relatively clean, certainly no give-away footprints by the door. However, we have been able to establish that the fingerprints throughout belong to the nurses, their patients and one or two visitors, all members of their families. Tell Pel, he'll be delighted, his killer is not co-operating with easy clues. I can't hurry things along as you suggest, it would render our work useless, we might just as well guess, estimate, conjecture, presume or speculate – you wouldn't want that, would you? I'll be in touch,' the scientist snapped and put the phone down. Darcy gave Pel the news and set off with Pujol to see Marie-Hélène Aynard, the dead man's widow.

Her pretty face was pale, accentuating the charcoal circles under her eyes. She'd obviously slept very little in her grief for her husband. Darcy noticed that her designer jeans and turquoise sweater concealed a curvaceous body; her shoes, however, were scuffed and worn down at the heel. Showing them into the attractive *salon* of a modern villa, she gathered up an armful of discarded toys and went to make fresh coffee. As they added sugar to their cups, she crouched on the sofa opposite and began weeping.

'What will I do now?' she sobbed. 'We were so happy. He was such a good, generous man. Two years he'd suffered, two years we've waited for a transplant, hoping they'd save him, we've been through hell and back, and the bank manager being a bastard.' She leaned forward and collected a box of paper handkerchiefs from the low table between them. 'There was a kidney ready for him six months back but when we got there, they found he wasn't completely up to scratch, just a sniffle, a tiny temperature, and we had to come all the way home again, our hopes dashed. It was his turn, he could've been called again any minute and, well, now . . .' She blew her nose, leaving the sentence unfinished.

Darcy nodded sympathetically while Pujol hid behind his thick glasses, always embarrassed by an emotional female. 'He must have known his nurse quite well after all that time,' Darcy suggested as lightly as possible.

'She was sweet.' Marie-Hélène sniffed. 'I sometimes popped in for a chat, see how Hugo's dialysis was going – you know, keep him company. We'd have breakfast together.'

'How often?'

Darcy glanced up at Pujol's abrupt interruption. It showed his lack of experience and sounded tactless, but he let it pass, wanting to hear the answer.

Marie-Hélène frowned. 'Sorry?'

Pujol cleared his throat. 'Er, how often did you pop in for a chat?'

'Well, I don't know really. Once a week at least, although I must confess it's been less lately. Seeing Hugo connected to that machine had begun to make me feel sick, it was a constant reminder that he was . . .' She sniffed, mopped at her brimming eyes. 'Listening to his blood being pumped round those tubes through the filters . . .' She took a deep trembling breath, trying to control the tears. 'Actually, I hadn't been for a couple of weeks. I couldn't stomach it any more.'

'Did you talk to your husband about your feelings?' Darcy asked.

'Yes, of course, he understood, said it didn't matter.'

'I'd like to go back for a moment to Adrianne Fabres,' Darcy suggested. 'You say she's sweet – would you enlarge on that, please?'

'Well, she was also kind and generous. Do you know, I admired a Chanel jacket hanging on the door once, and she gave it to me there and then, saying she'd had it for ages and was fed up with it. She quite often gave me clothes like that, we were about the same size, except for our feet.' She laughed sadly. 'We had a hilarious morning once playing Cinderella. I went to her lovely home to try on shoes she was throwing out, but I just couldn't squeeze into them, so she made up for it by insisting I took a Dior dress.' Marie-Hélène looked down at herself. 'You don't think I could afford all this, do you?'

'She's a friend?'

'Yes, I suppose she is, for both of us. We needed and appreciated having someone who understood the situation. But it wasn't just that, she's more than a nurse, she's our confidante, you can tell her anything. Poor love, is she any better?'

'As far as we know, she's hanging on,' Darcy said. 'If you hadn't been to the surgery recently, would you still consider her as your confidante?'

'I . . . I, well no, I guess not. But it wasn't because of her, we hadn't had an argument or anything, it was just that machine.'

'I expect your husband still confided in her though?'

'I expect he did. I know they discussed things, he'd tell me about their conversations when he got home. Hugo adored her.'

'You didn't mind your husband adoring another woman?'

'She was his nurse! When I say adore what I mean is, well, like an older sister if you know what I mean.' Darcy knew what she meant although older sisters weren't usually present while their younger brother masturbated himself to ejaculation. Was it really the dialysis machine that disgusted Marie-Hélène Aynard or something she suspected, or had seen? She'd been to the nurse's lovely house, her own home was practical. Jealousy? A dangerous emotion that became destructive when she found out the nurse was trying to steal her husband? If she'd found out.

'You know, she was generous in the way she cared for her patients,' Marie-Hélène was saying. 'For instance, she always brewed up hot drinks and bought them *chocolatines*. She didn't have to, she was just like that. If it hadn't been for her I think my husband would have given up long ago.'

'It must have been difficult living with a man who was so handicapped by illness.'

'Our life together had changed beyond recognition. When we

first came here we looked forward to a secure future, Hugo hoped to huy himself into the dental partnership. As it was, he fell ill and gradually stopped working altogether. I had to find a job sooner than I'd planned – we've two children, you see. Yes,' she sighed, 'living with a sick man wasn't easy, but not as difficult as living without him.' Blinking hard, she was unable to stop her eyes overflowing; dabbing at them again, her mouth quivering, she fought to regain control. 'You're right,' she admitted bravely, 'it wasn't easy, he was very weak, unable to socialise, unable to eat, drink and be merry, life was very restricted. But we coped, or rather I coped, with the kids, the house, the car, the finances, the boredom, the lot. We couldn't even go out for dinner, I had to prepare his meals specially, weighing every morsel he ate. He was always tired, he went to bed before the children, I'd tuck them in and wander round the house wondering what the hell to do with all the hours the evening held. I'd watch television if there was something worth watching, or read, or mend, or iron, I once washed the kitchen floor three times, then I'd crawl into bed beside him and pray that tomorrow would be the day they'd call to say it was his turn for the transplant and a new lease of life.' She sighed again heavily, her face creased in sorrow. 'And now he's dead, for ever.'

Finding Alain Fabres wasn't at his wife's bedside as they'd expected, de Troq' and Nosjean went to their home, not far from the village of Fontaine les Lacs. It was an impressive barn conversion with a swimming pool in a well-stocked garden, but unfortunately Fabres wasn't there either. They were told by a hand-wringing cleaning lady that he'd gone to work.

Once again in the crowded city centre, they found his modern office under the bold blue sign of a well-known estate agents who had offices throughout the area. The secretary who greeted them was middle-aged, smart and efficient; they waited while she dealt with two phone calls and an obstreperous farmer who didn't seem satisfied with the compensation he'd received, and who unfortunately reeked of manure. As he left, she smiled, apologised and started spraying air freshener liberally. De Troq' flipped open his identification, the red, white and blue stripe unmistakably announcing the law. 'We'd like to see Alain Fabres,' he told her.

'I'll see if he's free,' and she disappeared behind a wall of filing cabinets into another room.

As they were shown into the room, Fabres looked up at them, then rose to shake hands. Although he wasn't a particularly handsome man, he went with his house, carefully groomed. His brown hair, his manicured fingernails and his expensive suit were neatly cut; on his little finger he wore a heavy gold signet ring. Under normal circumstances he would have had the air of an affluent businessman; today, understandably they felt in the circumstances, he looked haggard, his movements disjointed, a distressed human being with his mind elsewhere.

'Just a couple of questions, monsieur,' de Troq' said.

'Of course. Perhaps I should apologise for my behaviour yesterday, I wasn't myself – after all, what was his name, ah yes, Chief Inspector Pel, he was only doing his job. He must have thought me very rude.' He sank back into his chair. 'But, God, who would do such a thing?' He picked up a biro and fiddled with it, tapping it occasionally on the desktop.

'That is what we intend to find out,' de Troq' reassured him. It wasn't going to be an easy interview. They started slowly, checking times, posing questions to which they already knew the answers in an attempt to put the fidgeting Fabres at ease.

'How many dialysis patients does your wife treat?' Nosjean asked, glancing up from the notes he was making.

'Half a dozen or so, I'm not sure. I'll find out if you like and let you have their names. Adrianne keeps duplicates of her records at home. She's a rural nurse sharing the practice with another girl, Crystal Combes. Actually, it would probably be quicker if you ask her.'

They agreed they would. 'The two nurses must know their patients well?' de Troq' suggested cautiously while Nosjean wrote.

'Adrianne certainly does,' Fabres shrugged. 'In the morning she does the dialysis. Each one takes a couple of hours to complete. Inevitably they chat while she gets it going and as it finishes, sometimes in between too if the patient doesn't doze off – that's what usually happened.' The biro clattered out of

41

his fingers. He stared at in in surprise for a moment before retrieving it and continuing the gentle tapping. 'Then there are her general patients in the afternoon,' he went on. 'She does the rounds, giving injections, changing dressings, that sort of thing.'

'Was she particularly friendly with any of them?' de Troq' tried again.

'All of them.'

'Monsieur,' Nosjean said quietly, 'did she see any of them outside visiting hours?'

'She may have come across them in town, doing the shopping, but she always said we shouldn't mix business with pleasure. I agreed, we didn't mix with my clients either, it can lead to embarrassment. Oh, dear, it's hard to believe.' He covered his face with his hands. 'I'm sorry.'

'How long did you spend at the hospital?'

'Virtually all night, but I only caught a glimpse of her.' Fabres wept. 'I went home early this morning, there seemed no point in staying. Then the phone calls started, friends, people from the village and bloody journalists. So I came here, at least here my secretary can protect me to a certain extent. The hospital know where I am. I want to be left in peace. I can't bear the thought of her being . . . being mutilated like that.'

As the team came in that evening they were despondent. They'd walked themselves off their feet covering every inch and every house in Fontaine les Lacs, and still no one remembered seeing – or, even more extraordinary, hearing – anything suspicious, which was incredible considering the noise a shotgun makes and the fact that it was fired twice. However, the negative reports had to be typed up anyway. Pel was despondent too. He'd been hoping for a hint from the forensic lab and so far they'd offered nothing, which was bad news – it was taking time which meant Leguyder would very probably collar him just as he was ready to leave with a hefty document the size of the Paris telephone directory and would keep droning on until the small hours of the morning.

As Pel was wading through the reams of reports, ticking off the names of the inhabitants of the village as he came to their statements, and gasping at what he hoped would be his last cigarette at the Hôtel de Police for that evening, the phone rang.

'Ah, Leguyder,' he sighed, 'I thought it might be you.'

'I'll be late for dinner because of your bloody murder,' the scientist complained.

'It was indeed bloody,' Pel agreed. 'How about giving me your news in résumé form?' he suggested hopefully.

'I don't think that would be wise but I will give you something to think about. Boudet fastidiously bagged the body's hands for protection before removal for the post-mortem, and on removing the plastic they discovered he was holding an earring.'

'They didn't mention it.'

'They did in their written report,' Leguyder retorted. 'Do you ever read them? In any event,' he went on haughtily, 'it is their job to analyse the body and the contents thereof, not objects adhering thereto. Acting correctly, they sent it to me.'

Pel gritted his teeth and waited for further explanation.

'It's a silver hoop, three centimetres in diameter,' Leguyder continued smugly, 'usually held in place by slotting the open end of the ring into the other side, hence completing the circle through the ear.' He paused. 'You understand, of course, the difference between ears that are pierced and ears that are not?' Pel nodded to himself, yawning, his jaw creaking with boredom.

'Pel! Are you there? Have we been cut off? Damned phones, always on the blink.'

Pel finished his yawn and propped his head on the palm of his hands. 'I'm still listening.'

'Ah good. This was for pierced ears and was, I concluded, pulled from the ear with some force. There was evidence of minor injury to the wearer, a spot of blood visible under the microscope, on the connecting wire, which I should add was broken.'

'Ah,' Pel replied succinctly.

'I'm in the middle of DNAing a scraping of the nurse's spilt blood to see if it was hers.'

'D and Aing?'

'Forget it. I'll call you when I've finished.'

Pel sighed at the sordidness of murder enquiries. 'What about the pellets?'

'Calibre twelve, thirty-four grams, very common, the cartridges can be bought just about anywhere, used for everyday hunting of hares, ducks, small game, up to young *chevreuil*.'

'And a couple of poor sods in the middle of a blood transfusion.' Pel frowned. 'Anything else?'

'I haven't finished yet! Everything else's been put to one side, you've no idea what it's like down here, we're snowed under what with drunken drivers, road accidents, industrial accidents, paternity suits – mind you, now that we can DNA, for your information that means deoxyribonucleic acid . . .'

Pel gently disconnected, grabbed his packet of Gauloises and, while he was still stuffing them in his jacket pocket, ran for the door, in case Leguyder phoned back.

4

'Annie!'

Pel was in a foul mood. It had started the evening before with Madame Routy wearing a brand new pair of hobnailed boots and stamping about on the *carrelage* floor like a regimental sergeant-major. She'd terrorised him, taking advantage of his wife's absence. Madame Pel had gone to console an ageing aunt who was preparing for her final departure and proposing to leave her worldly goods, which were considerable, to a local politician. His wife felt that while a generous donation would be acceptable, it was her duty to persuade the immense fortune into more deserving hands: cancer research, AIDS, homeless children, a starving village or two in the Third World, the down and outs of Paris and London, the Pels perhaps – anything but a politician. And although the consequences of her departure were obvious, Pel was forced to agree. He'd suffered his housekeeper until she disappeared to her quarters having served him a revolting *pot au feu* of limp vegetables floating in greasy dishwater and grey gristle masquerading as meat. To combat her television, going at full volume, he'd switched on his own and sat nursing his indigestion until almost midnight. The American cop movie – seventy-five per cent of all televised films were American – had infuriated him; all tough types shooting their mouths off, and their guns, and getting the girl, the one with legs that went up to her armpits, twice as much hair as any normal female, and who spent the entire hour and a half scantily clad, pouting at the young muscular policemen, because every one of them was young and muscular. None of them wore specs, was going bald and had an impossible addiction to Gauloises. The plot was unbelievable with spectacular car crashes and fist fights which would have left him, or his men, unconscious if not dead but from which the hero walked away smirking, not a mark on his pretty face. Plus the fact that the film had just got to an interesting bit when it was interrupted by adverts for hamburger joints, fizzy drinks, hair gel and a deodorant, all with American names he couldn't pronounce. He'd slept badly in his fury at the colonisation of his beloved homeland and arrived at work with his temper simmering to find Annie's flame-coloured hair missing from the sergeants' room. No Annie, no coffee.

'Annie!' he bellowed again.

'Delayed, *patron*,' the punk Huguenot, Officer Jourdain, informed him.

'Damn, blast and hellfire!'

'Coffee's on its way.'

'Don't bother – it'll be undrinkable.'

Jourdain disappeared to reappear a moment later. She placed his mug amongst the papers on his desk. 'Decaff with one sugar, *patron*,' and she left the room.

'Definitely been briefed,' Pel muttered as he sipped the perfect, reviving beverage. 'Just right, damn her.'

Leguyder slid through the closing door and sat opposite the obstreperous policeman. 'I was passing so I thought I'd pop in and give you this morning's analytical results personally,' he said importantly.

'Give by all means, all donations are gratefully accepted,' Pel replied unwisely, 'then pop out again, I've got things to do.'

A strangled gasp came from the forensic scientist. 'So have I,' he snapped, 'so pay attention!' He paused dramatically to make sure Pel was concentrating. 'My information concerns the ear-ring Aynard held; I compared it with the DNA of the two victims. As you will appreciate, there were plenty of nucleated cells present at the scene of the crime – '

'D and A, nuclear cells, what the hell are you on about? It sounds like some futuristic prison in danger of exploding nastily.' The words of science were beyond Pel. New ones were added every day, and it was impossible for a poor plodding policeman to keep up with them.

'DNA stands for deoxyribonucleic acid, as I tried to tell you yesterday evening before we were unfortunately cut off – you really ought to have your phone looked at, it's always happening. Where was I?'

'Having a go at the blood all over the surgery,' Pel said, already bored.

'Correct. DNA analysis gives a genetic profile on the donor, it's better than fingerprints, only identical twins have the same. In fact, in England they have used this knowledge to create identical twins, although of different generations. Have you heard of Dolly?'

'Eh?'

'Dolly the sheep. They took part of a sheep's breast and through molecular genetics were able to recreate the same genetic profile in a foetus which was then implanted into a living ovine uterus to mature. The resulting lamb is identical to the sheep from whose breast the sample was taken. Brilliant, *n'est ce pas*? It's called cloning.'

Pel had heard of cloning, the idea had been around quite a while.

'Of course,' Leguyder went on, 'molecular work takes time, extracting and purifying the DNA, cutting it into fragments, sorting the fragments by length, splitting and transferring the DNA, attaching radioactive probes and finally making a print for analysis, but it is one hundred per cent accurate, it pinpoints the owner precisely.'

Pel yawned. 'I know another bit of D and Aing,' he said. 'My man Misset: his brain's cloned from a chicken.'

'D-N-A, for God's sake, man, listen! It could revolutionise your job, certainly revolutionise the presentation of evidence in the criminal courts. All I need is a trace of semen, saliva, hair roots, bone or of course blood, and I can match it perfectly to the guilty party.'

Pel's mind was clearing. 'Do you mean to say that with a single hair root you can tell me who it belongs to?'

'If I've got the DNA of a suspect there is no question of doubt with my findings. In the paternity suits that I'm often called to deal with, I'm given a specimen of nucleated cells from the baby, plus specimens from the mother and the suggested father, and I can tell them whether or not he is in fact the male who impregnated the mother at conception.'

Pel grimaced. 'Is that what it's called nowadays?' he asked. 'A roll in the hay sounds much more fun.'

At last Leguyder left, and Pel relaxed with a cigarette. They now knew that some hanky-panky was definitely going on in the surgery before the nurse and her patient were blasted to smithereens. Pel had hesitated over the suggestion the two pathologists had made, but Leguyder had finally come to the point and told him the broken silver ear-ring found in Aynard's closed fist had been pulled from Adrianne Fabres's ear. The picture was clearer: Aynard had been lying on the bed stroking the nurse's ear, while she, they had to accept, was participating in certain activities provoking his sexual arousal. The murderer entered suddenly; she lifted her head in surprise, pulling her ear-ring out on Aynard's curled fingers, and was shot. Aynard was shot immediately afterwards, still holding the broken silver circle. Had it been discovered under different circumstances, the absurdity of how they passed the time during dialysis might have raised a smile; as it was, the idea was rather macabre. There were plenty of husbands and wives being unfaithful – the divorce courts were full to bursting and the police were often called out to domestic scenes of violence where an infidelity had been discovered. Unfortunately, that sort of thing didn't remain secret for long, someone else nearly always knew or suspected the affair and couldn't resist sharing the information with a neighbour, who in turn would pass it on, and so on. It seemed extraordinary that neither the grieving spouses of the victims nor the population of the village had made any comment about the affair.

Pel also knew precisely what had done the damage, not that

47

it helped. Everyone with a gun in the area would be questioned. It would probably take all week – hunting was every Frenchman's right, anything from songbirds to bunny rabbits, from brightly plumed cock pheasants to hideous hairy wild boar. As Leguyder had cheerfully pointed out, between 700 and 750 million shots were fired per year in their pursuit. Unearthing the guns would be no problem, you just had to knock on practically any rural front door, but the one that had made holes in Aynard and Fabres would be well hidden or well cleaned. It was an impossible task. A search had been made, around the surgery, in the public dustbins standing at the ends of the village streets, behind hedges as far as the stream; the muddy water had been dragged, and they'd gone beyond, into a field of sown corn, but they'd found nothing. Now the search was being extended, into the three lakes after which Fontaine was named, into the public gardens to the south, the esplanade on the eastern edge, the cemetery to the west and of course the rubbish tip at the northern extremity. Pel didn't expect them to turn it up so simply but it had to be done in case their killer had been careless.

And why had no one heard anything? Shotguns made a hell of a noise, not something the average human being could even pretend not to hear first thing in the morning on the edge of a still sleepy village. Cars didn't backfire any more; there was no railway within twenty kilometres, no airport, no factory, just the village and the fields surrounding it. It was too early in the year for a massive harvester to be on the road. A tractor? It was just possible if it had been pulling an empty trailer, old enough to rattle over every bump, but the road went nowhere except through the village and out the other side; a farmer needing to cross it would take the lower, straighter road, missing all the difficult narrow turns between the houses. However, it would be worth making sure.

While the surgery was slightly apart from the village, it wasn't all that far from the inhabitants of Fontaine having their breakfast and setting off for work. And how did he get away? No one had seen a third car parked outside, just the nurse's and Aynard's. Across the fields? He could have arrived that way too but Leguyder had found no twigs, no leaves, no earth at the entrance to the scene of the crime. Pel paced round the

48

room a couple of times, puffing vigorously; coming to a stop by the window, he gazed into the street below in search of inspiration.

After the surprising warmth of March, when everyone thought summer had arrived early, April had appeared clothed in grey, bringing ominous dark clouds in from the north. It had drizzled on and off for days and that morning Dijon woke to the softly tapping fingers of steady rain, falling from a thick black canopy overhead. Now it was a deluge, saturating and solid, flattening pedestrians to the sides of buildings or sending them running into doorways to find shelter. Across the street the awning that had given shade to the terrace of the Bar Transvaal was filling up dangerously; as the owner started winding it in, it deposited gallons of water gushing on to the pavement, narrowly missing Misset who was just strolling into the road.

Pel flung open his window. 'In my office! Five minutes ago!' Misset, flapping his arms in panic, cantered towards the building. A brain cloned from a chicken . . . The idea appealed to Pel.

The unfortunate Misset appeared, dripping on to the carpet, stuttering out excuses for being caught in the café during working hours. 'Just checking something, *patron*.'

'What?'

'A story in the paper, thought it might give us an idea for the shooting.'

'And?'

'Well, it was an article on a new law being passed in America, in, er, in . . . I can't remember which state, but they've passed this law to make it illegal to let off shotguns when a female reaches orgasm.'

'I don't believe you.'

'It's true! I'll go and get it if you like.'

'I mean, I don't believe that's what you were doing across the road. I believe you were feathering your nest with a hot coffee and hoping not to be seen out of the henhouse by the old fox Pel!'

Misset looked confused.

'I don't give a damn what they do in America before or after orgasm. Go and peck for clues somewhere useful.'

As Misset slouched out into the corridor, Pel shook his head. What would the Americans think of next?

The day brought nothing new except extensive puddles accumulating in every undulation, and grumbling pedestrians huddling in a crowd in the doorway of the Hôtel de Police. One or two filtered through to chat to the duty sergeant, but in general it was calm. The men came in drenched. One by one they made their short verbal report to Pel before setting about their typewriters with determination, getting it all down on paper, in triplicate, and praying there wouldn't be an emergency that night; they were all looking forward to a good steaming shower, a decent meal and a long dose of shut-eye.

Angelface Aimedieu rang through from the hospital. 'They're operated again, *patron*, but no change – Adrianne Fabres's condition is still critical.'

'Stick with it,' Pel replied. 'If she utters it may be significant – one word, it could be all we need. I'm coming over to see the surgeon.'

He climbed into a voluminous mackintosh, swam into the street and paddled towards his car. Squeezing the drips from his trouser ends, he muttered, 'Too much weather, always too much sodding weather,' and drove, squinting between the windscreen wipers, through the storm to the hospital.

Big Bardolle, the team's very own Hulk, was on his way to relieve Aimedieu and almost collided with his boss at a crossroads of wide antiseptic-smelling corridors. 'Look where you're going!' Pel growled. '*Poids lourds* carry speed limits, you know!'

'Sorry, *patron*,' Bardolle boomed. 'Didn't realise it was your right of way.'

'It's always my right of way,' Pel told him, looking anxiously at the dozens of signposts to all the different departments. 'Left or right?'

They took the lift up to the third floor to *Soins Intensif* and eventually spied Aimedieu through a window, sitting reading a magazine beside Adrianne Fabres's bed. There were three other patients in the room, all of them unconscious, all of them connected by tubes to drips and by wires to terrifying machinery with small flashing lights, monitoring heartbeat, blood pressure and respiration. In the centre of the room, behind the desk, a nurse kept watch over her patients with the help of a number of computer screens. Bardolle's large finger pointed at a prominent notice on the door: 'NO ENTRY. Knock and wait.' They followed the instructions and soon the nurse allowed Bardolle in, Aimedieu out, and indicated to Pel where he might find the doctor in charge.

He was tired; Pel noticed the deep lines of fatigue etched on his face. 'We've done what we can,' he said, 'but it's touch and go.' He drew Pel to the side of the corridor and sank gratefully into a chair. 'There were large clusters of shot in the upper abdomen and left elbow, the arm was grossly deformed, the joint and surrounding flesh were pitted with shot, there were multiple fractures, it's a real mess. I removed the shot as best I could to alleviate swelling and help prevent infection.' He sighed, running a hand through his tousled hair, then seeing Pel extricate his packet of cigarettes from its hiding place, he suggested they continue talking in his office. Once the door was closed he begged a Gauloise and sucked soothingly.

'I didn't think you doctors smoked,' Pel commented.

'Shouldn't,' he admitted. 'Trouble is, it's hard not to sometimes.'

It didn't make Pel feel much better to know policemen weren't the only ones who were forced to consume vast quantities of tobacco due to stress at work. 'Adrianne Fabres,' he prompted sympathetically.

They both sat down before the doctor continued. 'Pellets were also removed from her breast and surrounding area, left-hand side. There were a hell of a lot of them – look.' He pushed himself to his feet again and went to a series of X-rays clipped to a row of light boxes. At the touch of a switch they flickered and ignited. 'See that? A neat row, one behind the other in a vein.'

'Looks like a train waiting in a tunnel,' Pel agreed.

The doctor's hand swept across the prints. 'The destruction was widespread. We've had to remove part of her stomach and the pancreas, then the spleen. We rebuilt her arm but it's her chest and lungs that have got me worried, plus the inflammation round her heart.'

'What are her chances of survival?'

51

'God knows. Strictly speaking,' the doctor sighed, turning away, 'she should be dead already.'

Angelface Aimedieu had gone and with Big Bardolle in position, Pel left them to it. Stepping from the lift into the immense entrance hall of the hospital, he stopped and looked around. The building was quietening down for the night. The small shops selling magazines and newspapers, tobacco and writing paper, razors and soap, games and cuddly toys, were closing. There were a number of wheelchairs parked by a coffee machine, their inhabitants comparing injuries, and a man with a tracheotomy was gurgling through the tube in his throat as he enjoyed a cigarette. The chief inspector watched for a moment, fascinated to see the smoke drawn in through his mouth and escape through the plastic hole in his neck, then, as the man's head turned in his direction, Pel walked on embarrassed and depressed.

He stopped at the double doors, remembering something, and taking the hall at an ungainly trot managed to catch the woman sitting behind *Accueil* just before she locked up. Shortly afterwards found himself grinning like a kid at the lovely Kate.

'Pel!' she cried, flinging up her arms. 'What a super surprise.'

He shuffled his feet. His hospital visiting was restricted to interviewing victims of violence; confronted with beautiful women who'd just had babies, he wasn't sure what was expected of him.

Darcy stood up. 'Come and see my sons,' he said proudly, showing his bad-tempered boss the small pink bundles sleeping peacefully, minuscule hands curled into tiny fists.

'Jolly nice,' Pel said humbly. 'Got all they should have?'

'We've counted fingers and toes, all present and correct.'

'Do I get a kiss or don't I?' Kate teased. 'I was the one that did all the work.'

Pel obliged then wondered what to say. 'Well, I suppose I'd better be getting along – don't want to be late for supper.'

'Madame Pel's back?' Darcy asked.

Pel's heart sank. 'No, it's taking longer than expected, there's only the monstrous Madame Routy and her cauldron of bat's wing soup to greet me.'

Kate laughed. 'Order a Chinese,' she suggested brightly.

'We'll eat it here. I've got your bottle of champagne hidden under my bed.'

'Have a party here?' Pel looked horrified.

'Why not, it's a private room. My parents paid for it knowing that Darcy is no ordinary husband, being a detective that's never off duty, and my other two sons, nicknamed the Riot Squad, are not conducive to recovery in anyone else but me. Go on, no one'll mind. If they do you can threaten to arrest them!'

She was contagious and, encouraged by the delightful possibility of ringing Madame Routy at the last minute to say he wouldn't be home for supper, knowing it would annoy, Pel agreed. Later he even consented to hold one of the babies. It was a terrifying experience – he was scared stiff he'd break it.

5

Alain Fabres looked aghast at Pel, then accusingly at Pujol. For a moment he stared at them, furious. 'No, I did not know!' he snapped indignantly, then his anger seemed to seep away into new distress. 'You're wrong,' he said more calmly. 'There was no liaison between my wife and her patient, Hugo Aynard, some gossip's put you up to it. It's just not possible, she's a nurse, it's very important to her, she gave up a life of luxury to go back to it. We love each other, we're very happy. Look around you,' he went on, opening his arms to indicate the surroundings in which they sat, their home, 'she's got everything money can buy. I love her, she's a wonderful wife.' His hands fell on to his knees. 'That's not to say, of course, that we don't have our little tiffs,' he admitted quietly. 'All couples have their arguments, but we do love each other. No, Chief Inspector, you are definitely barking up the wrong tree!'

'How long have you been married, monsieur?'

Fabres thought for a moment. 'Nearly eight years.'

'Any children?'

'I don't see what that's got to do with it, but no, no children, perhaps that's why we got on so well,' he suggested. 'Children complicate couples, don't they?'

'They can,' Pel agreed, thinking of Nosjean. He'd once been a shy young man who blushed in front of girls; when he'd found himself married he could hardly believe his luck. Since their daughter had been born, he looked more and more harassed. His thoughts switched swiftly to Darcy, an incorrigible collector of beautiful women, bed-hopping and horizontal jogging being his favourite sport. Until he'd met Kate, and now they had twin sons and contented grins. 'On the other hand,' Pel contradicted himself, 'they can be known to complete them.'

'Well, it wasn't a problem for us,' Alain Fabres told him. 'We both have successful professional lives and used our spare time to enjoy ourselves to the full.'

'Doing what?' Pel was sure other grown men didn't waste precious leisure hours playing with computerised boxes or waging war on their housekeepers the way he did.

'Why?'

'I'm trying to build up a picture of all the people concerned, that's all.'

'Oh, I see. Well, we used to go out quite a lot, to the cinema, to eat in restaurants, and to exhibitions of modern art. We collect it.' He swivelled in his chair to indicate an oil painting hanging behind him.

To Pel it looked like badly scrambled egg in a bowl of insipid tomato soup. 'Very nice,' he managed.

'In the old days,' Fabres went on, 'we'd jog together, play tennis. I almost had a court built here, but I found my wife preferred lazing by the pool in fine weather. I still jog, not as often as before, but I've got to keep fit for her, she's a good-looking woman – men notice her, you know.'

'Doesn't that worry you?'

'On the contrary,' he smiled, 'I find it flattering.' Pel was inclined to agree. He enjoyed seeing the astonishment on strangers' faces when he presented his attractive wife, not at all the sort of woman one expected to be married to an uncultured tramp like himself. 'She loves me,' Alain Fabres said, 'our life together is very fulfilling. We spend a lot of time relaxing here, actually. Nowadays our favourite pastime is watching videos with a good bottle of Bordeaux.'

Bordeaux! Pel's eyebrows shot up: the man lived in Burgundy, a region that produced the finest wines in the whole of France, if not the world, and he drank Bordeaux – highly suspicious!

'Do you own a gun, monsieur?'

'Certainly not! My father had them, he was always bringing his trophies home for my mother to skin. I ate rabbit stew for years,' he added, lowering his eyes. 'It made me vomit.'

With a frown still firmly attached to his face, Pel told Pujol to drive him to the widow Aynard's house. Pujol adjusted his thick glasses, licked his lips and obeyed.

Marie-Hélène's reaction to the suggestion of her husband playing fast and loose with his nurse was almost the same. 'You're joking!' she cried. 'We've got two kids, he wouldn't have put their happiness at risk. Or mine,' she added as an afterthought, as if to convince herself. 'Okay, he was ill,' she continued, still troubled, 'at times it wasn't easy, but we often spent time lying side by side, while he rested, making plans for after the transplant, a family holiday and starting again, building him back up to health and strength. We talked and talked about the future, I think it gave him hope that there would be one. No, Chief Inspector, I don't believe you, and anyway,' she said more firmly, relieved to have proof it was untrue, 'he couldn't. The last time we tried to, you know, make love, was last year. It wasn't successful. But it didn't matter, there's more to marriage than that, isn't there? I loved him just as much, I was waiting . . .' Her words trailed off as she realised that all her waiting had been in vain. 'I miss him,' she sobbed, 'oh dear, I miss him. I don't know how I'm going to make the children understand that Papa's never, ever coming home again.'

Pel sat patiently while she wept, pulling tissues from a box on the table to mop up her reddening eyes. It wasn't always easy to make grown adults understand the terrible finality of death, and he was grateful he'd never been faced with her heartbreaking problem. However, once her tears had slowed to a dribble, he continued his questions and asked her if they owned a gun. She chokingly replied with another question: 'What on earth for?'

Pel finally left her in peace and went to see Crystal Combes,

Nurse Fabres's partner in Fontaine les Lacs. She received them in the kitchen of her small house, terraced into a narrow street just off the village square. 'Poor Adrianne,' she said. 'It's chaos without her. All the dialysis patients are having to be bussed into the city while our surgery is sealed. It's causing no end of problems, and I'm worked off my feet trying to keep up with double the calls in the afternoon. I can't wait for her to come back.'

'It may be quite a while,' Pel pointed out.

'Yes, I know, I was in touch with Intensive Care this morning. I've decided to get a temporary replacement, I can't go on like this, it's exhausting.'

She was fond of her partner, they'd worked together for seven and a half years and knew each other well. 'She was conscientious, all our patients adored her, she's being sorely missed. I truly can't think of anyone who'd want to hurt her.'

Pel told her what had been suggested was going on in the surgery when the shooting occurred.

'Good God!' she said laughing. 'What a load of baloney! It's incredible, what imagination!'

'Did she never talk about Hugo Aynard?'

'Of course she did, frequently, he was a patient. We talked about all of them; how their treatment was going, how their families were coping, what we could do to improve a difficult situation, like offering to put them in touch with home helps, getting the kids taken to school by a neighbour, things like that, anything to ease the workload of whoever cared for a patient twenty-four hours a day. It's not simple looking after someone who's basically dying, not to mention the emotional stress. Yes, we talked about him, but if you mean did she insinuate ... No,' she shook her head, 'never.'

'What about her private life?'

'It was private,' Crystal replied. 'It was only by chance that I even found out she's divorced, it was written on her *Fiche d'Etat Civil* in the office files. When I mentioned it she said it was over and done with and that was that. She met Alain, her present husband, before we went into partnership, she said it had been refreshing to meet someone so unsophisticated.' Pel raised an eyebrow. 'That's what she said. When I met him, I was surprised too. But he was head over heels in love with her, you

could see it in the way he looked at her. I commented afterwards that he wasn't in the least unsophisticated, quite the
opposite really and she replied, It's surprising what a decent
haircut can do for a chap!' She smiled easily at Pel. 'They don't
mix socially with the locals, perhaps they don't need to, perhaps it was a deliberate decision. If I had their money I'd move
out of the village. As it is I'm constantly disturbed at night.
You know, the old boy down the road's run out of Doliprane
and he's got a headache, the kid's got a cough and is keeping
Dad awake, Gran stubbed her toe on the way to the lavatory
and have I got an Elastoplast, always frantically urgent!' She
managed a tired laugh. 'If I moved further away it would make
them think a bit, as it is I'm the convenient nurse next door.'

Pel was thinking hard; they were getting nowhere very fast.
He and Pujol, frantically polishing his specs, met Big Bardolle
outside the cordoned-off surgery where he was standing chatting to the two gendarmes who'd taken the call when the
shooting had been discovered. Bardolle had once been a village
policeman himself and he got on well with members of the
gendarmerie, often easing snippets of what they considered to
be useless information out into the open when Pel's rank
terrified them into dumbness. When they saw the chief inspector stroll across the tarmac towards them, the two uniforms
immediately stood to attention.

Slowing to a stop, deep in thought, Pel extended a hand. The
gendarmes' arms hovered half-way to a salute and hesitatingly
dismissed the formality, almost missing the opportunity to
shake such an important hand. 'Okay,' Pel said, once they were
officially at ease, 'you two go and stand in the street at the
entrance to the village, and listen – I want to know what you
hear.' As they set off, he accompanied Bardolle, who was
carrying a shotgun loaded with blanks, to the surgery and told
Pujol to take up his position behind the war memorial, bellow-
ing after him, 'And stop fretting over those things! It's your
ears you should be cleaning not your goggles.'

'Don't forget,' he called to the disappearing bulk of Bardolle,
'shut all the doors except the one to the room where the
treatment was taking place.' Bardolle nodded and Pel lit up
under the gently rustling trees between the memorial and the
low whitewashed building.

He was about to remonstrate with himself that the new campaign of giving up smoking was worse than useless, perhaps he'd have to accept the consequences of heart failure, lung cancer and chronic bronchitis, and that was just for starters, when he heard two loud reports. 'Ha!' he said and turned to look back at Pujol. He gave the thumbs up but shouted, 'Only just.'

The two gendarmes were still standing idly in the middle of the street gazing towards them. Pel beckoned to them and they hurried forwards. 'Well?' he said.

They looked confused. 'Well, what, sir?'

'Well, what did you hear?'

'Oh, has it happened?'

'Didn't you hear it?' Pel yelled. 'Were you concentrating, or yapping about the girlfriend?'

'Sorry, sir,' the older one stammered, 'but we didn't hear anything.'

'Go back and we'll try again.'

They tried three times, but they still didn't hear the shots.

'Well,' Pel sighed as Bardolle emerged, 'there we have it, the triple glazing on the porch door and the entrance are extremely effective – the factory that makes them is to be congratulated. Now we know why no one heard a bloody thing!'

As the working community of the city prepared to join the bottlenecks of traffic on to the bypass, hampering their homeward journey, Darcy pushed open the door to Pel's office. He was carrying another fistful of reports. Pel glanced up and waved him into a chair, snatching up a cigarette in the same movement. 'Any news from the hospital?' he asked.

'Adrianne Fabres's husband visited her again late this afternoon but went away looking as grim as usual. She hasn't said a word, she hasn't regained consciousness.'

'Who's on duty there tonight?'

'Bardolle, he volunteered.'

'Fine.' Big Bardolle's stamina was as impressive as his physique. Pel made a note and sat back expectantly. 'Fontaine les Lacs,' he said. 'What have we learnt so far?'

'The questioning has been methodical, on foot, door to door.

We've made a good start on the electoral roll but we're four men short and it makes a surprising difference, one thousand and fifteen inhabitants takes time.'

'Stop prevaricating, Darcy, what have you turned up?'

'Nothing.' He placed the pile of papers on his desk. 'Except corns and blisters all over our feet.'

'We've got to get a sniff soon, the trail's rapidly going cold. For the rest of the week I want everyone on it, absolutely everyone.'

The following morning Pel's team assembled themselves in the sergeants' room. Weary and fed up but ready for more, they waited with anticipation for instructions. One good thing: at least it wasn't raining.

Pel arrived behind a thick cloud of blue smoke; with the situation as it was he'd temporarily given up giving up. Darcy followed him through the door. They'd been through the assignments, making the necessary adjustments to free the men involved in the less important investigations. The lists of names still to be visited were depressingly long.

Rapidly they went through the other thousand pending cases and rapidly Pel dismissed them and gave his orders. 'We've split the murder enquiry into two halves, those working here in the city or elsewhere, and those who stay by day in the village. Everyone must be found. The village itself has been divided into sectors. You will be working in pairs as usual, one asking the questions, watching for reactions, taking in details, one writing the answers, to the word, looking for hidden innuendoes. Misset, are you listening?'

Misset jumped, shot to attention and dropped his dark glasses clattering to the floor. No one sniggered. 'Sit down, you ass!' Pel said, then turned to Darcy. 'You'd better have him with you otherwise he'll fall asleep on the job.'

'Oh, thank you very much,' Darcy replied sarcastically, making the alteration on his duty roster.

Pel cleared his throat and continued addressing the room. 'Reports will of course be written before leaving the Hôtel de Police this evening while it's all still fresh in your minds. Personal observations and opinions are to be added separately, not on the official document – all I want on that is fact. Copies to the *procureur*, the *juge d'instruction* concerned, and me. I think that's about it. Hang on!' he shouted as chairs were scraped back. 'Before leaving, collect your list of names. You must ask each name, each question. No skipping, thinking you've covered it already with another member of the household. If, during your interviews, an unknown name crops up, you will add it to your own list and find that person and repeat the questions, patiently and politely. As well as the people living in the village, you will also notice the names of friends, acquaintances and clients of the two victims. Don't miss any-one, question both husband and wife, and if information is offered by children, listen. Children often notice things adults don't and have been known to eavesdrop at locked doors when they shouldn't. Telling tales is exactly what we're after.'

As Pel went back to his office, the whole team gathered their belongings together for a very long day. The only ones excused from the arduous schedule were Big Bardolle, who'd been on duty all night at Adrianne Fabres's bedside, no change; Angel-face Aimedieu, who was sitting there now; Debray, their computer expert, who could make pages of insignificant infor-mation come up with a surprising common denominator, given there was one; and Pel. He went to the airport, boarded a plane and flew to Paris to see the nurse's ex-husband, believing it was always possible he'd suddenly turned up again in Adrianne's new life. They'd divorced ten years ago, but . . .

It hadn't been difficult to find him. Crystal Combes had supplied his name from her files; Minitel had done the rest, giving two addresses, one work, one home, and two phone numbers. An efficient secretary, responding quickly to the words 'Police Judiciaire' and 'attempted murder', gave Pel an appointment at 1345.

The ex-husband, who turned out to be a specialist in plastic surgery, was busy, charming, shocked and saddened, in that order, when Pel presented himself in his office and told him why. 'It is always disagreeable to hear of anyone being shot and maimed,' he explained, 'but I haven't seen Adrianne for nine and a half years, since our divorce was final – in fact I have to confess I didn't even know where she was living, no need. We'd fallen in love, married, had three good years until Adrianne told me she was bored being a housewife and was leaving. We separated and divorced. Two years later I married

60

again. We have two children,' he added proudly. As they parted, he shook Pel's hand. 'Give her my regards. I hope she'll be out of hospital soon.'

Pel flew back to Burgundy that evening, relatively satisfied he'd had nothing to do with the shooting.

By the end of the week all the reports were in, every name on their lists had been tackled, and it brought nothing but a stronger feeling that the victims, Hugo Aynard and Adrianne Fabres, were well liked and had been happily married to their respective spouses.

Pel was tearing his hair out, what remained of it. He'd been to see the families' solicitors to find out if money was the motive and discovered the Aynards were mortaged to the hilt.

'Hugo was a nice chap but unwise in financial matters,' he was told. 'You understand I'm telling you this as a friend of his, not as his legal adviser?' Pel nodded, knowing all he was going to get was general information almost anyone could find out. 'When he moved here six years ago,' the solicitor went on, 'he was newly qualified and newly married. He had no savings and was refused a mortgage by his bank for the purchase of a house. The dental practice he was joining offered to lend him the money on very good terms and he jumped at it. Unfortunately they didn't insist on a life insurance policy to cover the loan and although I advised him to consider it, he didn't feel it necessary. They are being sympathetic, as they always were during his long illness and inability to work, but well, the debt remains. Then there's the car; the bank agreed to lend him enough for that just before his kidney trouble started. Most of the interest has been paid but the capital remains and must be reimbursed. From what he said, the bank isn't being as nice about it – he came to me to see if I could do anything in view of his fragile condition. Unfortunately I couldn't. He signed the contract, and where money is concerned there are no mitigating circumstances. His poor wife must be very worried.' It was probably the understatement of the year.

The Fabres's solicitor, after a certain amount of bullying, had finally stated, 'I cannot give you details of a will in Adrianne Fabres's name because one does not exist, therefore, if she dies,

61

it will be her next of kin who inherits.' Pel had assumed that meant her husband, Alain, but he was wrong. 'They are not married,' he was told. 'Fabres is Adrianne's maiden name which she reverted to after her divorce. Alain Fabres was also born with that name, you know how common it is, there are more Fabres in the phone book than Duponts. I suppose there is no harm in telling you that her parents were killed in a car accident many years ago and the only surviving relative is an older brother. He lives in Canada.' So it wasn't a question of large bequests.

'If only the nurse would recover sufficiently to talk,' Pel scowled at Darcy. 'Surely she'd tell us something useful, if not exactly who was holding the sodding gun.'

'Or if we could find the sodding gun.' Darcy had just come from the hospital, seeing his brand new family, and being a conscientious man had dropped into Intensive Care for the latest on Adrianne Fabres. She was still teetering between life and death and, as he'd left, the surgeon had told him they would be making another attempt to remove the remaining lead pellets clustered dangerously close to her heart.

'They're operating again this evening. Let's hope after that there'll be a definite improvement and we'll be able to question her, because for all our efforts Fontaine les Lacs is not revealing its secrets.'

As Pel closed the file on his desk for the day and struggled into his coat, the phone rang. He hesitated before answering. It was Angelface Aimedieu. 'Sorry, *patron*,' he said sadly, 'we no longer have a witness. Adrianne Fabres died a few moments ago. They were getting her ready to go to theatre and there was a sudden panic, people running in all directions. Ten minutes later it was all over, she never said a word.'

Pel sighed. 'Come home,' he said. 'You've got some typing to do.' He replaced the phone and sat heavily back in his chair. They'd waited ten days for the nurse to speak. Now she was dead, the only chance remaining was that an autopsy would reveal something they didn't know.

When he arrived home, his wife recognised the signs of strain and gestured to Madame Routy to disappear. While she accepted that their continual war was necessary, perhaps even good for them both, most of the time, there were days when an amnesty had to be declared and Pel protected. She knew, as did the whole of France, of the brutal shooting of a nurse and her patient at Fontaine les Lacs thanks to the television crew who'd filmed there, but Madame, unlike the general public, knew her Pel and, because of this, suspected that that wasn't all, that there was something odd about the case that left him silently thoughtful throughout his evenings at home. She served him a drink and sat on the arm of the chair beside him. He sipped, slipping his hand round her waist. 'It's a nasty one,' he confided. 'Things are not what they seem.' She smoothed the remains of his hair into neat lines, unconcerned that her husband's head was going bald; it was what went on inside that fascinated her.

'Why does a woman make a pass at another man?' he asked, thinking of attractive Adrianne Fabres going cold in the hospital morgue.

'Boredom,' his wife replied immediately.

'Explain.' He was looking interested.

'In my experience,' which was considerable, running as she did the most fashionable and expensive hair salon cum beauty parlour in the city; for some reason, when her clients paid vast amounts of money for her services, they also had a habit of confiding their innermost secrets, 'when we're young we dream of being swept off our feet by our hero – tall, dark and handsome, short, blond and cuddly – we all have our own idea of what he's going to look like. I imagine men have the same sort of dreams, *n'est ce pas*? Carole Bouquet, Sharon Stone, Kim Bassinger. Eventually we get married for one reason or another, most of us have children and that's it, the rest of our lives stretch out in front of us filled with weeks and months identical to last year, the same as next; half the year saving up for Christmas, the other half saving up for the summer holidays. The couple know each other well and don't make the same effort as they did at first, compliments are forgotten, manners slide, they live almost on automatic pilot. One day someone gives them a wink and hey, presto! They come alive again. It's flattering, exciting, daring – also, if you ask me, damned stupid, but that, according to my clients, is the way it goes.'

'But women who have everything,' Pel asked, remembering the Fabres' expensive home, 'is it the same for them?'

63

'Probably worse. They don't have to struggle to feed the family, pay the rent, they have no real goal, life can be simply an amusing game.'

Pel thought about it: his wife was probably right, she usually was. Then he frowned. *Nom de Dieu*! Had she been dropping hints about his lack of attention? 'Geneviève, *mon coeur*, I'll try harder.'

She laughed out loud and kissed him affectionately. 'Oh, Pel! Don't worry, boredom is one thing I shall never suffer from. You can be quite a handful at times, my dear, even infuriating, but never boring!'

He smiled, then wondered whether he should – his wife had accused him of being infuriating. He went on smiling, he liked being infuriating, and apparently, wonder of wonders, she still loved him. He wasn't quite sure how it had happened. Personally he wouldn't have given himself house room.

Adrianne Fabres's body was delivered to the pathologist's white-tiled rooms early the following morning and Cham, along with Boudet, set about their gruesome dissection. When the bells of the city's churches chimed midday, they were ready to reveal their findings to Pel.

He snatched up his Gauloises as soon as he saw them and puffed without guilt as he listened to the doctors' report: '. . . frothy fluid in the air passages . . . yellow in the chest . . . orange in the lungs . . . leakage of stomach contents into . . .' Pel inhaled deeply. '. . . led to infection and in spite of subsequent treatment it spread to the liver and pericardial sac.'

Pel exhaled, glad it was over. 'So she died of an infection that developed in hospital,' he said absently.

Cham's eyes flashed. 'No,' he corrected firmly. 'When she was admitted to hospital, she was dying from the gunshot wounds. Surgery was undertaken in the hope of saving her life, such as it may have been. Our autopsy showed that this surgery was carried out correctly, everything was done that was humanly possible to maintain life, but her wounds were too devastating, the vital organs too damaged. She was riddled with pellets. We removed many more during the post-mortem

64

from her chest, particularly around her heart. Although they showed up on the X-rays they were practically impossible to find in the operating theatre because they were embedded in swollen tissue. I want there to be no misunderstanding,' he went on cautiously, 'particularly for the lawyers later, the hospital worked near miracles. They are to be congratulated, not blamed. Her death certificate will show,' he ended, 'death from complications arising from wounds caused by gunshot.'

Pel nodded, understanding his caution. 'Thank you for being so thorough,' he said magnanimously. 'It's more or less what I expected.'

'There's more!' Cham exclaimed. 'Not that it'll change much but you ought to know.'

'If it's more of your guts and bile, I think I'd rather read it.'

'No, nothing like that but interesting all the same,' Cham reassured him. 'Adrianne Fabres had undergone a hysterectomy, her uterus was absent.'

'When?'

'Difficult to be precise, but more than ten years ago. The method of incision was revised around then, hers was – '

Pel interrupted, 'So that's why they didn't have children.'

'And she had also undergone quite a lot of plastic surgery.'

Hardly surprising, she'd been married to a bloke specialising in it, Pel thought and flicked his cigarette at the overflowing ashtray, sprinkling cinders on to the carpet. He stamped at them, hoping to avoid a full-scale fire.

'She'd had a silicone implant in her breasts,' Cham went on, wrinkling his nose at the acrid smell of smouldering nylon. 'I don't think you've put it out properly.'

Pel stamped again, then, collecting the bottle of water from his desk, poured a good measure on to the floor.

'And,' Cham continued, amused, 'she'd had liposuction performed on her thighs and buttocks.'

'Lip what? Explain.'

'A process for removing cellulite, excess fat, an expensive way of slimming. She also had a torn earlobe but that must've been the ear-ring Aynard was holding. Anyway, there you are,' he said, placing the report on Pel's desk. 'It's all in black and white if you want to read it for yourself.'

'What about the wound?' Pel asked, dropping a handful of blotting paper into the puddle underneath his desk. 'Can you tell me her exact position when she was shot?'

'As we thought, she was facing her patient. She must have lifted her left arm to protect herself and turned slightly away from her killer. The gun was lower than the wound.'

'So if our murderer wasn't used to handling a gun, the first shot was fired without proper aim being taken.' Pel gave up on the mess at his feet. Disgusted, he lit another cigarette. 'He quite obviously intended killing them but it looks as if the gun went off sooner than he expected. Aynard was dispatched immediately afterwards from shoulder height.'

It was a double murder. The houses, offices and cars of the two grieving spouses had already been searched, in case – in spite of what they'd said – the gun had been hidden there, or the cartridges disposed of. So far they were the only suspects, doubtful ones at that.

On instructions from the Chief Prosecutor, they were now brought to police headquarters. In the presence of the Chief of Police, the examining magistrate and Pel himself, they were extensively interviewed; it was hoped that this would intimidate them sufficiently to put them on edge and cause them to make a mistake. Through their tears, they repeated everything and more, cursing the police's inquisitiveness, denying their insinuations, and finally in Aynard's case, threatening legal action if they weren't allowed to mourn in peace. Their misery spread through the corridors of the Hôtel de Police and a feeling of sadness settled in the offices. Catching criminals was all very well but hounding men and women who had lost their loved ones was gruelling.

Ten days later they had no further information, no gun, no other suspects, and the mourning families were seen to be gradually pulling themselves together and carrying on as normally as possible.

By then the police knew the deceased well; they'd been admired and respected by the community in which they lived, no one had a word to say against them.

'It's odd, isn't it?' Darcy said as he and Pel leafed yet again through all the statements that had been taken. 'When it was suggested that there had been deviations in their lives, we were met with disbelief, or at most a shrug of the shoulders.'

Pel studied the comments his men had copied carefully on to paper. ' "I suppose that sort of thing does go on but not them," ' he read out loud. ' "She was a nurse!" "He was dying, poor man! You only had to look at him, a walking skeleton." "No, not them." ' He tossed the statements on to his desk. 'It's ridiculous!' he said. 'No one's that nice!'

Darcy sighed. 'In a way, you know, it's heartening to find village tongues stilled for once and the vicious gossip non-existent – usually they revel in it.'

'But it doesn't help us much, does it?' Their enquiry had come to a dead halt.

6

The Chief wasn't pleased. He called Pel to his office as the April showers turned into comforting May warth. An ex-champion boxer, he was an impressive man, uncomfortable trying to fit into other people's furniture which was always too small or too frail to hold him, but very comfortable fitting into his role as Chief of Police in a big bustling city. Most of the time. Pel could, if he tried really hard, make the Chief weep, but while he was a difficult little bugger, he was an excellent policeman. Thanks to Pel, their crime statistics were among the best in the country, if not the best, which was good, it meant Monsieur le Procureur left him to get on with his job without too much finger-wagging and interference. However, his job was coming to an end, his retirement was due at the end of the year, and when asked to nominate a successor he had naturally proposed Pel; he was the obvious replacement. The Chief was somewhat amused by the raised eyebrows and exclamations, although he was less jovial when persuading the powers that be it was truly no typing error.

When the shooting at Fontaine les Lacs had occurred, pro-fessional eyes had turned in Pel's direction to watch his handling of the case. To the Chief's relief there'd been no blunders, not even Misset had put his foot in it, and for a while everything had gone as it should have. However, time had slipped by, it was now over a month old and still there had been no arrest. The Procureur had mentioned it again that morning, and it had been the subject of conversation at a public dinner the previous evening. Very soon Monsieur le Ministre de la Justice would be sticking his nose in. And then there'd be real trouble.

Pel pushed open the door, puffing peacefully on a Gauloise, doing his impression of a steam train shunting into a siding.

'How's it going?' the Chief asked hopefully.

'It's not.' Pel was short and to the point.

'The Public Prosecutor is impatient for an arrest.'

'Aren't we all,' Pel agreed. 'Unfortunately what Monsieur le Procureur doesn't seem to realise is that to make an arrest we have to have some idea who did it and that involves more than sticking a pin blindly into a list of suspects.'

'The local elections are making everyone rather edgy. Promotions are being considered – he was intending to second my proposals, but he informs me he must now hesitate.'

'So let him hesitate.' Pel shrugged. 'I don't have the time to worry about the bleatings of officialdom waving its little flag.'

'This case could affect your future.'

'Every case affects my future,' Pel growled, 'and my health!' He stubbed out his cigarette viciously and reached into his pocket for another to prove his point. 'This case is no more or less important than any other murder case, tell that to Monsieur le Procureur. Remind him that a kid of sixteen was dumped on a bloody freezing night at the Roman dig, with her head bashed in, and when she was found a fortnight later, she was stone cold and extremely dead. On his instructions, we temporarily shelved that enquiry to work on the shooting at Fontaine les Lacs. Tell Monsieur le Procureur we're doing our best, but there are only so many hours in a day and only so many days in the week, so while he has the time to hesitate over a signature or two, I and my men are still out tramping the streets.' He sucked hungrily on the end of his cigarette. 'In fact,' he went on, 'you can tell Monsieur le Procureur he can go and boil his head as far as I'm concerned.' The Chief sighed. Sometimes Pel was his own worst enemy.

As Pel left the Hôtel de Police that evening he was in a foul mood. Interfering officials who sat on their fat backsides chewing the ends of their expensive fountain pens wondering, To sign or not to sign, that is the question, should be flogged, nothing like a good flogging to bring a man to a quick decision. He stopped at the bottom of the steps to sniff: summer was on its way! Through his gloom, the smell of newly planted geraniums filtered. He wrinkled his nose, frowning – there was no mistake, it was geraniums and newly turned earth, and looking up and down the street he could see the balls of colour hanging from the many iron lamp posts.

'A demain, patron.' Nosjean's voice was dull as he bid his boss good evening and set off down the road. For a moment Pel watched his hunched shoulders as he weaved his way through the lingering pedestrians. There was something up with Nosjean; he no longer reminded him of a young Napoleon on the Bridge at Lodi – more like Napoleon after his defeat at Waterloo. Pel sighed as he turned in the opposite direction. Fatherhood didn't suit Nosjean; the second pregnancy had ended after three tricky months, adding further complications to their already faltering marriage. Nosjean and Mijo were not the happy young couple they had been.

It was almost with a hop, skip and jump that Pel arrived at his car, unlocked it, started its engine and kangaroo-hopped out into the crawling traffic. All evil thoughts concerning public prosecutors had been abandoned. He was feeling smug; his marriage had survived far longer than he'd expected, and looked like surviving a great deal longer. He smiled to himself, swerved, narrowly missing a bicycle – yes, he decided, he was definitely getting the hang of it after . . . how many years? He couldn't remember and, realising it was entirely due to his wife's good nature and intelligence that they were still married, he huffily shook a cigarette from the packet beside him, lost two down the side of the seat and finally managed to light up, flapping a hand wildly as he attempted to clear the blue fog that now obscured the windscreen.

*

69

The April showers had set the farmers complaining about floods and crop failure; the hot May sun that followed made them talk of drought and crop failure. When June arrived the schools prepared for the end of a year exams, while parents prepared themselves for the long summer holidays, and local politicians churned out pamphlets and posters, generally wasting a great deal of paper. The farmers were still complaining but less noisily – June was a busy month, spraying the vineyards against insect infestation, de-weeding the alleyways between the rows of baby grapes, servicing the harvesters in readiness – and Pel was creating merry hell at the morning meeting.

'. . . don't think just because everyone else is preparing for a month at the seaside that you can ease up! I've seen you gazing lovingly at the calendar and your allotted patches of pleasure – well, it's not on! I want results, at least one or two!'

'The bank robbery was a success,' Darcy pointed out. 'We got them all. Coming up for trial in September, an open and shut case.'

'Nothing's an open and shut case!'

'And the supermarket at Talant,' he went on, 'we got them too.'

'It's not enough!'

'*Patron*, be fair, for once there isn't a great deal left. As usual, it's slowly going quiet for the sweaty season.'

'That's just why I want action! The blighters pack their bags and leave to do their dirty business elsewhere. It's now we need to pounce, while they're not expecting it. Be vigilant as they spread the suntain oil on their despicable bodies, welcome them home from the hols with a nice arrest and a long stay behind bars.'

The team sighed inwardly. Life was never easy with Pel. They'd be aching, irritable and exhausted before leaving for a short break with the wife and kids, so aching they'd be unable to play football on the beach with their sons, so irritable they'd shout at their daughters, and so exhausted they'd be incapable of making love to their wives. What a life!

They still had a million and one minor crimes on the books: frauds and swindles, marital bliss coming to blows, poison pen letters, neighbourly jealousies, commercial antagonism, robberies and pilfering, nothing unusual, plus of course the stiff found at Alesia by the archaeologists, and the double shooting at Fontaine les Lacs.

While chasing round the countryside for information that might lead to another arrest, the members of Pel's team, and Pel himself, regularly stopped in or around the village. It was beginning to look very pretty with the summer flowers, their startling fluorescent colours blooming from thousands of window boxes lining the streets. The gay parasols were out on the pavements in front of the two bars where they would sometimes drink a well-deserved beer. More often than not they just browsed, antennae up, in the hope that something would turn up, an unguarded comment, a memory that had surfaced, a child's chatter that contained a hint, but all they found were shops revving up for the season, full of trinkets and souvenirs for the swarms of tourists that would make their pilgrimage to the edge of the lakes – the community was looking forward to another bumper summer raking in the money. And of course the sycophantic faces of candidates hoping to be elected to the local councils smiled sickeningly down from the newly erected hoardings.

The only thing of any interest was that Marie-Hélène Aynard had put her house on the market and was looking for something cheaper. Pel went to see her with Pujol in tow. She looked exhausted; her hair was hanging unwashed round her face as she heaved a huge basket of washing on to the kitchen table. 'I just can't afford to stay here,' she told them miserably. 'I can't pay off the loan. They've been patient, ever so patient, but the repayments will cripple me.' She started folding tiny underclothes into piles in front of them. 'I've got two little girls and only a part-time job. The *allocations familiales* help now I'm on my own but it's not enough. I'm in debt up to my ears. I can't go on like this.' She sat down with a bump and hid her strained face behind her hands.

A few days later Nosjean, his unhappy marriage still causing him to frown, told Pel he'd seen Alain Fabres driving around in a smart BMW. The Préfecture had confirmed he'd sold his second-hand Audi and his deceased wife's new Peugeot.

'Nothing will replace my wife,' he said, inviting Pel in for a drink that evening, 'but there was no point in having two cars sitting in the drive to remind me every time I came or went that I'd never see her again.' It was an acceptable explanation but even so the following morning Pel bought a copy of *Argus* magazine to look up the prices of BMWs. He nearly fell off his chair when he discovered they cost up to 770,000 francs depending on the model. He telephoned the Préfecture to check the *carte grise* in Fabres's name. They informed him the new vehicle was a two-year-old 525. Turning to the relevant page of *Argus* again, he found it was worth approximately 100,000 francs which appeared to be far more reasonable considering the almost new Peugeot would have been traded in at well over half that amount, the Audi practically making up the rest. He slipped his notes into the file and closed it again.

The murder of young Patti was still unsolved. While her file remained unchanged, Pel's men hadn't given up; they went in turns for a stroll round the Roman remains, chatting to the men and women engaged in carefully uncovering the foundations of the dwelling of the soldiers of Julius Cesar. When the body had been found it hadn't been easy for the police or Forensics to make their usual searches, hampered as they were by history. 'Julius Cesar was defeated in 52 BC,' it was pointed out to Pel, 'therefore you must appreciate what we're dealing with here.' 'And I'm dealing with a murder,' he'd roared but it hadn't helped much.

Nosjean in particular found a strange peace pottering between the crates of carefully packed and labelled fragments of ancient pottery, silently staring out over the surrounding green fields that stretched lazily towards woodland, the dipping valleys and the horizon touching a deep blue sky, asking himself philosophical questions about life and death, origins and eternity, marriage and men, particularly policemen with discontented wives. He loved Mijo but didn't know how to help her. When he got home in the evening what he wanted was a kiss, a cold beer and a cuddle with his daughter, not 'You're late, your supper's in the oven, Erika and I are going to bed.' He was tired of her complaints, justified though they were, tired of sitting alone at the kitchen table eating a lukewarm meal, tired of not daring to switch on the television for an hour's relaxation in case the noise would disturb his sleeping family on the other side of the paper thin walls of their tiny flat. By the time he'd walked round the Roman ruins, he was tired of his own problems and inevitably began pondering the down-to-earth puzzle that sat on the site like a ghost: why had someone beaten up a sixteen-year-old girl and dumped her there to die?

And Misset, caught nodding off at his desk, had been handed the list of members of Le Peuple de Soleil et Lumière and told to check them. Although the Main Ray, Viguier, had kept his promise and sent them on fairly quickly, no one had had time before. However, it suited Misset nicely. Taking the list down to the computer room, he spent a couple of days with one of the girls going through their records. After that, he would take it to the Préfecture and do the same. Then the Hôtel de Ville – the Mayor's secretaries were quite accommodating. In fact, if he worked it well, with refreshments in his favourite bars to revive him, he could spin his bit of research out for the rest of the summer.

They weren't a bad bunch, Pel thought, signing his team's time sheets, noting the extra unpaid hours every one of them spent poking about. Even Misset seemed occupied. They only needed stirring up occasionally. He could trust them while he took a few days' well-deserved break – after all, he reasoned, he'd already postponed it twice. Darcy'll hold the fort. They're basically a hard-working lot of blokes, even Annie and the Hugenot, Jourdain, although she still looked as if she'd been playing with electricity.

He slipped out of the building by a back door and walked into the sultry city. At nine in the morning it was already hot, not unbearably so as it would be in July and August, but hot enough to make Pel run a finger round the inside of his collar and wish he'd put on a lighter jacket. He strode along the pavement with one thing in mind. In the early morning lull he'd decided now was the moment; if he left it till later, the day would take off leaving him gasping for breath and trying to catch it up, and tomorrow would be too late. Tomorrow he was going over the mountains.

He stopped outside his favourite tobacconist's, looked left and right to make sure no one was watching, and slipped into its cool interior.

'Monsieur Pel! I expected I'd be seeing you soon.' The shopkeeper greeted him like a long-lost brother. 'Now is the season. I've got everything you'll need, come into the back and see my beauties.' Pel followed the enthusiastic man into a small room containing large refrigerators. 'There, look at them!' He opened the lid and lifted out a tub of squirming maggots. 'Fresh today! Will you want red ones or white, or perhaps a cocktail of both?'

Pel gave his order and turned to browse amongst the rods. He was sorely tempted to buy a new one. A week's fishing could be harrowing if his neighbour caught more than him, and he usually did. He selected one that looked most likely to win, added a reel to it on the counter, chose the fluorescent line, the books of hooks, half a dozen spare floats and a couple of packets of sweet-smelling powder to tempt the prey towards their trap, 'and two hundred cigarettes, you know the brand,' he said as the happy face behind the counter rang each item up on the till.

Going back into the street, he was scowling at the small coins in his hand. 'I've been robbed,' he muttered, adjusting the carrier bag on his arm.

7

They got off to an early start with Pasquier at the wheel. While Pel didn't trust teenage drivers he had to admit his own efforts with a car were a public danger and perhaps Yves would be less hazardous to the other motorists. And soon he wouldn't be a teenager, about to turn twenty any minute, sensible young chap, studying medicine, bright and intelligent. And good-looking, lots of blond wavy hair, Pel's looked like seaweed stranded on a rock at low tide. Yves didn't wear glasses. And he was tall and slim. Within the first five minutes of their journey Pel had decided that if he didn't like his next-door neighbour as much as he did, he'd dislike him intensely.

74

They sped off down the motorway under a clear blue sky, arriving in the foothills of the Pyrenees in comfortable time to find a cheap hotel for the night. Because of the excellent weather they decided not to take the tunnel the following morning but to carry on along the frontier and cross the mountains by a smaller road, hence benefiting from the extravagant views they were bound to see as they ascended to almost three thousand metres and descended the other side into Spain.

By lunchtime they were crawling through thick fog fighting to see the road in the dipped headlights. They hadn't passed another car for over an hour. Yves squinted through the windscreen and braked suddenly to let a herd of wandering sheep cross the road. Pel lit yet another cigarette and glared at the stupid animals, who were preparing to settle down on the tarmac for a communal siesta. A little further they discovered a couple of pigs wandering about on the white line, round and pink and totally unconcerned at their arrival. Then they came upon a crowd of ramblers who appeared to be having an argument on a dangerous bend, maps and arms making waves in the swirling fog. 'I think I preferred the sheep,' Pel commented as the hiking boots and bobble hat brigade resentfully cleared a path for them to pass. 'Or the pigs,' he added.

Not much further on, Yves stopped again. 'Sorry, Pel, need to take a leak.' The two men climbed out of the car into the cold grey clouds that curled menacingly around them.

Pel stood by the vehicle while Yves climbed over some rocks towards a trickling stream, and when he turned back to the car he nearly jumped out of his skin. He let out a shriek which brought Yves scurrying down the loose shale. 'What in heaven's the matter?' he said anxiously as Pel clutched his heart and panted.

'Bloody cow crept up on me. I turned round and we were face to face.'

They caught the cow up shortly afterwards; she was plodding nonchalantly along the verge going at almost the same speed as them. Pel waved his fist and reached for a Gauloise.

Two hours later they were at last below the obliterating clouds, and an intense sunlight blinded them as they gazed down on to an empty plain. 'It looks like a flipping desert,' Pel said. 'Not a house in sight.'

However, there were a few ramshackle villages and they at last found a bar willing to feed the weary travellers. Then the holiday really started. They unpacked their fishing tackle and spent the rest of the afternoon playing with small silver fish in a splendid turquoise river. Pel relaxed, believing life was worth living after all.

That evening they found a restaurant that looked as if it would have rooms to rent and settled themselves for a rest.

'I'd give my right arm for a cold beer,' Pel said, leaning back in his chair.

'This is Spain,' Yves said. 'I'm having sangria.'

When the waitress came to take their order, she naturally didn't understand a word of French. Although Pel tried all the words he knew for beer in various languages, she shook her head, unable to grasp what he was getting at. In exasperation he led her to the bar and pointed to an advert for Kronenbourg. 'Ah,' she said at last, *'cervesa!'*

'Good God,' he muttered as he came back to the table. 'I've been about a bit, never had any trouble before, trust the Spanish to have a word that doesn't remotely resemble *bière*.'

Yves efficiently ordered an adequate meal and Pel began looking forward to a good night's sleep. But there were no rooms. At midnight in desperation Yves pulled into the parking lot of a Quick Palace Motel. All they needed was a credit card to gain entrance. Pel refused to do business with a machine so Yves did the honours, acquiring not only entrance but the codes needed to open their rooms.

He was peacefully pulling the covers up to his chin when an urgent knock came on his door. Struggling out of bed, he opened up to find Pel standing forlornly in the corridor.

'Forgot the code,' he said simply. 'Went for a pee and I can't get back in my bloody room.'

On their second night in Spain, after a peaceful day's fishing on the edge of a bright blue lagoon, they wandered into a town to find a traditional hotel for the night and came upon a funeral procession. It seemed as if the whole district had turned out. Leading the crowd were three priests, two small elderly men either side of a much taller, younger man who looked ill at ease in his robes. He shrugged from time to time, resettling the heavy gold-encrusted chasuble square on his shoulders. Behind them the coffin followed, supported on sturdy shoulders and surrounded by weeping women, their heads bent under black mantillas: then lastly the men, clasping hats to their chests, trailed off into the distance.

Pel and Yves removed their battered hats respectfully to watch. As the priests disappeared into the candlelit interior of the church they began chanting, and the mourning townspeople took up the hymn until the street was filled with the tragic song of death. Then the heavy doors closed with an echoing bang, shutting the two foreigners out.

Yves pushed Pel along the street. He knew him too well – watching funerals could lead to discovering things about the deceased, which may lead to Pel scratching his head, turning obstinate, if not plain bloody-minded, and insisting on asking a lot of questions, and that would be the end of their fishing trip.

They crossed the wide dusty square and in spite of the sorrow that inhabited the town found a small hotel open for business. It was a scruffy place but as it was the only one available, they decided to make do with the room they were offered. It had two single beds and further along the dark corridor they found the communal bathroom badly in need of a dose of disinfectant.

Yves took in the torn wallpaper and stains round the ill-fitting windows. He grinned, pulling at the stiff grey sheets. 'Hope there aren't bugs in the bed.'

At three in the morning, Pel turned over yet again, setting the springs under him twanging muscially. 'If they don't shut up soon,' he muttered, 'I'll damn well fetch the *guardia civile*.'

While the women from the funeral party had slipped off into the shadows, the men had congregated outside for a long discussion. Gradually they'd filtered into the bar below to argue. Pel couldn't make out what the animosity was about but it got louder as the night grew older. Cars and motor bikes buzzed raucously to and from the square, always accompanied by raised voices, then a fight broke out downstairs; a couple of tables were overturned and glasses crashed to the floor. Shouting, the barman threw everyone out and to make his point released the metal shutter that sealed the entrance. It rattled down, making the building tremble as it crashed to the ground, but the argument continued outside until at long last, probably just before dawn, Pel suspected, the town went quiet. Five minutes later a delivery lorry turned up and the driver leant on the bell, yelling for help with the unloading of his crates. Pel counted the crates as they were pushed, dragged and kicked on to the premises. When he got to ten, he threw back his sheet, shot out of bed and threw open the shutters, letting the glaring sunlight pour into the room. '*Je me casse!*' he snapped at the slumbering body of Yves Pasquier, and pulling on his clothes he left, slamming the door behind him.

When Yves joined him downstairs, he was sulkily sipping at a large cup of coffee and toying with an enormous croissant. 'Sleep well, did you?'

Pel scowled. 'Shut up and listen!' he hissed.

Yves did as he was told, accepting with pleasure what the barman put in front of him. There seemed to be a row going on. A small bent old man was taking the brunt of it. The other three men, and the barman, were calling him all the names under the sun. The old man bellowed insults back at them.

It looked as if it would develop into another scuffle when the men abruptly fell silent, turning towards the door as a large silhouette made its way out of the sun-filled square into the bar.

'The priest,' Yves whispered.

He was even taller than he'd appeared on the day before. No longer wearing his ceremonial robes, he was nonetheless dressed in black from head to foot, a charcoal grey cardigan draped casually over his broad shoulders. The barman served him coffee as he pulled a high stool up to the counter and perched to drink it. Still no one had spoken. He clanked his cup into its saucer, took a packet from his trouser pocket and placed a cigarette in his mouth. Three lighters clicked into action.

'You are a fool!' he said to the old man. 'When will you learn to keep your trap shut?'

The old man shuffled backwards. 'You of all people should believe me.'

'I, of all people, refuse to listen to your fantasies and fiction. You watch too many cheap films late at night. Vampires indeed! The poor child died of asphyxia, you heard the judge as well as I did, she choked on her own vomit!'

Pel paid the bill and, gathering his overnight bag up, he pushed Yves towards the door. 'Did you hear that?'

They sat in the car going over what they'd heard, making sure they weren't mistaken.

'So what?' Yves asked. 'You're on holiday.' He had a sneaking suspicion Pel was about to become disastrously involved. 'And anyway, this is Spain,' he said more firmly. 'It's nothing to do with you.'

'Follow me.' Pel climbed out and set off at a trot. The priest had come out of the bar and was walking away. Pel went in hot pursuit.

He followed the priest into his church and waited silently as he knelt in prayer. Yves came to a stop, wondering what the hell they were up to. When the priest rose at last, Pel stepped forward. 'Father,' he said quietly, 'may I speak with you?' He beckoned to Yves. 'Listen carefully, I may need you to translate,' he said.

'Well?' Pel asked as they left the town. 'What did you find out?'

'I found out that you speak Spanish a damn sight better than you let on. All that fuss about ordering a beer!'

'I wasn't concentrating.' Pel waved his objection aside. 'Tell me what you heard in the church. I want to be sure I got it right.'

Yves changed gear. 'He said the funeral was of a sixteen-year-old girl. Her dead body had been found by a shepherd who brought it down to the town. The police say she died of asphyxia after vomiting as a result of alcohol, but the old boy – who's a cleaner of some sort, *non*?'

'That doesn't matter, go on.'

'The old boy saw the body while it was waiting to be embalmed. He said her neck had the mark of the devil on it. That was where Father Lopez raised his voice and said it wasn't the mark of the devil, the silly old fool, he's off his rocker, always preaching death and doom, the end of the world is nigh. Now he believes in vampires and is trying to persuade them to open the tomb and hammer a wooden stake through the girl's heart to stop her becoming a zombie.'

'You've missed a bit out.'

'Which bit?'

'The bit when the priest was called to the morgue to give the girl his goodbye speech, forgiving her all her sins, remember?'

'Oh yes, hang on, let me get past this lorry.'

Pel waited with a frown on his face then, as Yves eased his foot from the accelerator, he turned expectantly to him.

'That's better, at least I can see where I'm going. So, he was called to do his stuff and saw the mark with his own eyes. He said even though he told the old man to shut up about it, it was quite obviously a human bite. He said he could have almost counted the teeth.'

'That's what I thought,' Pel said, satisfied.

While Yves fished, Pel said he wanted to catch up on last night's lost sleep. He lay back on the stony beach on the edge of the river and closed his eyes. From time to time he'd sit up and stare into the water and Yves knew he wasn't resting, there was something troubling him, something that would mean the long journey back to Burgundy would be spent in silence with only the occasional halt to phone the Hôtel de Police. He could almost hear Pel's brain whirring and he knew it wouldn't stop until he'd solved his puzzle. Resigning himself to the inevitable, he reeled in his line, packed up his rod and collected his paraphernalia together. 'Come on, Pel. If we set off now and drive through the night, you'll be in the office tomorrow morning.'

8

'De Troq' can't be on holiday! He's the only one that speaks fluent Spanish!' Pel yelled. 'I rang and told you to stop him!'

'I tried, *patron*,' Misset replied dully, 'but all I got was the answerphone.'

Pel went purple with rage. 'You mean to say that you left a

message?' The words hissed through clenched teeth. 'You prize idiot! Get out of my sight!'

Misset slipped from the silence hanging heavily over the sergeants' room. For a moment no one spoke as Pel simmered, then he turned on his heel and the room seemed to breathe again.

'Look where you're going!' Pel bellowed, bouncing back after colliding with someone in the corridor. It was Baron Charles de Troquereau de Tournay-Turenne, their impoverished aristocrat. 'You're supposed to be on holiday!'

'Jourdain found me as I was leaving last night,' de Troq' explained. 'She caught up with me as I was about to take a ticket from the motorway machine.' He smiled graciously at the girl. 'She drives likes Alain Prost.'

Pel whirled round. 'Why didn't you tell me?'

The Huguenot didn't flinch. 'You didn't give me a chance, sir! I had the idea from your brief call that there was a panic on, so I set off to find him, sir!'

Pel sighed. 'Thank God for women,' he said, still boiling, 'and stop calling me sir! Now,' he went on more calmly to de Troq', 'the Spanish vampire.'

De Troq' followed Pel into his office, calling for Darcy as he went, and by midday the police and pathologist's reports relating to the dead girl in Spain had been faxed into the Hôtel de Police in Dijon. De Troq' collected the papers together and went directly to the Puppy's desk. The Puppy's name was Rigal, but he had earned his nickname as a result of his constant cringing whenever their boss shouted, which was most of the time. Pel retaliated by telling him to go back to his basket. In an effort to become invisible, Rigal answered phones and practised his typing, much to the pleasure of men like Big Bardolle, who had hands like shovels, far too large for the new electric keyboards, far too large in fact for any keyboard; hence the Puppy was a whizz with the word processor.

While de Troq' translated the text into French, Rigal's nimble fingers flew across the keys.

Pel put down Patti's file and studied the resulting document with interest. 'They were the same age,' he said to de Troq', 'our cadaver at the Roman dig and the girl Gomez, and they both had savage love bites. Take these over to Doc Cham for a medical comparison.' He handed him the Spanish photographs. 'He may have some comment to make.'

As de Troq' disappeared, Pel heaved himself to his feet, lit a cigarette, forgetting it was too early to smoke, and went to seek vengeance for his interrupted holiday on some unsuspecting victim. But he couldn't find Misset anywhere. He wandered down the corridor thinking hard and, finding himself near the room where Debray worked, he thought he might as well find out how their computer buff was doing. He crashed through the door and came to a halt by his chair.

'Busy collating information turned up on Le Peuple de Soleil et Lumière, *patron*.' He didn't turn round, the blue cloud of Gauloise smoke had effectively announced his superior's arrival. 'The Sunshine and Light lot whose naked dancing girls disturbed your pig-killing peasant.' Pel coughed, collecting his thoughts. He'd forgotten about them. He'd read the report Cheriff had handed him in March; apparently there'd been nothing illegal going on at the sect and he'd added it to his out-tray having marked it 'Check history and for criminal records in membership list, then no further action.'

'Not much to tell really,' Debray went on. 'It was established relatively recently in Holland, spreading to Belgium and France last summer. They sent out disciples and an association was declared in Paris on 13th June that year, so it's legal, they have the right to preach and recruit. So far it's a small organisation with only a few hundred members in each country, nothing like the Moonies or the Krishna tribes, but it's growing. They hope to spread the Light throughout the world. Viguier, the Main Ray here, was in Holland with them when his elderly uncle died and left him the farm at Pont le Vieux. He suggested setting up a community. Naturally they agreed – until then they only had a small settlement near St Dizier up north. Viguier is a graduate of French Literature at the Sorbonne; he was a teacher for a couple of years until he dropped out. There was nothing official but I dug up a couple of hiccups in his career. He offered private tutoring to one of his students. He wasn't paid, claiming he only wanted to help the girl succeed in her *baccalauréat*, but her father stopped it, he didn't like her going to his flat.'

'Is that all?'

'Yes. The girl left school the following year with a good *bac* and the subject was dropped. On a second occasion the parents found a diary and discovered their shy seventeen-year-old daughter was in love with her teacher, Viguier. He denied making any advances but again there was a question mark left over the incident. He left the school after a third girl, known as a women's rights militant, claimed he'd tried to seduce her. Naturally he denied it but he disappeared in a matter of days, leaving everyone to draw their own conclusions. He turned up in Holland a few years later with a band of wanderers – hippies, I suppose you'd call them. That was when he became involved in the People of Sunshine and Light.'

'What do they do?' Pel asked. He had little regard for people who needed a sect to give them confidence.

'They worship the sun, believing its heat is the centre of life and love. They preach the word believing it will bring light to our darkened planet.'

Pel flicked ash into Debray's empty paper cup. 'How jolly,' he said gloomily. 'Nothing more exciting than that?'

'Their worship of the sun is done by dancing naked . . .'

'What a surprise.'

'. . . to absorb the maximum of its rays, presumably that's what your farmer saw, and once the word has been spoken by the Main Ray, in our case Viguier, while all his little sunbeams are catching their breath, they retire after twilight to share their love.'

'Just an excuse for an orgy. Anyone ever been arrested?'

'Actually, they seem to be a very discreet group, keeping themselves to themselves. Ours is the first complaint against them on record.'

'And that wasn't official, just a peasant who found what was going on rather disturbing.' He ran a hand over his balding head. 'It can't be made official either, he wasn't supposed to be there, poaching on someone else's land. Look,' he said, checking once more that he did actually have a little hair left, 'store the stuff, will you? One never knows. Then find out what you can on vampires.'

Debray swung round. 'Vampires?'

83

'Yes, that's right,' Pel replied, turning to leave. 'Vampires in Europe since, let's say the last ten years.'

'Do you mean le Vampire d'Azara, the blood-sucking bat? Or the undead from Hammer Horror films?'

'The undead.'

'They don't exist,' Debray said bluntly.

'You and I know they don't exist,' Pel retorted, 'but how many people think they do? What, why, who, where, okay?'

Pel left Debray scratching his head. He was delighted – usually it was Pel who was totally confused after looking at or listening to one of his complicated computer reports. They were no easier to understand than Chinese.

Thirty-one kilometres away, as the crow flies, in Fontaine les Lacs, the Mayor's secretary, Christine Delmas, was making herself a cup of coffee. She was sick of the elections and they'd only just started. She stirred sugar into the cup and took it back to her desk. Monsieur le Maire had just left and she was thinking, Good riddance. He was a local shopkeeper who'd campaigned aggressively for the position six years previously and, having enjoyed the glory of being a dignitary, was not going to give up easily. It never ceased to amaze Christine that idiots could be and were constantly elected. She sipped her coffee and, looking up as the door opened and banged shut, she realised there was going to be trouble. Madame Martin was always trouble.

'I know my rights,' the woman said, banging her fist on the counter between them.

'*Bonjour*, madame,' Christine said sweetly.

'Eh? Oh, *oui, bonjour*. Everyone else's got a signpost. I've been forgotten.'

'I assure you this is not the case.'

'They're just jealous, that's why, because my *gite* makes more money than theirs.'

'It's not a question of jealousy, madame, all the *gites rurales* and the *chambres d'hôte* within the boundary of the village are clearly marked.'

'Then why not mine?'

'Yours is five kilometres outside the village, madame, and

84

Monsieur le Maire's decision was that further than three kilometres was not our responsibility.'

'Deliberate! Good thing my boys tacked a bit of cardboard to the telegraph pole or we'd be missed. Had a young chappie in the spring thanks to that. The weather's ruined it, no more than a soggy bit of paper now.'

'I'm afraid, madame, it is up to you to replace it.'

'*Démerdez-vous*? That's what you're saying, isn't it? It's always the same, whatever I ask for it's always "*Démerdez-vous*." Well, you'll see if I don't, biggest bloody signpost for miles.'

Christine sighed. 'Perhaps now would be the right moment to inform you that it must not exceed regulation size or you'll have to apply for planning permission.'

'*Putain*! The Mayor should be hanged!' Madame Martin left in high dudgeon, mumbling expletives to herself all the way down the stairs, and it was only that evening while the Mayor's secretary was packing up to go home that she remembered what the angry woman had said.

Cham had studied the translated autopsy report and looked carefully at the photographs of the girl's corpse. Having compared the Spanish bite with the one on the body at Alesia, he agreed the marks on the two girls looked the same, 'but,' he pointed out to Pel, 'just because the dentition appears similar doesn't mean it is, these are faxed copies,' and he picked up a black and white. 'I'd have to see the originals or the bite itself to be sure one way or the other.'

'What about the autopsy report, what do you make of that?'

Cham was cautious. 'Without actually examining the body, I shouldn't really comment.'

'Give me a hint,' Pel encouraged.

'Well, the cause of death was registered as asphyxia, suffocation after vomiting. It has happened,' he said. 'Janis Joplin and I think Jimi Hendrix died like that.'

Pel frowned. 'Who the hell are Janis Joplin and – '

'It doesn't matter, the point is, they'd been abusing both drink and drugs.'

'She was drunk, wasn't she?'

'There was certainly enough alcohol in her blood to indicate that she had been drinking quite heavily but to vomit and not react you need to be in a semi-comatose state, absolutely blotto, unconscious.'

'Drugs?' Pel asked.

'Evidence of marijuana was mentioned.'

'Enough to render her unconscious?'

'There were only traces,' Cham pointed out, 'and anyway marijuana is a soft drug, it makes you sleepy, contented. If it had been Ecstasy I'd have said it could have been at least partly responsible for her death, that's a dangerous one, but marijuana? I doubt it.'

'So you're not satisfied with their conclusions?'

'Oh, God, Pel! That's not what I said. This conversation is strictly off the record, I haven't seen the corpse . . .' Cham's voice trailed off briefly. 'However, by the look of her neck I'd say something strange was going on before her death, there's a certain amount of bruising around the area which in my opinion is not connected with the bite.'

'Could swabs be taken from it? She was buried forty-eight hours ago.'

'We managed it with Patti Fauré at the Roman dig thanks to the freezing weather but I doubt it with this one. The Spanish are pretty thorough with the preparation of their dead. Bodies are "made up" so death is slightly more attractive for the relatives and friends who wish to pay their last respects – it's normal to keep the coffin open at home before the funeral – so I'm pretty sure they'd have filled the abrasions before covering it all with skin-coloured cream. However, the bite itself might be enough, if it hasn't been damaged.'

'What about a vaginal swab?'

Cham flicked through the pages on the desk in case he'd missed a vital remark. 'There's nothing about rape here,' he said at last, 'and that would depend on the method of embalming.'

But Pel wasn't going to be put off. Two sixteen-year-old girls had lost their lives, one at the end of January just outside his own beloved city – the reason and the perpetrator were still a mystery to him – and the second in June, in Spain, and she was lying in a sealed concrete chest of drawers in the back yard of a Spanish church.

'De Troq'!'

An expectant face appeared at his door; de Troq's fine nose was unavoidably that of an aristocrat. Pel glanced at his highly polished shoes, then at his own scuffed suede affairs sitting apologetically on his feet. It was no good, barons were born not made, Pel would never look noble. He disliked going out on an enquiry with de Troq', it made him feel like something the cat had dragged in after one hell of a chase, crumpled and stained and fraying round the edges.

He beckoned for de Troquereau to enter. 'Same town,' he said, 'but this time I want you to call a priest, chap named Lopez.'

9

'Well? What did he say?' Pel was pacing the floor in his office. De Troq' had been a long time on the phone to Spain, asking the relevant questions, jotting down the replies and continuing the discussion. Pel had stared at his scribblings but was unable to decipher the peculiar squiggles and finally gave up in favour of pacing while consuming Gauloises nervously, like a schoolboy behind the bike shed.

'He said,' de Troq' studied his shorthand notes, 'that Mariana Consuela Gomez was bright. She was the middle of three children and was often unfairly brushed aside being the only girl. She was expected to baby-sit the younger brother and wait hand and foot on the older one plus dealing with their meals and most of the housework. Both parents work in a factory miles away in Huesca.' He looked up to explain. 'Women's liberation wasn't heard of in rural Spain until very recently. One mustn't forget that twenty years ago, a married woman there wasn't allowed to open a bank account in her own name. However,' he continued, looking again at his notes, 'her teenage rebellion began at Christmas, not this year, last year, when for the first time she didn't follow them to mass, but she continued to go to confession intermittently until a couple of months ago.' De Troq' turned a page. 'Obviously he didn't tell me what she confessed, in fact he grew more reticent after having referred to the confessional. She seemed determined to attract her parents' attention by outrageous clothes and behaviour, although in the priest's opinion, what she wore and what she did was perfectly normal for a child of her age from a poor home, bombarded by articles in glossy magazines and romantic television programmes. She was, he believed, like many of her generation caught up in our fast and grasping world – particularly there where freedom of expression has been sudden since Franco's death. He thinks she was simply desperate for love and affection.'

'What did he say when you announced we were thinking of asking for an exhumation order?'

'He offered to go and see the family.'

'Did he indeed! Any idea why?'

'He said,' de Troq' read, ' "Nothing will bring the poor child back, she's at peace at last, but if your interest will avoid another innocent girl joining her, I will do what is necessary." '

Pel raised an eyebrow. 'When I repeated what was written on her death certificate, death by asphyxia et cetera, he replied, "I am neither a doctor nor a detective, only a spiritual guide for those who choose to follow. If you have the power to uncover the truth, I shall pray for you." '

'Fat lot of good that'll do!'

The June sky was clear azure, the garden peaceful. Pel sat on the terrace watching yellow butterflies float in the distance over the flower border. He was ruminating on the request he'd made to the *juge d'instruction* that afternoon. Digging up dead bodies was always gruesome. He wondered whether permission would be granted to remove the young Spaniard from her concrete tomb: they had very few facts to give weight to his argument of 'suspected victim of wilful murder; modus operandi suggests connection with the unsolved murder of Patti Fauré, et cetera.' The bruising on her body, noted by the Spanish doctor, could have occurred when she fell drunkenly and rolled down the hillside, coming to rest where she was found. She could have died in the circumstances stated, having been dazed by the fall. But what about the bite? Was it the same man that had bitten Patti? Was this man the murderer of Mariana Gomez? *If* she was murdered – so far no mention of foul play had been made. The one huge stumbling block was that Gomez was in Spain, out of his jurisdiction; it was officially nothing to do with him at all. Except for a possible link with the body at the Roman dig. Not only that, Maître Castéou had disappeared for a month's holiday, which meant Brisard, a pompous fool in Pel's opinion, would be handling the request for a second autopsy and would very probably turn it down because of the international legal complications. He too was involved in the local elections and wouldn't want to put a hair out of place. Brisard and Pel had declared war a long time ago, each trying to out-manoeuvre the other. Mostly Pel won; he'd found out, by accident, that Brisard visited a policeman's widow in Beaune when he should have been at home with his family. Making reference to her, while studying Brisard's silver-framed photo of his wife and children, gave Pel the edge to any argument. Would it be worth going to see him? Intimidation always worked better in person.

A crashing from the kitchen interrupted his thoughts. 'Madame Routy!' he shouted. 'You're sacked!'

'*Merci, mon capitaine!*' came back through the open window.

'Stupid woman,' he muttered then, catching a glimpse of movement in the next-door garden, he rose to see Yves emerging, tall and bronzed, into the sun. His thick blond hair was in a tangle and he was wearing nothing but a towel wound round his waist. Pel despised him, he looked perfect for the role of a Greek god.

'Oh, hello, Pel,' he yawned. 'Didn't see you at first. Sun's bright, isn't it?'

'Tiring holiday?'

'The holiday would've been fine if I hadn't gone with a lunative detective who made me drive non-stop through the night because he was homesick for his office.' He rubbed his eyes. 'I've only just got up, been sleeping it off.'

'I thought you were going for a swim,' Pel said indicating the towel.

'Oh, that. I can't find any clean clothes, Mum did her rounds and collected everything that was lying on the floor to do the washing. My entire wardrobe's gone.'

'Put things away, my boy – organisation, that's what you youngsters lack.'

'Don't you start.' Yves turned to go back into the house.

'I don't suppose,' Pel called beseechingly, 'you've got a cold beer, have you?'

'Madame Routy breathing fire, is she?'

'I just sacked her.'

'Again! Come through the hedge then, I think I saw a couple in the fridge.'

Pel was just settling down with his frosty bottle, watching with distaste as Yves tackled a bowl of chocolate cereal drowned in milk, when the phone rang next door. A second later his housekeeper's head poked out, shrieking for him. 'Monsieur Pel! *C'est* Darcy!'

Pel went back towards his own house. 'And the whole bloody neighbourhood knows.' Yves shrugged and went on eating.

He snatched the instrument from Madame Routy's hand and clasped it to his ear. '*Oui!*'

'The Mayor's secretary rang from Fontaine les Lacs,' Darcy told him. 'There was a stranger wandering about the village in the spring. She doesn't know who he was but she does know where he was staying.'

'Then get over there.'

'De Troq's already on his way with Jourdain. Do you want them to pick you up?'

'What's the punk doing going out on an enquiry like this?'

'Gaining experience,' Darcy replied casually, 'plus, she was the only one available, the office is virtually empty.'

Pel sniffed. 'De Troq' knows the score, he'll ask the right questions. If they get into difficulty or have anything to report, I'll be here all evening.'

De Troq' drew the car off the road under the shade of the plane trees in front of the Mairie. As promised, the secretary was waiting for them; she came forward as they started opening their doors. 'Monsieur Troqueau?'

'De Troquereau, madame,' he corrected her politely, unfolding his wallet to reveal the police identification as proof.

'I'm Christine Delmas. I hope I haven't called you out on a wild-goose chase,' she apologised, 'but, well, I just thought . . .'

'Would you like us to drive you home?' Jourdain suggested. One or two locals were already looking enquiringly in their direction.

Christine took them into a comfortable farmhouse and, pushing the debris of the last meal to one end of a large table, she poured them a glass of mint each and begun recounting her interview with Madame Martin.

'How did we miss her?' de Troq' asked no one in particular. 'We went right through the electoral roll.'

'The Martin family isn't on it,' Christine told him. 'They refuse to vote and consequently they refuse to be registered as voters. They're rather a law unto themselves, very rustic, if you know what I mean.'

As they drove away, following her directions for the Martins' farm, de Troq' glanced at the new member of the team and smiled. 'Did you enjoy your mint, Jourdain?'

'It's a bit like drinking toothpaste,' she smiled back, 'but it was refreshing.'

'Sorry to be so predictable,' de Troq' went on, 'but how did a girl like you come to be in the Police Judiciaire?'

'Same way as a bloke like you, *baron*.'

'Okay, point taken, but why?'

'Why not?' she laughed. 'Actually I wanted to be a racing driver first, then an explorer. The police was my third choice but as they were the only ones prepared to take me, train me and pay me, it clinched the deal – I need to earn my living just like you. Plus the fact that my parents said if I wasn't going to get married like the other girls in our village, I'd better do something useful with my life.'

'So you don't want to get married?'

'*Mais si*, but not yet, not just because it's the thing to do.'

De Troq' concentrated on the road ahead, considering what she'd said. 'Neither do I.'

Jourdain turned in her seat to look at him. 'Is it on the cards?'

'Very much so and I was wholeheartedly in agreement – unfortunately, as the date approaches, Véronique's family has been putting pressure on me to leave the police and join the family firm as a junior director.'

'A good opportunity maybe?'

'They make rivets!'

'Oh, shit. What does Véronique say?'

'She worries about the dangers of chasing criminals. It's understandable, Nosjean was shot a few years ago. Kate, Darcy's lady, was knifed, either of them could have been killed. But I know I'd be miserable behind a desk chasing paper. And if I was miserable I'd make a rotten husband.'

'My father told me never to do something for a man that I wouldn't do for myself.'

De Troq' frowned. 'He's obviously a very wise man.' He swung the car from the country lane into a short bumpy track towards a smart farmyard. The hedges were clipped, the verges newly mown, white pots of pink geraniums and oleanders were arranged in a neat line round a paved yard that looked as if it had been swept, washed and polished as well. A brass knocker shone from a newly painted door. De Troq' lifted it and waited to be answered.

Madame Martin blinked at the police identification then told them to follow her. After crossing a gleaming entrance hall towards a handwritten notice saying '*Privé*' they were shown into a large scruffy kitchen where the family were gathered for supper.

Madame's husband, an ample slovenly man with two days' growth of beard attached to his ruddy face, grunted as they were introduced and the two lank adolescents slouching either side of their father lowered their heads further into the soup bowls. Parked a little way from the group was an ancient grandmother, a wisp of white hair hanging over her forehead. She didn't seem to notice de Troq' and Jourdain, or anything else that was going on around her. Madame Martin pulled two wooden chairs away from the wall for them and went back to spooning watery soup into the puckered mouth of the old lady.

As de Troq' opened the batting, politely asking if they'd had many visitors that year, Monsieur Martin interrupted. ''Ere,

Mother, stop yapping and fetch the grub, never mind 'er,' he indicated the oldest member of his family, 'you can drip feed 'er later, or,' he said with an ugly grin, 'get one of them police types to do it while you look after your darling 'ubbie.' He glanced at his watch. '*Putain de merde*! The match's starting in a minute!' and he left the table to switch on the television.

Madame Martin fetched the steaks, as thick as tractor tyres and almost as big, a barrowload of chips and a bucket of green beans. Without turning from the applauding television where the teams were coming on to the pitch, the men piled food in front of them and started eating. While they watched, shovelling food into their mouth, Madame Martin wheeled the old lady into position so she could see too, and crept round to where de Troq' and Jourdain were waiting.

'Now you see why,' she whispered, 'I take in paying guests. Look at them,' and she waved her arm in the television's direction. 'That's the only thing they're interested in. If I had my way it would be abolished.'

'Football?'

'Television!'

She was efficient, if rather aggressive, with her answers and she remembered the artist who'd come to stay in the March: 'Nice chappie, ever so polite,' she said. 'Came to paint the countryside round here for his exhibition.'

'Where was it being held?'

'Ooh, I wouldn't know, he never said, nice paintings though, he showed me one or two, ever so colourful. Told him so, thought he might give me one as a souvenir but he didn't, maybe next time.'

'Will he be coming back?'

'I don't know, he didn't say, he left unexpectedly. He'd paid until the end of the month but he went on the 25th.'

The day of the shooting. 'Did he say why?' De Troq' opened his notebook.

'No, just that he'd finished and it was time to be off.'

'How did he seem?'

'Whad'ja mean?'

'Calm, happy, worried?'

'In a hurry, didn't even want to wait and eat lunch, there was *rôti de porc* too, bought it special.'

With his pencil poised, de Troq' asked the million dollar question: 'What was his name?'

'The *rôti de porc*?' she cackled. 'Only joking, we called the artist Monsieur.'

'Did he ring to book, perhaps he left a name then?'

'No, he just turned up, saw our sign. My boys pinned it up because the flipping Mayor's deliberately decided to exclude us. The village folk are jealous, that's what it is, if I told you all the trouble I've had – '

'Did he receive any mail?'

'No.'

'Did he leave anything behind?'

'No.'

'What about his car?'

'It was white with a Paris number.'

'92?'

'No, 75.'

'Did he say which *quartier* he came from, if he was going back there?'

'No.'

'Did you talk to him at all?'

'Of course, in the morning when I served him breakfast. I also gave him his picnic lunch, extra cost of course, all nicely packed in a shoulder bag, home-made pâté, cheese, bottle of wine, fresh bread – '

'Is that all?'

'No! I made him a salad as well and added fruit and a thermos of coffee!'

'I meant, is that the only time you spoke to him?'

'No, we had a chat in the evening too, when he came in for supper. Not in here, across the way there, in the guests' dining-room. Said he liked my cooking but he didn't eat much, always left something on his plate, not like my lads, now they've got good appetites – '

'Did he talk back?'

'Well, no,' she said slowly, 'come to think of it, not much.'

'Did he tell you anything about himself, where he worked, if he was married, what his parents were like, if he had any children?'

'Well, no, I don't think he did.'

De Troq' sighed: it had started off too well. He decided to try another line. 'Does your husband hunt?'

'Yes!' She seemed delighted to be able to answer in the affirmative for once.

'Did you talk about that?'

'No.' Her smile slipped again.

'Your visitor didn't ask about game round here, discuss what guns your husband has, perhaps ask to see them?'

'Ooh, no.'

'He does have guns, I suppose?'

'Yes!'

'May I see them?'

She looked doubtful but, after a moment's hesitation, she shrugged and led them into the scullery. De Troq' persevered with his questioning while he examined the three rifles, thankful to get away from the raucous football match. 'So he didn't borrow one?' he asked, lifting out a shotgun the same calibre as the one used in Nurse Fabres's surgery, but it was clean, the inside of the barrel shone silver, the wooden stock gleaming with polish.

'No, never,' she said as if they were stupid. 'Artists paint.'

When he'd completed the list of questions, adding more as they occured to him, he thanked her for her co-operation and led Jourdain out to the car. Madame Martin watched them leave with a puzzled expression on her face.

'That got us a long way,' Jourdain commented, 'didn't it?'

'I get the impression,' de Troq' replied, 'that if someone says hello, she says the rest.'

'I don't suppose she gets much conversation out of her nearest and dearest. What a crew!'

They went on discussing the Martins until they found themselves not far from Pel's house at Leu, and although de Troq' didn't agree with the suggestion of making their report in person, he was finally persuaded by the enthusiasm of his colleague.

'Go on, it'll liven up his dull little life,' she said confidently. 'Poor old thing, sitting mulling over who he can shout at next!'

It was a surprise when Madame Pel opened the door. She wasn't the dreary housewife Jourdain expected. With a flicker of the eye she took in her neat figure in a tailored dress, her discreet make-up framed by perfectly cut hair and her cheerful smile: she was an extremely attractive woman, and she looked happy to be married to the *patron*!

'*Et voilà*, Monsieur le Baron!' Madame exclaimed. 'De Troq', what a pleasant surprise.' Clicking his heels, he bent to kiss her outstretched hand.

They found their boss on the terrace hunched over a Gameboy which was attached by a lead to a second miniature computer in the hands of Yves. Madame Pel put her finger to her lips. 'Serious stuff, this Tetris game,' she whispered. 'When he plays he stops grumbling and he doesn't smoke, so I can only encourage it.'

'I win!' Yves held up a hand in triumph.

'You cheated,' Pel cried.

'Impossible, you're a bad loser!'

Pel laughed. 'You wait, I'll get you tomorrow.' He turned to see who'd arrived, and his scowl slid effortlessly back into place. 'What the hell are you doing here?'

10

'A small white car, but not too small, *immatriculé*, 75, brilliant! There must be millions in the capital! They'll never find it, it's hardly worth asking. Tall and thin, looked in need of a good meal,' Pel repeated, 'grey hair and beard, almost white, and steel-rimmed glasses. Amazing, she actually opened her eyes long enough to take a look at him.' He sniffed. He could say a lot with a sniff; this time it meant, Well, it's not much but it's a start. 'Send it to Paris, you never know. Tell Debray to get over there with his magic box, she might be able to put a face together for us. If she does, send that to Paris too. What about fingerprinting his room?'

'She's spring-cleaned it, always does after a guest leaves, and judging by what we saw it'll be spotless.'

'All the same, it's worth a try.'

'*Patron*,' Jourdain said, 'this is only an idea, but could we bring her to Debray at headquarters?'

'Why, for crying out loud?'

'I'm sure she'd enjoy a trip into the city, and while she was out of the way the fingerprint boys could do their job. It would be faster for them not to be constantly interrupted, she has a tendency to chatter.'

Pel glanced at de Troq', who nodded. '*D'accord*,' Pel agreed. 'Organise it. You realise this opens things up again? We're going to have to do another house-to-house in case anyone else remembers this elusive artist.'

As they left Jourdain looked back over her shoulder, still surprised by Pel's elegant home and attractive wife. 'She's a bit out of his class,' she said.

'Don't you believe it, he's in a class of his own,' de Troq' replied, chuckling. 'I must confess we were all taking bets as to how long she'd put up with him and we all lost, they've been married eleven years and she still adores him.'

'Opposites attract?'

'Heaven knows what it is that attracts one person to another.' He smiled at her cautiously. 'How about a bite to eat? I'm starving.'

Having dealt with the rest of the lingering paperwork on his desk, Darcy left the office and went singing into the street. He still couldn't believe it, he was the father of two sons, all in one go! Kate as usual was taking it in her stride, dealing with the older boys, feeding the babies. She was tired but that was understandable – the nights were punctuated by tiny cries of hunger. Nosjean's wife, Mijo, was permanently worn out and Nosjean didn't look much better. His beautiful Kate always managed a beaming smile when he arrived, whatever time it was, kissed him and made him feel like the most important chap in the world, after the kids of course. He sang most of the way home, proud and happy with his life.

When he arrived at their house, he stood and breathed in a lungful of warm woodland air floating through the trees on a gentle breeze. A couple of birds clattered up from the bracken as he slammed the car door closed. He loved coming back to their hiding place in the forest, to the chatter and laughter of the children, to Kate . . . If only she'd marry him – he'd have to work on it. And Rasputin, their monster dog, who knocked him flying every evening. 'Down, you dirty bugger!' Too late, two huge paw marks were printed on to his shirt front. He put out a hand to fuss the dog who was squirming in ecstasy at meeting his master.

'*Salut*, Daniel.' Kate's older sons came tearing out, leapt on to their bikes and sped off down the earthy track leaving a trail of dust behind them. Inside Kate was sitting at their long oak table looking worried; Mijo was sitting opposite, her eyelids swollen, her cheeks pink.

Later, when they'd settled the Riot Squad into a peaceful slumber, Darcy handed Kate a tot of brandy. 'So what was Mijo crying about?'

Kate curled into a corner of the sofa nursing her glass. 'She can't take being cooped up any more in their cramped little flat with Erika, she's not an easy toddler. She's on her own a hell of a lot, she resents Nosjean being out and about all day, that he's never home on time, that he works with pretty women, and that the office is more important than the family.'

'That's quite a list!'

'My guess is she's got a bad dose of post-natal depression, magnified by the miscarriage; she feels unloved and useless.'

'What's the remedy?'

'Heaven knows. She wants to go home to Mum, who I might add is encouraging her.'

'Poor Nosjean,' Darcy frowned. 'I wondered what was up, he's been distracted lately. You know I'm going to have to tell Pel, don't you?'

'I suppose so, but maybe you could have a word with Nosjean first.'

'If the occasion rises, I will, but we're fairly busy at the moment, everyone's off in different directions.'

'Fairly busy is nothing for you lot,' Kate laughed. 'You've been home on time twice this week. You just don't want to meddle.'

'What do I say?'

'You'll think of something.'

'I just have,' Darcy said brightly. Kate raised her eyebrows inquisitively as he stood up and came towards her. 'It's a long time since we made love.'

Kate giggled as he pounced. 'At least twenty-four hours!' she teased but Darcy took the glass from her hand and silenced her with a kiss.

'De Troq'!' Pel was punching buttons on his phone as if he hoped to win the jackpot. 'De Troq'! Get in here!' They'd know who it was shouting, he was the only one in the Hôtel de Police who bellowed so eloquently. Having tried all the extensions, he slammed the receiver down and lit a comforting cigarette. When he'd come into the office that morning, Darcy had been waiting for him and it was only after their conversation about Nosjean that he'd noticed the rejected request for exhumation of Mariana Gomez's body sitting on his desk. Expecting it, he'd worked out his next move.

De Troq' appeared in the doorway, clean and polished. 'Ring the priest Lopez, tell him about this.' He waved Brisard's short negative note. 'See what he says, find out if he's prepared to get more involved.'

'What about Madame Martin? I was just getting ready to leave.'

'Hand it over to . . .' He looked down at the duty roster and the cases each man was handling, 'Cheriff. Tell him to pass the latest lists from the Sunshine and Light lot on to Misset again. It's only a question of checking through the new arrivals Viguier sent us – he managed the last one, it keeps him out of mischief.'

Madame Martin was thrilled to take a ride in the unmarked police car. She'd taken off her apron, added a hideous hat and, collecting a handbag the size of a suitcase, banged the front door closed. She talked all the way into the city and along the winding corridors to Debray's office, and didn't stop once while he worked on creating a portrait of her artist from the few details she remembered. However, after a noisy hour she was satisfied with the result. 'That's about it,' she said. 'Course, it's not easy to say really, it was quite some time ago, but it's not bad. Could I have a glass of water, my throat's rather dry, must be the pollution in built-up areas. All those car fumes, far better to live in the country. I was saying to my menfolk only the other day . . .'

Pel stared at the portrait. It hadn't matched with anyone in their files, Debray had checked. It meant a nation-wide search. He marched from his office into the sergeants' room to find Nosjean fiddling at his desk. 'Fax it to Paris, we sent a description yesterday, use the same reference, then get it to all other *département* capitals throughout France,' he said. 'Mark it "No press", I want it kept out of the papers for the moment, we don't want to tip him off we're on to him. We'll let them have it if there are no immediate results – he must be found. How did he meet the nurse, Adrianne Fabres, or Hugo Aynard? Check with Fabres's husband and Crystal Combes. There were no unidentified names in the surgery files but find out if they treated a casual caller who wasn't written up, I'm sure it happens from time to time. And get on to Aynard's dental practice and his widow. Oh, and chivvy up Fingerprints as soon as they get back from the farm, see if they've found anything useful.'

'*Oui, patron.*' Nosjean's voice was dull as he took the picture and laid it on his desk. '*Tout de suite.*'

As he was leaving, Pel stopped. Unhappy marriages made unhappy men, and unhappy men were not trustworthy policemen. Darcy had enlightened him about Mijo's problems, adding that he'd tried broaching the subject but had been dismissed with a shrug and the comment, 'Damn it, it's not my fault.'

There was no one else in the sergeants' room for once, so, closing the door, he went back to sit opposite Nosjean. Pel offered him a cigarette which he took and lit, inhaling deeply. Pel watched as the smoke dribbled out of Nosjean's nostrils: he was wearing a look of defeat, the sort that they'd both seen on the faces of minor criminals who'd been well and truly caught. It was ugly on one of his team. He banged his fist on the table. Nosjean jumped, his eyes wide, suddenly alive. 'Snap out of it, Nosjean!'

'*Comment? Quoi, patron?*'

'You know what I mean! You've had a long face for weeks now. Your personal problems don't concern me until they follow you in here. Your mind's not on the job and it should be. If you're not thinking straight you could be a liability.'

'Mijo's leaving me,' Nosjean said dismally, lowering his head again.

'Then tell her to buck up! I can't tolerate time-wasters. Good God, Misset's bad enough, but at least he's useful for the dreary stuff, you look fit for nothing.'

'I don't know what to do, *patron*.'

'You can stop whining for a start!' He disliked being so unsympathetic but knew he had to be, his men must be one hundred per cent on the ball. There had been occasions when they'd been faced with a madman holding a knife threatening to slit a throat, or looking into the barrel of a trembling gun – he couldn't afford risking the safety of them all because one man wasn't up to scratch. Being a policeman could be danger-ous, it was certainly extremely time-consuming, the divorce rate was high in the force, but they all knew it when deciding to join. Hard though it was to face when the chips were down, that's what it was all about, it was the gamble all of them took. Pel sighed. He was surprisingly fond of young Nosjean and it saddened him to see him in a mess.

By the end of the day, Fingerprints reported that the stranger's room was clean, as was most of the rest of the house; all they'd been able to lift were the fingerprints of Monsieur and Madame Martin and their two sons. The old lady, they said, never moved from her wheelchair. Pel left the office disappointed. His men had done the rounds in the village – the petrol station, the bars, the restaurants, the shops, and the surrounding farm-ers in case he'd been sitting in one of their fields to paint – but no one remembered the artist. Paris gave them a negative reply to the portrait Madame Martin had built up and requested more details on the small white car, which they couldn't give. Crystal Combes confirmed that neither she nor Adrianne Fabres had treated a stranger. It was unethical, she'd said; all their patients had to be referred to them by a doctor.

After their initial excitement the lead had taken them nowhere. The grey-haired man who'd lodged at the Martins' farm for nearly a fortnight, who'd left in a hurry a few hours after the shooting, had disapeared into thin air; he was no more than an indistinct shadow. They were going to have to publish the picture and Pel knew what that meant, millions of helpful idiots calling in to say they'd seen him from Abainville to Zuytpeene. But it had to be done in case one of them was a genuine sighting.

Pel drove home thoughtfully, leaving a trail of motorists shaking their fists in his rear view mirror. Just beyond the city centre a traffic warden recognised his car; the balding head and spectacles peering through a cloud of smoke just behind the windscreen were unmistakable. He stopped the flow of cars in all directions, waved Pel through, saluting as he passed, then, breathing a sigh of relief, allowed the *circulation* to continue normally.

The following morning, as most of the team were leaving, Misset was slouched over his desk devouring the antics of the Soleil Sect, thinking perhaps he'd join up – it sounded like just what he needed to keep him away from his wife, the kids, the mother-in-law and the bloody poodles. Rigal, as usual, was sitting contentedly in the corner typing, and Jourdain, being the newest recruit, was struggling to put some order into the paperwork that was piling up on the filing cabinets. Although they'd all been concerned with the brutal shooting at Fontaine les Lacs, they'd also juggled investigations into dozens of other breaches of the law; every interview had been put on paper in triplicate and the young punk was painstakingly sorting them into the correct dossiers. As the phone trilled, she was standing by Misset's desk, hesitating over the written statement he'd taken in connection with a lost canary. Misset sighed at the interruption and lifted the receiver.

'Don Evaristo Pel? *Jefe de Policia Francesa.*'

Misset's eyes opened. 'Eh?'

'Don Evaristo Pel? Don Carlos dos Troquereau?' the agitated voice pleaded.

He winked at Jourdain. 'Got a prankster here.'

She whipped the phone from his dithering hand. '*Si, signor,* I'm listening,' she said in perfect Spanish. 'Father Lopez? Just a moment, please, I'll put you through.'

Pel listened to the priest. '*Momenti por favore,*' he replied, wondering whether it was right, and dashing into the corridor he shrieked for Troq'.

It was Jourdain who answered. 'Left twenty minutes ago for a robbery at Les Chartreux.'

'Hell's teeth, I need him to translate. I don't suppose you speak Spanish, do you?'

'*Si, patrón,*' she said briskly and followed him back to the office.

The three-way conversation took time, but eventually Pel nodded. 'Tell him we need the request from the family to interfere in writing, signed by a magistrate.'

Jourdain complied and shortly afterwards rang off. 'Go on then,' Pel said almost pleasantly, propping his head on his fist. 'Tell me all about it.'

'He went to see the Gomez family and explained that you'd become interested in the case and why. At first they were hostile to any more stirring up of trouble, they'd had enough, specially after some old codger had suggested hammering a stake through their dead daughter's heart, they wanted her left in peace. But, when he implied that perhaps her death wasn't the way it seemed, that someone else may be involved, they changed their minds. The parents were feeling responsible for Mariana's waywardness, not paying enough attention to the girl because of the boys.'

'If she was murdered, however,' Pel proposed, 'it's no longer their fault, the blame lies elsewhere.'

'Having reached the same conclusion, Lopez said little more. As he pointed out, nothing will bring the girl back but the idea of being less responsible was helping them decrease their guilt. They asked if you would handle the case, Lopez didn't suggest it.'

Pel sniffed. 'I'm sure he knows how to put ideas into people's minds without them realising it.' He scratched his forehead. 'I can't go, damn it, this lead in Fontaine les Lacs is too important. If we do find this artist chappie it could be the answer to all our prayers. When de Troq' comes in, tell him to come and see me, and,' he added, 'as you seem to speak such good Spanish, you'd better get a bag packed too.'

'Yes, sir!'

Pel sighed. 'Let Doc Cham know too, he'll be going with you. As soon as I've got the request in writing I'll go back and nobble Brisard, we still need the permission from this end to interfere. Bugger the elections! I'll put him in thumbscrews if he refuses the second autopsy this time.'

As Jourdain left, there was a knock on the door and Sarrazin, the freelance journalist, entered. 'Lots of activity around Fontaine les Lacs yesterday,' he said as he sat opposite Pel. 'What's going on? Got someone in your sights? Darcy wouldn't tell me a thing, so I've come to see the top dog.'

'Woof,' Pel replied gloomily.

'If it's nothing,' Sarrazin went on, 'you know me, I won't invent, but – '

'Like hell!' Pel interrupted. 'You make up your stories as you go along.'

'My editor writes my headlines, he doesn't think mine are eye-catching enough, but what I write underneath is what I'm told.'

Pel had to concede he'd stuck to the bare details when he'd reported the shooting originally. 'D'accord,' he said and explained who they were looking for and why, stressing they needed forty-eight hours before the photograph was published in a national daily.

Sarrazin took it all down in his notebook, carefully adding the artist's portrait, then he reached across and pinched a cigarette. 'And what about the Soleil et Lumière members? I've had a whisper that you're interested in them. Same case?'

'No, it's not!' Pel bellowed. 'We just want to keep tabs on who's in the area.'

'That's not what I heard,' but he closed his notebook and stood up.

'Sarrazin.' Pel pushed his specs up on to his forehead and frowned. 'Where did you hear the whisper? Let me in on your secret and I won't arrest you for robbery.'

'Robbery?'

'If you hadn't noticed, that's my Gauloise you're smoking!'

'So it is,' the journalist smiled. 'My profound apologies.' He fished in his jacket pocket. 'Here, fair exchange no robbery,' and he threw a book of matches on to his desk as he slipped out through the door.

Pel's frown deepend as the newspaperman disappeared. The enquiry into their neighbourhood sect had been unofficial – how had Sarrazin found out? For years he'd suspected Misset of earning a bit of pocket money by feeding information to the press but had never been able to prove a thing. Perhaps this time he might.

11

Misset sat in his car blinking at the early morning mist that was rising off the fields on either side of the road. The sky above was already pale blue tinged with gold as the sun burned through. He reclined the seat and relaxed; this was going to be an easy one, keeping an eye on a group of religious nuts and making a note of their movements. He wasn't sure why he was doing it – he thought Pel had lost interest in the Sunshine Sect after he and Cheriff had been to see the Main Ray and the first list of members had been checked – but Darcy had collared him first thing with the surveillance instructions, telling him to keep out of trouble for a couple of days to let the old man cool off. He'd muttered something about leaks to the press and Misset had obligingly disappeared.

He glanced round and, satisfied that he was well positioned, relaxed again. He'd pulled into a lay-by not far from the entrance to the property where Le Peuple de Soleil et Lumière had set up home. Behind him were the communal dustbins where the inhabitants of Point le Vieux came to put their rubbish; in front, the road continued past the beginning of the driveway he was supposed to be watching. Their signpost, a buttercup yellow sun on a blue background, was clearly visible in spite of the overgrown hedge. Definitely a cushy number, he thought. Hippies don't get out of bed until midday; he felt confident a quick doze would be in order.

He heard a dog bark and, surprised by its closeness, opened an eye, moving it from right to left, but could see nothing. It barked again. Turning in his seat to look through the back window of the car, Misset saw a large hairy mongrel tied behind a dustbin.

*

As the morning meeting came to a close, Darcy and Angelface Aimedieu, armed with a photo of the mystery artist, set off to requestion Aynard's wife. When they drew up outside her house, Marie-Hélène was hanging out washing in the garden. Seeing the car, guessing who they were, she abandoned her basket and walked over to the fence. 'More questions?' she asked wearily.

'Just one or two.'

'You'd better come in, we'll have some coffee as usual.'

They followed her inside and sat in the kitchen as she fiddled with crockery beside the sink. 'You know,' she said sadly, 'I still can't believe what you imply was going on between my husband and Adrianne. I've gone over and over it in my mind, it's stopped me sleeping at night, and now I'm sure you've made a mistake, they can't have been having an affair.' She wearily placed three stout glasses on the table. As she poured the coffee, her mind was obviously elsewhere – a dark puddle formed round the first glass. Looking at it with misery, she passed the jug to Darcy. 'You'd better do it,' she said, 'I don't think I'm capable.' She turned her back and wept quietly into a handkerchief, her shoulders trembling with distress.

'Hypothetically,' Darcy suggested gently, 'what would you have done?'

'I don't know. I've thought about it so often it's becoming obsessional.' She sounded exhausted. 'In the end I don't think I'd have done anything much. He was a sick man, what little pleasure he got out of life he was entitled to. I decided I'd have talked to him about it. What else could I have done? I'm sure it wouldn't have been intentional adultery, more a surprise, if you know what I mean, a surprise to find that he could after all.' She blinked fiercely, fighting her tears. 'We loved each other.'

Darcy had to admit it sounded like a plea from the heart, genuine enough, but he'd heard one or two like it out of the mouths of cold-blooded murderers. Calm family men who claimed to love their wife and children, who'd been sent down for sexually molesting or murdering them. The police couldn't yet rule out *crime passionnel*: the marital partners of the nurse and her patient were still suspects, in spite of their search for the artist. Facts were what the police worked on. This woman's husband had been in a state of sexual arousal when he died; he had been fingering the nurse's ear. The fact was that there was no doubt about their liaison, whatever anybody said. However, that wasn't the only thing they'd come to discuss. He took the computer portrait out of its envelope and pushed it across the table, watching Marie-Hélène's face for any reaction. She might not have done the shooting, but she could have employed someone to do it for her.

'Who's this?' she said.

'He's believed to have been in the village around the time your husband was shot.'

She looked again, studying the face carefully. 'I've never seen him before.'

'Think carefully, madame.'

'I wish I could say otherwise, that this nightmare would come to an end, but I can't, I'd be lying.'

'This man was staying at the Martins' farm until the day your husband died.'

'Martin?' She frowned, trying to remember something. 'Hang on, that name means something. They weren't patients or anything, by the state of Monsieur Martin's teeth I don't think he'd ever been to a dentist.'

'So how do you know them?'

'I don't, but if I remember correctly he rang one Sunday, while my husband was still fit enough to work, and said he had a *rage de dent*. Usually, although it was inconvenient, Hugo would meet the patient at the surgery and treat him, but Monsieur Martin told him he'd had toothache all week and he didn't want it to spoil his day off. Well, my husband saw red. People do that you know, take painkillers for days then ring up at the weekend. Hugo said it was impossible and that he'd see him first thing the following morning. Half an hour after he'd put the phone down, Monsieur Martin turned up here demanding treatment immediately. He got a couple of paracetamol and was sent away again. Honestly, you should have seen his teeth, black stumps, no wonder they hurt – well, he went off shouting abuse and we never saw him again.'

Aimedieu looked up from what he was writing. 'What sort of abuse?' he asked angelically.

'Oh, you know, incompetent, butcher, just because you wear

a white frock instead of a man's blue overalls, you think you're God's gift. He threatened to ruin him.' She managed a weak laugh. 'It wasn't funny at the time though.'

'What happened after that? Did he keep his appointment on the Monday morning?'

'Well, no,' Madame Aynard sighed, 'he didn't turn up. Hugo had a call from the dentist in the next village. Martin had badgered him for ages that Sunday until the poor man finally gave him a jab and extracted the tooth in question. He was ringing up to say thank you for nothing.'

'Was the other dentist angry?'

'No, not at all, it was just a joke, they were friends.'

'Would you give me his name, please?'

As they went out to their car, Darcy turned to Aimedieu. 'We'll check it,' he said. 'Who knows? We'd better see the Martin man too.'

At the other end of Fontaine les Lacs, Nosjean and Pujol were having the same conversation with Alain Fabres. He, like Marie-Hélène Aynard, continued to deny the love affair. 'Adrianne wouldn't have,' he stated, 'she had no need, we had an extremely good and satisfying sex life.'

'And your wife was of the same opinion?'

'Of course she was, she told me often – and anyway, a man knows whether he gives pleasure or not, *n'est ce pas*? She had no complaints.'

'What would you have done though,' Nosjean insisted, 'if you had found out she was being unfaithful?'

'I'd have been shocked! And upset. Then I think I'd have wondered what I'd done wrong. We'd have worked it out, I'm sure we would.'

Nosjean dropped the subject. He'd been told to ask and note Alain Fabres's behaviour and answer. He moved the artist's picture from its envelope and handed it over. Fabres took the photo to the window to examine it closely, smoothing the palm of his hand over one side of his head. He sighed. 'No,' he said at last, 'I haven't a clue. Was he the one who . . .?'

'For the moment all we want to do is establish his whereabouts and speak to him,' Nosjean told him.

'So there's no proof?' Fabres asked sadly.

'Not yet, sir.'

He handed back the photo. 'Well, good luck. It would be such a relief to know Adrianne's murderer has been brought to justice, to feel the case is finally closed, that all this horror is over and done with.' He looked down at his hands, studying his fingernails. 'I might then manage to begin living normally again. You can't imagine what it's like, it's hell not knowing.'

They also asked about the Martins and Fabres remembered his wife had been called out to give a series of injections to the grandmother. 'She handed it over to Crystal Combes, the second nurse in the practice, half-way through but I honestly couldn't tell you why.'

As they left, a shining grey metallic Mercedes drew up outside the house and they were introduced to La Vicomtesse, Béatrice de Maupou. 'One of my valued clients,' Fabres added while she adjusted a collection of gold jewellery in a tangle round her neck. She got the knot sorted out and smiled widely. 'Call me Béa, everyone else does.'

Bardolle arrived at the gendarmerie's locked gates just after ten. Having pressed the button and introduced himself over the intercom, he was finally allowed into the courtyard, up the steps under the French flag and into the square building. He was shown into the Adjutant's office where a heap of record books were stacked ready and waiting. They mostly contained accounts of neighbourly disputes: a farmer who'd ploughed up a metre of land that belonged to someone else, a dog that barked all night keeping the next-door house awake, a gang of children pinching fruit from a tree overhanging the road, a rowdy teenage party, that sort of thing. What Bardolle was looking for was any sighting of their stranger who'd stayed at the Martin's farm in March. It was odd no one had noticed him. Had he been secretive about his stay? Could he have been a peeping Tom, a watcher of children, a loner who spied through windows or into back gardens? Had anyone reported him hanging around where he shouldn't have been? Pel's instructions were fixed clearly in his mind; it was going to be a long morning.

When the men began trickling back that afternoon, Pel was storming up and down the corridors. Darcy and Nosjean had both phoned in to say there seemed to be some link between the victims of the shooting and the Martins – they were going to find out exactly what. He was impatient for their return. Was this the break they'd been waiting for? Where did the mystery artist come into it? He'd been staying at the Martins', so what? Madame Martin had led them to her house, to her lodger, or had she inadvertently led them to her own kith and kin? He also wanted to know where bloody Misset was, he hadn't yet been able to tackle him about the leak to the press nor had he shouted properly at anyone all day. The only one left in the sergeants' room was Rigal the Puppy and he wasn't much fun for yelling at, he always had his typewriter to hide behind.

When at last Darcy arrived, he shook his head. 'We've been right round the village again, no one saw the artist. However, we did get to see Monsieur Martin. He hates Hugo Aynard's guts. We finally found him down in the valley harvesting with his sons – we had a hell of a job persuading him to switch the damn machine off. Mucky little blighter, isn't he? He wasn't in what one would call a good mood either but did admit to having a row with Aynard and threatening him. He finished by saying, "Good thing he's gone, useless bunch of *cons*, them dentists."'

Pel raised his eyebrows as Nosjean joined them. He was looking slightly more perky, the trip into the country had obviously done him good. 'I've nothing to add about Fabres,' he said, 'except that he has flashy clients. Negative on the artist, but a query on the family who he stayed with. We went to see Crystal Combes who took over the care of old Gran Martin. She confirmed Adrianne had started looking after Gran at the beginning of a ten-day course of treatment way back in September, and had refused to continue. Apparently, Monsieur Martin was present on the second and third occasions – he'd come in early for lunch and insisted on gossiping, trying to find out

110

about her other patients. He said he'd seen Aynard at her surgery when he'd been working in the field behind and told her,' here Nosjean read from his notes, 'not to mess with that one, he's a nasty piece of work.' Nosjean looked up. 'What else he said we don't know but Crystal replaced Adrianne as the visiting nurse. She met the whole lot of them eventually and although Monsieur Martin was a "nosy old toad" it didn't particularly bother her.'

Pel was scowling. 'This damn investigation keeps changing direction. First we have a straight shooting which turns into a probable *crime passionnel*, then we turn up a mysterious painter who's vanished, *et maintenant alors*, it looks like a stupid squabble between a case of toothache and a dentist. I think,' he concluded, 'this definitely calls for a comprehensive turning over of the Martin house and outbuildings, though what I'll put on my request for a search warrant is anybody's guess – no magistrate in his right mind will believe it.' Pel shook his head doubtfully. 'Darcy, draw up the papers for me to sign. I'll take them personally to Brisard, see if I can bully him a bit.'

'What about Bardolle?' Darcy asked. 'He was poking about at the gendarmerie.'

Bardolle had turned something up. A young couple necking behind a tree had become aware of someone watching them. They'd jumped to their feet shouting and he'd disappeared. The following day they'd noticed him again; this time they'd gone to the local bobbies. Their visit had been logged but no official complaint made, the kids didn't want policemen asking embarrassing questions in front of their parents. However, Bardolle had their names and addresses and had gone looking for them. It hadn't been easy; the families of both were convinced each one was with a respective friend innocently playing hopscotch or practising on his skateboard. He finally found the two groups of girls and boys draped over the benches on the esplanade, a long shaded walkway, behind the village. They were loyal to their friends and wouldn't budge when asked where they were.

'Look,' Bardolle explained, his deep voice friendly. He understood how the youngsters of a village defended one another against adult interference, particularly when it was the law. 'They've done nothing wrong, perhaps something very helpful. They went to the gendarmerie in March about a man they'd seen in the wood. I'm following it up, that's all. Don't worry, I won't cause trouble, I just want to know if this was the person.' He pulled a now rather crumpled picture from his pocket and let them pass it around.

'Well . . .' A tall girl hesitated. 'It's a bit delicate, see.'

Bardolle smiled sympathetically. 'I don't care a button what they were up to when they were interrupted. I only want to know who they saw.'

'What about their parents?' A beefy boy came forward protectively.

'I've already been to see them.' There were one or two sharp intakes of breath. 'I showed them the picture too. Don't worry! I didn't say anything that could be misconstrued, just that, as intelligent, alert younger members of the community, they might have seen him.'

The beefy boy grinned. 'I guess it's all right then.'

'They've gone to the *pigeonnier*,' the girl said. 'We'll take you if you like. We've got a secret code – they won't come out unless they hear it.'

Bardolle tramped off after them. Once out of the confines of the village, he noticed a packet of cigarettes appeared and was handed round. All of them puffed professionally as they crossed a stream, pushed their way through a hedge and marched round the edge of an immense field. They'd been walking for well over ten minutes when they stopped; beyond a rickety gate on the other side of a pond stood the remains of a *pigeonnier*.

The roof was missing and its walls ended in an uneven line just above the first floor. It had been hidden behind the trees they'd followed along the edge of the stream, and now Bardolle looked towards the crumbling stonework positioned on a gentle upward slope in an abandoned paddock of startling red and white flowers. The beefy boy whistled a short tune, ending with a note that was high and long, and a moment later another boy's head peered over the broken wall and a second short tune came in reply.

They clambered over the gate, circled round a pond through

112

the tall daisies and poppies, and halted by a hole in the wall that had once held a door. A couple emerged, their hands entwined. They were very young and both blushing. Bardolle came out of the crowd. 'Sandrine? Julien?'

'What did you bring him for?' Julien's voice was aggressive.

'*Pas de panique!*' the beefy boy replied. 'It's to do with the bloke in the woods.' He pointed to a copse on the other side of the spacious paddock.

Bardolle fished in his pocket again. 'Did he look anything like this?'

Sandrine's eyes opened wide. 'That's him!'

'Are you sure?'

'As sure as I shouldn't be caught here with Julien!'

12

'*Patron!*' Bardolle's foghorn voice was only just under control.

Pel jerked the phone away from his ear. 'Breathe in, Bardolle, and whisper what you've got to say.'

'Sorry, *patron*, but I think I'm on to something. I've got a couple of kids who actually saw our tall grey stranger!'

'Slow down and explain.'

'Two youngsters went off for a quick snogging session and were disturbed by our artist chap, twice. The second time they went to the police. The local gendarmes, however, didn't seem very interested – they said they'd keep their eyes open and ticked the kids off for trespassing – so they decided to do their own bit of sleuthing. There's a whole crowd of budding bloodhounds here, they hid themselves in the wood to see if he'd come back. He didn't but they inadvertently discovered where he was painting! On top of a flipping *pigeonnier*! They had a meeting that evening to discuss what they should do and decided to deal with their peeping Tom themselves but he never came back.'

'Perhaps it's just as well if they were intending to confront him.'

'I've persuaded the local chaps to seal the place off and keep guard. They were none too keen seeing as night was falling, but if you could put a word in it'll stop them going off when the hedgehogs and owls come out to play.'

'Hedgehogs?'

'They make a hell of a racket in the dark, believe me. Them and the rest of the nocturnal inhabitants of the countryside, it's enough to frighten the life out of you.'

'Get two of them on the job, they can hold hands. I'll fax the request. Once it's on paper and signed by me they'll have no option but to do it properly. And Bardolle,' he added, 'be there at first light to show Forensics where the *pigeonnier* is.'

'*Oui, patron*!'

'What about these kids? You'd better have them available for more questioning.'

There was a brief silence before Bardolle replied, 'Er, *patron*?'

'*Oui, quoi*?'

'Their story is that they were mushrooming in the woods.'

His chief inspector smiled. 'I'll remember.'

Pel called Darcy and Nosjean back into his office. 'Things are moving on the artist,' he said. 'You'll have to go to the Martins' place without me tomorrow, four of you should be enough. Brisard has surprisingly agreed to the search warrant. You're due to start at 0800 hours, so don't turn up before, but there's no time limit after that. Thank God for Article 56 of the Code de Procédure Pénale.'

When they'd left, Pel rang Leguyder and got the answering machine. He left a string of expletives and a short message: 'Where are you, damn it? This is bloody urgent! Fontaine les Lacs first thing tomorrow morning!'

He pulled the thick file marked 'Aynard/Fabres, Murder, Fontaine les Lacs' towards him and, opening the cover, started reading. Had the artist really got anything to do with it? Or had he just happened to be there? Or was it a personal vendetta between Martin and the dentist with a kidney problem that had been reignited by some unknown incident? But why shoot Adrianne Fabres as well? Because she was in the way when the gun went off? They'd decided it had gone off too soon, fired from the waist by someone not used to handling guns. Martin? Unlikely. Peasants had acquired the right to hunt when the law was changed after the revolution in 1789, they'd been brought up to it for generations. Had he gone only to frighten Aynard, get his own back, and been surprised to find the nurse doing what she was doing instead of sitting innocently at her desk with her back to him? So surprised he'd pulled the trigger accidentally? Adrianne Fabres hadn't liked Martin – she'd handed Gran over to Crystal Combes. Why? Was it a pretty nurse not enjoying the attentions of a vulgar farmer, or something else? Could Martin have got to the surgery and away again without anyone seeing him? It was quite a trudge from his farm. On the other hand he could have travelled across his own fields in a tractor, no one would have noticed that. Except that in March he'd have damaged precious newly sewn crops. Or was there a footpath round the fields? Could the mysterious artist have used it? It was possible, no one had seen his Parisian number plate in the village. But why shoot the nurse and her patient? If he was a peeper who liked hurting people, and Pel knew only too well they existed, he wouldn't have needed a reason beyond being a bloodthirsty psychopath. But if he crossed the fields to the surgery on foot, there would have been some evidence on the floor there. And where the hell had the weapon gone? Who had held it? Who had hidden it? If it was hidden.

Pel's head was filled with unanswerable questions which he wanted to discuss. He lifted the phone wearily to call for Darcy. There was no reply and, realising he was the only one left at his desk and that he could do nothing more that night, he stuffed his pockets with the remaining cigarettes and went home.

Nosjean was lonely. Mijo had finally caught the train home to Mum. The days were okay, he had plenty to keep him occupied, but he dreaded the empty flat that was once filled with his wife's moods and the baby's crying. Bad as it had been, it was preferable to the silence they'd left behind. Delaying the inevitable dreary evening, he walked slowly along the warm streets, idly gazing into shop windows. The restaurants were already open, allowing inviting odours to waft into his path – perhaps he'd treat himself to a decent meal. He'd lost weight, Mijo hadn't wanted to cook much this last month. 'What's the point, you're never here,' she'd shouted, pointing to the oven where he'd found another plate of tepid noodles topped by tinned sauce. He decided on finding a properly prepared *boeuf bourguignon* and a bottle of Mâcon. Bugger it, he thought, I'm not driving anywhere tonight, I could, if I really wanted to, indulge myself with a good wine. It'll help me sleep in that huge cold bed.

Turning down a side street he made his way to a La Marmite, a small restaurant noted for its gourmet food. However, as he approached the open door, a car parked outside caught his eye, a BMW he recognised. Right behind it was a shining grey metallic Mercedes. Disappointed, he pushed his hands deeper into his trouser pockets and headed off to another restaurant, not wanting to embarrass Alain Fabres with his presence. He hesitated, turned and made his way back again, then, beckoning to a waiter, asked if in fact Fabres was dining there. *'Sur la terrasse,'* he was told.

He went into the discreet bar and ordered a beer, and while he was drinking, looked out to the busy walled garden where a dozen people were already eating. In one corner, sitting under a colourful parasol, Alain Fabres was patting Béatrice de Maupou's hand. She was smiling. Nosjean swallowed his beer, paid and left. De Troq's place wasn't far away. He wanted to ask him something.

De Troq' answered the bell, speaking into the intercom, his voice distorted through a cheap microphone. Nosjean didn't reply at once, there could be someone up there with him. He was still shy in his personal life and knew there was nothing worse than having an intimate evening spoiled by a colleague turning up to talk shop, and de Troq' was engaged to be married to a posh bird who tended to look down her nose at Nosjean.

De Troq' asked again, 'Who's there?'

He sighed and announced himself – anything was better than missing Mijo. The door's lock buzzed and he let himself into the ancient building, imagining as he climbed the wide curling staircase what it must have been like when it was a house with only one family living there. It must have been huge; each floor had been divided into four flats. De Troq's was on the top floor and he was waiting as Nosjean arrived, apologising for the intrusion.

'Have you eaten?' de Troq' asked immediately.

'Er, no, actually I haven't, just on my way.'

'We'll eat together?'

'Well, all I wanted to do was ask you something.'

'Ask while we eat, I was just putting the finishing touches to the meal when Véronique cried off.' He shrugged. 'She's woken up to the fact that she'll be marrying the police force if she marries me, because I'm not leaving. She's got cold feet and is calling my bluff by breaking our engagement.'

'She'd get on well with Mijo,' Nosjean said miserably. He gave de Troq' a twisted smile and they both grinned.

'At least we can enjoy the very fine Beaune I bought,' de Troq' said, 'without being interrupted by wedding plans.'

'Or wet nappies.'

Nosjean finally asked his question as they were enjoying the last of the wine with a piece of ripe Camembert. 'Béatrice de Maupou?' de Troq' said. 'No, I don't know her but my mother will, she keeps tabs on all the titles. I'll phone her.'

'I get the impression that my mother,' he laughed, five minutes later, 'while she doesn't approve of Béatrice, does quite admire her. She was the elderly Vicomte's housekeeper cum live-in nurse who took him to the Mayor for a short ceremony and became his wife. He hung on for another decade and finally died a couple of years ago. However, Mother says that while she didn't approve of the marriage at the time, Béatrice did make the old boy very happy, he would have reached a century in September. And even though she was entitled to be called Madame la Vicomtesse, she never has been and never will. Apparently, they once sat next to each other at a function and although Mother tried hard not to talk to her, she had to in the end. When asked why she insisted on being called simply Madame de Maupou, Béatrice dug Mother in the ribs and said, "It's my husband I enjoy, love, not his blooming title." My dear mother, who is not known for her easy sense of humour, almost choked on her vol au vent.'

Nosjean told him about what he'd seen at La Marmite. 'I suppose Fabres's got the right to date another woman now,' he

commented. 'All the same, he was a bit quick off the mark –
it's barely three months since Adrianne snuffed it.'

Pel was up at dawn and, kissing his long-suffering wife tenderly on the cheek, set off for the city. Settling behind his desk
to go through the mail, he noticed one of the envelopes had a
Spanish stamp. He tore it open, struggled with the words
inside, then marched into the sergeants' room and handed it to
de Troq'. 'Take this to the *procureur*'s office and pick up the
mandat to cover our involvement. You're off to Spain! And let
Cham know, he's going with you so you'll need three air
tickets.'

'Three, *patron*?'

'Two police, one pathologist,' Pel snapped. 'The Huguenot
speaks Spanish, she's going too. It might help the Gomez
parents to have a woman on the job, but tell her that her
coiffure is not suitable for this sort of thing, she'll frighten the
life out of them, and,' he added, 'if she faints during the
autopsy, she's fired. *A propos*, I want you there and back by
tomorrow.'

Before he left, de Troq' told him what Nosjean had seen the
evening before.

'Interesting,' Pel agreed, 'although we can hardly consider
the man's behaviour suspicious because he was having dinner
with a rich widow – I've done the same myself. However,' he
continued thoughtfully, 'I'll have a word with Cousin Roger.'
Cousin Roger was the only member of Madame Pel's family
that he liked. They shared the same political views, believing
all Members of Parliament to be idiots; the same tastes, good
food, good wine, always Burgundian; and the same insane
habit, smoking. He was also one of the city's accountants and
had been known to lay his hands on information a policeman
couldn't get near without a court order.

Having bellowed at everyone he could find at the Hôtel de
Police, he gave the front page of the papers a quick inspection,
nodding at the now released portrait of their missing artist,
then, filling his pockets with the essentials for the day, mostly
lighters and packets of cigarettes, plus a notebook and a handful of biros, he made his way towards the stairs and the exit.

118

He found Bardolle in the café on the *place* at Fontaine les Lacs. He was drawing a map. 'It's not impossible,' Bardolle told him. 'Our artist could have come from the *pigeonnier* and round the edge of the field without being seen, the trees make a good screen, then jumped the stream to land almost directly behind the surgery.'

'If he was an athlete,' Pel pointed out.

'I tried it,' Bardolle smiled, 'and got a wet sock for my trouble.'

Pel ordered a cup of coffee and asked why the kids who'd been disturbed by the artist hadn't come forward before. 'They're a group of seven or eight youngsters,' Bardolle explained. 'They live up to ten kilometres from here. They all go to the same school in the city and meet on the esplanade to discuss their problems. However, because the village has become wealthy in recent years thanks to tourism, the kids who live actually in the village have found themselves with money in their pockets and swimming pools in their back gardens. Our group are from the farms scattered about the surrounding countryside, and they haven't been touched by the change. They still help on the land, pick the grapes, bail the hay, castrate the corn, and don't mix with the villagers who think of them as lowly peasants. It's easy to tell the difference; one gang whizz around on flashy scooters called *beewees*, while our lot continue to repair and repaint their parents' old mopeds.'

A large Renault Traffic drew up in the little square: Leguyder had arrived in his mobile laboratory. The scientist jumped nimbly from the cab and headed straight for the bar. 'I thought I'd find you in here,' he snorted. 'You leave me offensive messages in the middle of the night and when I, as a dutiful member of the Forensic Science Department, responsible for many men doing important work for the whole county – not just the police, you know – when I arrived as ordered, what do I find? The chief inspector sitting chatting in a bar.'

Pel sighed, glanced wearily at Bardolle and stood up. 'I've been waiting hours,' he lied. 'Now you're here let's get on with it, shall we?'

Although he too would have liked a cup of coffee, Leguyder realised he'd been outmanoeuvred and stamped out after them. Bardolle climbed into the car and led them through the winding streets to the esplanade. 'This is where we leave the vehicles,' he said, reaching for a pair of binoculars on the back seat and hanging them round his neck. 'We do the rest on foot.'

'How far?' Leguyder asked.

'About ten minutes or so.'

'How am I supposed to carry my equipment?'

'Oh, for God's sake, stop bellyaching,' Pel said. 'There are two of us and two of you, you can't have that much to take. Surely cameras and plastic bags don't weigh that much?'

'You don't understand! Forensic analysis is an extremely precise science, we don't just take pretty pictures and shovel everything in sight into dustbin liners.'

Leguyder loaded them all with boxes and containers, insisting it would all be needed. Bardolle took most of it, being built like a sideboard, Pel took as little as possible and the lab assistant took the rest. Leguyder carried a video camera that he fussed over intolerably.

When they reached the *pigeonnier*, he started filming. The two limp guards looked dolefully at Pel. 'Can we go now, please? We haven't slept a wink.'

'You weren't supposed to be sleeping!' Pel bellowed, but they did have bags under their eyes so he waved them away.

As Leguyder and his assistant went inside the derelict building, the camera still whirring, Pel turned to Bardolle offering him a cigarette. 'He does make a meal of it,' he said. 'Filming is a very good idea, particularly at the scene of a crime, but today I think he's rather overdoing it. His fastidiousness can be a pain in the arse.'

Leguyder's head appeared over the crumbling wall. 'I thought this was supposed to be where an artist worked?'

'It is.'

'It looks more like a bedroom, there's a mattress up here.'

'That's the kids,' Bardolle boomed back. 'They took it up there after the artist had gone.'

Leguyder disappeared again. 'Why?' Pel asked, quietly enjoying the scenery shimmering in the sunlight, the chirruping of frogs from a nearby pond competing with the rasping song of hidden crickets, and a blissful Gauloise between his lips.

'They saw where the artist was working, had a meeting and

came back the following day. He'd gone but they went up to see if he'd left anything. All they found was a better place for necking than the woods. They're sheltered from the wind, sitting or lying down they can't be spotted from the ground; they can, however, see for miles in all directions up there. If anyone approaches, they have enough time to leg it for the trees before they're discovered.'

'What do they do when it rains?' Pel asked.

By the time Leguyder had finished, a group of youngsters were making their way round the pond towards them. Bardolle introduced Sandrine and Julien to Pel as the scientist packed up his belongings.

'Can we go up now?' Pel asked.

'You can do what you like,' Leguyder replied huffily. 'I've got work to do,' and, heaving a number of containers on to the hunched shoulders of his assistant, he started off towards the gate.

Pel gazed at the view from the top of the *pigeonnier*. 'Okay, Sandrine, Julien, tell me what happened.'

They retold their story as Pel went on staring into the distance. When they'd finished, he asked them to go into the wood to the exact location where they'd been . . . he hesitated . . . collecting mushrooms. They grinned at him and started down the crumbling stairs.

They waited while the couple disappeared through the trees, then heard a shout indicating they were in position. 'I can hear them clearly but I can't see them,' Pel said. Bardolle handed him the binoculars.

'Hmm,' Pel said, 'they're still practically invisible, but perhaps it was enough, together with a few squeaks and giggles, to raise the curiosity of a man sitting alone up here, enough to make him go down and take a look.'

Pel swung the glasses round and stopped dead. 'Holy Mother of God!' His sights were fixed on the village; he could see the gap in the undulating roofs where the main street went into the small square; the esplanade with its tall trees on the far side; and on this side, over a high hedge with bold purple sprays hanging out from the greenery, he could also see a low white building set apart from the rest. 'Bardolle,' he said slowly, 'tell the kids they can come back, then walk into the village, to the surgery. I want you in the dialysis room with the shutters open, front and back. I'll join you there.'

While he waited, he was confronted with six expectant young faces. 'You went to the gendarmerie on 21st March, Sunday, is that right?' Julian and Sandrine nodded. 'What happened after that?'

'Well, we went to school on Monday and Tuesday, but on Wednesday, our day off, we went back to the woods over there and found out where the dirty old man had been hiding, we saw him up here, see. We had a meeting and decided to tell him what we thought. Well, we went to school on Thursday and Friday and Saturday morning but that afternoon, Sat'day like, we came over. He'd gone! We waited all Sunday too but he didn't come back, so, well, we decided to requisition the building.' Julien smiled, proud of using a long word.

It wasn't exactly what Bardolle had told Pel but the kids were certain. 'So the last time you saw him was the 24th, is that right?' he said, wanting to get the story absolutely straight.

'If that was the Wednesday, yeah.' Julien shrugged.

The shutter on the high back window of the surgery began to move as Bardolle wound it up. Pel picked up the binoculars again. 'Well, bugger me!' he whispered.

They trooped out of the *pigeonnier* and made their way back to the village. 'How long before we can use it again?' one boy asked.

'I don't know,' Pel replied deep in thought. 'I'm going to send a photographer back to take in the view. When he's finished and I've had the okay from the mad scientist who was poking about here this morning, you should be able to come back. I'll let you know.' He fished in his pocket as they reached the edge of the field. 'I don't know what your club is called,' he said, producing a hundred franc note, 'but I'd like to make a donation, you've been more helpful than expected. By the way, what do you do when it rains?'

They laughed. 'We get wet.'

Bardolle was waiting by the surgery. 'Shall I shut up again, *patron*?'

'Not yet, I'd like another look.'

There was patterned glass at the front, letting in light but keeping out prying eyes; at the back, however, the window was clear and clean. It was also well above head height, too high for a peeping Tom without a stepladder, and through it, all Pel could see was the top of the lilac hedge. He stepped back a couple of paces and bent his knees, bringing his eyes to almost the same level as the treatment bed where Hugo Aynard had been lying, and looked again. The top of the *pigeonnier* was clearly visible.

13

When Pel got back to the office it seemed as if a thousand bells were ringing. One of the interview rooms had been turned into an office with trestle tables and a dozen phones. He poked his head round the door to see how it was going; apart from Rigal, he didn't recognise the faces fielding the calls. There was no opening window in there, just a block of reinforced glass allowing the sunlight to penetrate, and the air was stale with cigarette smoke and perspiration. It was as hot as hell and almost as noisy. The moment a phone crashed down, it rang and was snatched up; notes were made and questions asked. The missing artist had been seen all over France and every sighting would have to be followed up as fast as possible on the off-chance that it was genuine.

Returning to his own more peaceful office, Pel unearthed de Troq's proposed timetable for the trip over the border: take off for Paris, 2005; Paris–Barcelona, 2125; hired car to travel inland; expected time of arrival, Huesca, midnight last night. Pel glanced at his watch. They should be well and truly on the job by now, setting off back any minute. And underneath was the information that Darcy and Nosjean, Aimedieu and Pujol had gone as instructed to the Martins' farm. He went through the team's movements, everyone busy, everyone on the ball, except Misset, of course – as usual he was nowhere to be seen and hadn't even bothered to let anyone know. His space on the duty roster was blank. Like his brain. Perhaps he'd run away from home, galloped off into the setting sun, disappeared into his own inefficiency for ever ... Pel sighed; it was pleasant to dream.

He pulled a pile of files towards him. Cheriff and Annie were dealing with the robbery at Les Chartreux. To date the dossier was clean and slim, containing few papers; it would fatten and become dog-eared during the week. No doubt their well-tanned colleague, two metres of handsome Arab, damn him, had taken their gorgeous redhead to ferret about in the antique and *brocante* shops, firstly to warn the owners about what might be turning up on their counters for sale, but also in the unlikely event that something already had.

As Pel shuffled the files like a pack of cards, trying to get them into order of importance and failing miserably, every one was important, he found himself wondering whether Cheriff and Annie would ever get married. He hoped not: marriage led to babies and babies led to, well, you only had to look at Nosjean to know what babies led to. Not only that, he'd lose a good policeman if Annie got pregnant.

Rigal appeared in his doorway, cowering in anticipation of Pel's fury. He shot him a look. 'And don't think being pregnant lets you off the hook,' he grumbled, then, realising what he'd said, he grinned to cover his confusion. Rigal thought his boss was in pain, suffering from agonising dyspepsia, and ducked lower, holding out a wad of papers as cover.

'Bardolle'll be here in a minute with a report to dictate,' Pel shouted, trying to regain some dignity. 'Give your lists to the uniformed branch, they can do the preliminaries.'

As Rigal bowed out, Pel started sifting through the files again, concentrating first on the girl found at the Roman dig. Was she really connected with Mariana Gomez in Spain? He pushed it to one side, he'd have to wait for the pathologist's opinion before deciding. He pulled forward Aynard/Fabres, at least that was moving again. He polished his glasses, lit a cigarette surreptitiously, pretending not to notice, blinked several times to alert his brain to impending action and started reading.

When the pealing church bells broke into his thoughts, he lifted his head. The corridors were calmer, the phones were quiet. Odd, he thought and, getting to his feet, realised why: that wonderful French habit, *la bouf*! Between midday and two the only thing that preoccupied a real Frenchman was filling his face with food. As he strolled towards the stairs, he wondered if many crimes were committed during the lunch hours. He thought not, eating was far too important an affair to be interrupted for something frivolous like a hold-up or grievous bodily harm, unless of course someone burnt the steak. He crossed to the main entrance; it was peaceful for the moment. He didn't expect it to last long but while it did, for once he would surprise his wife and take her to lunch.

The city was steaming nicely; the summer sun belted its heat towards the earth from an azure sky, turning the edges of the high buildings hazy; the streets were hot and relatively quiet, just the occasional puzzled holiday-maker trying the doors of the shops shut for the national pastime of consumption and digestion. He'd take his wife to a new restaurant he'd noticed. It looked just the place for a beautiful day like today; they advertised meat grilled over a wood fire and freshly made salads served on a terrace shaded by the large leaves of numerous mulberry trees. It was an attractive and agreeable setting for a woman who was likewise. Yes, he said to himself, she deserves it, whatever it costs. It had looked expensive – what the hell, I ought to make the effort. I'm useless at remembering birthdays and anniversaries, even Christmas sometimes. Thank God for Annie. If it weren't for her, our wives would complain a damn sight more – she always gives us the nod on the appropriate days. And another thing, if Annie and Cheriff –

'Pel!'

He stopped, a heavenly voice was calling . . .

'Pel!' No heavenly voice, it was the Hulk, Big Bardolle, lumbering along the pavement at full pelt like a charging bull, his nostrils flared and eyes bulging, while his thick muscular legs pumped, his feet pounding the pavement. He came to a halt. '*Patron*', he panted, 'they've found a gun!'

Darcy was still waiting as Pel picked up the phone. '*Accouche,*' he breathed, dabbing at his forehead with a sleeve.

'We're still at Martin's. Aimedieu turned up a gun in one of the pigsties.'

'Bring it and Monsieur Martin in, the gun to Forensics, Martin straight into an interview room.'

'When I radioed through, that's what we intended,' Darcy confirmed. 'However, in the last few minutes things have changed somewhat. He won't come, he's locked himself in the house with his sons and Gran. He's threatening to shoot the lot of us and them if we go near him!'

'Where's his wife?'

'Left early this morning.'

'I'm on my way.'

When Pel arrived, he found Darcy, Nosjean, Aimedieu and Pujol cowering behind their cars in the immaculately swept yard. All the shutters on the house were closed except one. Bardolle pulled up behind the other two cars and slid out to join his colleagues. Pel eased himself across from the passenger seat and tumbled on to the clean concrete, a loudhailer in his hand. 'Where is he?'

'Up there,' Darcy whispered, pointing to the only gap in the shutters. 'Have you brought the peashooters?'

'Behind the driver's seat but keep them out of sight. God knows what Martin'll do if he sees we're armed.'

They quietly sorted themselves out, Darcy and Nosjean discreetly loading the two guns, then Pel lifted the loudhailer to his mouth. 'Monsieur Martin,' he called, 'there are six of us now, don't do anything you'll regret. Put down your gun and come out, we only want to talk to you.'

'*Va te faire foutre!*'

Pel slowly stood up, his arms spread wide so Martin could see him. Nothing happened. So far so good. 'Monsieur, please put down your gun and we'll talk.'

There was an explosion from the house and a car window disintegrated into tiny cubes of glass. Pel threw himself to the ground.

'Reinforcements, *patron*?'

'Looks like we're going to need them,' Pel agreed. 'Where the hell's his wife?'

'Gone to market,' Nosjean told him.

'Everything packs up at midday, she should be back by now.'

As if in answer, a rattling *deux-chevaux* shuddered to a stop at the end of the drive and, after a shrieking conversation with the driver, they saw Madame Martin marching towards them carrying two heavily laden shopping bags.

Pel beckoned urgently to her. She crossed the end of the yard and looked down at the crouching police. 'What's going on? You can't picnic here, you know!'

The situation was explained quickly. 'Silly bugger!' she retorted. 'He's been at the *eau de vie* again.' Unperturbed, she set off towards the house. 'I try and keep it hidden but he always finds it in the end.'

'Madame, come back'

'Not blooming likely, stupid sod'll break something if I know him!'

'Come back!' but she already had the front door open and was disappearing through it.

In the minutes of silence that followed, Pel and his men tried to imagine what was going on inside. Pujol was poised with the car radio in his hand, ready to order reinforcements and ambulances as necessary. Darcy and Nosjean were poised with their police regulation revolvers, the entrance of the house in their sights.

They heard a couple of good hard smacks that resounded through the open window, followed by shouting and finally loud sobbing. A few moments later Madame appeared again, holding her husband at arm's length. He was nursing his jaw. 'There you are,' she said delightedly, 'no harm done, you can ask your questions now. That's what you're here for, isn't it?'

As their two adolescent sons slithered out and ran full tilt across the yard, she screamed after them, 'And don't think that's an end to it. You'll get what you deserve when you come in for supper!' Turning back to Pel, she added, 'They will too!'

With Martin wilting in a chair in a vacant interview room, under the guard of mighty Bardolle, Pel breathed a sigh of relief. Without thinking, he handed round his cigarettes; noticing all of them accept, even young Pujol, he regretted it immediately. 'Tell me,' he said, looking dismally into the half-empty packet.

'We arrived with the search warrant,' Darcy said. 'Madame was just leaving. She took a look at it and told us not to make a mess. The men were on their way to the fields and Gran was parked in front of the television watching cartoons, so we got to work.'

'Farms are filthy, aren't they?' Nosjean offered, looking at his dung-encrusted shoes. 'Roman digs don't smell.'

'It took us the best part of the morning,' Darcy went on. 'The outbuildings are like a rabbit warren, one led into another, and eventually we found we'd come round in a full circle. Nothing. That left the poultry run and the pigsty, round the back, so while we did the henhouse, I sent Nosjean and Aimedieu in to see the pigs.'

'Pigs stink.'

Ignoring Nosjean's comment, Aimedieu continued. 'I found the gun wedged between two beams. Nearly missed it – I was watching where I was walking.'

'And the pigs weren't friendly.'

'Nosjean had to fend them off while I climbed up to retrieve it,' Aimedieu explained, his face splitting into an angelic grin. 'He got bitten.'

'Then what?' Pel didn't want to waste time on farmyard tales.

'I called to Darcy who was picking feathers out of his hair and we took it back to the house.'

'Monsieur Martin had come back, he was in the kitchen with his sons,' Darcy went on. 'He had a bottle in front of him and was busy emptying it, the boys were watching television with Gran. Aimedieu showed him what he'd found and started asking questions. He appeared perfectly calm so I went back out to give you the good news. A couple of minutes later I heard a shot and Nosjean, Aimedieu and Pujol came tearing out.'

'When Darcy had gone,' Aimedieu explained, 'he suggested we all had a tot while we discussed things. He got up from the table and went towards the sink, for glasses I presumed. Then I saw a rifle leaning half hidden against the dresser. I made a move towards him but he grabbed it, lifted it to his shoulder and said if we didn't get out he'd shoot us. Nosjean tried reasoning with him but he wasn't listening. He let off one

128

barrel sending crockery falling like confetti from the dresser. We hopped it.'

'What about the gun he used?'

'All the guns in the house have gone to Forensics with the one we found.'

'Let's go and see our prisoner,' Pel said. But the telephone stopped him.

'You took your time!' he shouted through a crackling line from Spain. 'Having a holiday at my expense, no doubt.'

'*D'accord, patron*,' de Troq' replied calmly. 'We've got problems. The body of Mariana Gomez was exhumed first thing this morning and the second autopsy was completed an hour ago. Cham's taken all the samples he needs but the Guardia Civil are being obstructive. They will not authorise taking them out of the country.'

'Damn them!' Pel exploded. 'Can he do his tests in a lab there?'

'He could but it'll take time and I'm not sure they'll let him have access. The family's weeping and wailing at the arguing, the priest is doing his best but even he can't persuade the police to co-operate.'

'De Troq', you'll have to cope, I've got Brisard coming in to interrogate a suspect for the double murder. Flash your title about a bit, haven't you a relation or two down there who can pull strings?'

'I've a cousin married to a Spaniard. They live in Zaragoza – it's a couple of hours away.'

'Then use him! What are noble families for if not to help one another?' Pel sat back. De Troq' was infuriating at times with his aristocratic background and an education that allowed him to know history inside out, back to front and upside down, plus speaking half a dozen languages as if it was the most natural thing in the world. On the other hand, there were times when it could be useful. He could just imagine the faces in the Spanish police station when the Baron had done his stuff and a minister from Madrid rang demanding the release of the samples. He hoped it would be that easy.

The smile that had been growing immediately slipped from his face. Monsieur le Juge, boring Maître Brisard, had arrived to see Martin.

'What about the lawyer?' Pel asked, knowing one was required to be present.

'I thought he was here. One has definitely been appointed, I did it myself,' Brisard replied importantly. 'Perhaps he's waiting with the suspect. I'll go and see, get the preliminaries under way.' Pel wished the magistrate luck; in his opinion their suspect was on the brink of an alcoholic crisis, shouting and bellyaching then sinking into a depressed silence. Bardolle had had to restrain him once already when he'd tried to have a go at Darcy.

After a few moments frowning at the Aynard/Fabres file, he made his way slowly and thoughtfully to the interview room, hoping Darcy would hurry up with the stenographer. Standing outside the door was Bardolle.

'What are you going out here? You're supposed to be in there protecting Brisard.'

'He ordered me to leave,' Bardolle said.

Pel slammed the door open. Martin was squatting against the wall, his head in his hands, crying. Brisard was laid out on the floor.

'He doesn't know his own strength,' Madame Martin protested when she arrived. 'He didn't mean to do it.'

'But he did,' Pel insisted, 'and has now been charged with wilfully attacking a *juge d'instruction*, and that's for starters.'

'Ooh, blimey, I'd better get in there and sort the sod out.'

'Madame,' Pel said patiently, 'your husband had to be sedated by the police doctor. He was taken to 72 rue Auxonne in a prison van. I'm sure the guards will manage to sort him out on his arrival. You will not be permitted to see him. Monsieur le Juge, however, was taken to hospital in an ambulance.'

After answering Pel's short questions with very long answers, Madame Martin was allowed to leave. Pel was none the wiser. He made a résumé of the hour-long interview: 1. Aynard should be struck off (Pel sighed, he'd been more than adequately struck off); fancy not seeing patients at the weekend! 2. Nurse Fabres was a showy little piece and she didn't want her boys gawping at them bulgy protuberances!

Pel pushed his hands under his specs and rubbed his aching eyes. One false movement later and he'd flipped the glasses off his nose. In an attempt to catch them, he swatted them to the floor; pushing his chair back to find them, he crunched one lens underfoot. 'Damn, blast and buggeration!' He studied the glittering shards of glass tragically. Now he'd have to wear his spare pair, ten years old and with thick tortoiseshell rims – it would have them laughing in the aisles. If it hadn't been for that pompous ass, Brisard, he wouldn't have had to spend half the day listening to the twittering of Madame Martin. How could a man climb to the dizzy heights of being an examining magistrate and be so bloody stupid?

However, they had Martin well and truly under lock and key, it was only a matter of time before he confessed to the Aynard-Fabres murder. And yet . . . Pel turned the train of thought off. Doubts at this stage in the game were not good for one's sanity, and the Chief was waiting to see him.

As he groped his way blindly into his office, the Chief looked up and smiled, dropping his pen on to the top of his desk. He rose from his chair and crossed to the cupboard where he kept a small selection of bottles for visiting dignitaries, or sudden successes. 'Let's drink to Martin's arrest,' he said, sloshing whisky into two glasses. 'Bravo! At last we can close the case. Monsieur le Procureur is delighted; he's talking about promotions again.'

Pel squinted, trying to focus. 'I really don't give a – '

'Now, Pel,' the Chief warned kindly, 'don't say anything you may regret. Good God! I can't go on for ever, my retirement is looming, a replacement must be found and it looks once more as if my proposal will be accepted. Cheers!'

'Monsieur le Procureur, promotion, replacement . . . the politics in a police station is sometimes as baffling as the sods outside,' Pel mumbled as he tasted the soothing golden liquid. He tried to look his superior in the eye but without his specs it wasn't easy finding his head. 'Bah! Electoral candidates!' he said. 'You only have to see their rosy cheeks and twinkling eyes to know the lot of them are con men. I don't believe a word any of them say, and,' he added, 'I don't believe Martin killed Aynard and Fabres.'

The Chief spluttered. 'But he tried to shoot three of your men! And he took a pot shot at you. He's obviously unstable.'

'He'd been drinking.' Pel's voice was flat. 'Alcohol renders men either amorous and usually incapable, or aggressive. He's one of the latter variety.'

'Be reasonable, Pel,' the Chief sighed, sitting down again. 'Even drunk there was no reason for him to attack three unarmed policemen.'

'Maybe there was, they'd been poking about on his farm all morning. Peasants are proud, they don't like that sort of thing.'

'He'd hidden the gun, for heaven's sake!'

'I still don't think it was him.'

'Well, it's up to the *juge* now, he's the one that'll decide whether to charge him. What does Brisard say?'

Pel swallowed hard; apparently no one had told the Chief what had happened. 'Brisard isn't saying very much at the moment,' Pel said quietly to his glass.

'Ah, and why's that?'

Pel took a gulp at the whisky and told him. Even through his myopic haze, he saw the cheerful face turn gradually to a disaster area. ''Spose that buggers the promotion, *n'est ce pas?*' he added brightly, finishing his drink. The Chief was mouthing noiseless words. Pel decided he'd better leave.

Annie was in the corridor looking perplexed. '*Patron?*'

'Ah, just the person I wanted to see, if only I could.' He shook off the fuzzy image of the Chief considering committing suicide and handed her the smashed spectacles. 'Get them mended pronto, will you? I need a white stick without them.'

She smiled sympathetically and nodded. 'What about your spare pair?'

'I'm not putting them on in public!' He turned away. 'I've got to do some thinking,' he added as he wandered off.

'*Patron,*' Annie tried again, 'while we were going round the antique shops and jewellers for the robbery at Les Chartreux, Cheriff and I came across a bit of gold we thought we recognised.' She held out a small sketch she'd made. 'Ever seen this before?'

'I wouldn't know, even you're a blur. A lead, is it? Jolly good, you know what to do.'

'Yes,' she replied doubtfully, 'but we can't remember why or from where we recognised it.'

'Look in the files, everything's written down,' Pel called and walked away, confident in the efficiency of his team.

Annie watched the hunched shoulders as Pel worked his way down the corridor, hands in pockets, head bent deep in thought, a thin cloud of smoke playing round his ears, like photo's she'd seen of a volcano somewhere off the coast of South America. She'd rather hoped that his computerised memory would have come up with the answer in seconds, instead of having to spend hours going through millions of pages of reports. She sighed. Back to the drawing board – now was not the moment to pester the boss. She could almost hear his brain whirring, programmed to solve a new puzzle.

As he pulled up outside his house, Pel removed the Buddy Holly frames from his face and nearly tripped over his own feet. His wife met him at the door, smiling tenderly at her handicapped husband. She knew what had happened; Annie had phoned to find out which opticians had his prescription.

'I've already sacked Madame Routy,' she said softly as she led him through the house, 'to save you the trouble. There's a beer waiting for you in the shade outside. Make yourself comfortable. I'll join you in a minute, once I've checked she's not put too much bat's wing in the soup.'

Pel allowed himself to be guided on to the terrace, adoring his wife more with every step. She thought of everything, wonderful woman. Easing himself into the cushions of a wicker chair, he fumbled for his drink and, having found it, sipped. Bat's wing! *Mon Dieu!* It was true! He sank back and sipped again. Not to worry, his good lady had everything under control.

The bees were buzzing lazily behind him in the lavender bushes, the hollyhocks waved from the end of the garden and the dozens of hibiscus were preparing to burst into flower. Pel saw none of it, he could hardly see past his nose, plus he was trying like the devil to work out why he wasn't convinced of Martin's guilt. Very soon his head was nodding as he slipped into the blissful oblivion of sleep.

'Want another?' Pel shot up, spilling most of his beer. 'Oh no, you haven't finished that one,' and the fire-eating housekeeper crashed away across the paving stones.

'*Sorcière!*' he yelled after her. 'Yes, bring me another, the daisies drank most of this one! Then concentrate on your cauldron.'

It was his wife who brought it, apologising for the interruption. 'I'm sorry, Pel, but I was folding a soufflé together.'

Folding soufflés was beyond him, he always believed cooking was done in stout saucepans, not sheets of paper, but he let it slide. His culinary expertise stopped at spreading jam on his breakfast croissant, and even that was usually a messy business.

'You're looking tired,' his wife said kindly.

Pel told her about the Martin arrest, and Brisard's stupidity. She always took an interest in his work and often made interesting observations.

'So in return for being left with his toothache, the farmer shot the dentist and the nurse.'

Pel agreed it sounded preposterous. 'People have been known to murder for less,' he said.

'I'm sure they have, and I'm sure you're right,' but she didn't sound it. 'I went to see the Darcy twins today.' Diplomatically she changed the subject. 'They are a jolly couple and the older boys adore them. Kate wants us to go for supper, when you and Darcy have time of course.'

'Maybe next month, more likely next year,' Pel muttered, 'perhaps one day before I die.' His mind was elsewhere. They'd found the gun; Leguyder would confirm if it or one of the others removed from Martin's house was the weapon used. They'd got their man, a man who'd proved his violence, his ability to use a similar weapon for something inconsequential. He'd resisted arrest and attacked the buffoon Brisard while in custody. Pel had to accept the facts even though his seventh sense was telling him otherwise.

14

After a restless night, Pel arrived at the Hôtel de Police the following morning exhausted. While he consumed his coffee and the first cigarette of the morning, secretly before anyone saw him, he continued fretting over whether Martin should be charged with the double murder. A decision had to be taken during the next few hours. He tried to push his specs on to his forehead, it helped reflection, found they were still missing and cursed their absence – how was he going to be able to read all those reports? The spares were all right for driving but he daren't wear them in the office, it would reduce his men to hysterics. The door swung open, crashing back against the wall and making the windows rattle, 'I've spoken to Brisard,' the Chief boomed.

'How is he?'

'Shocked and dazed, nothing more, thank heaven. He'll be back in harness tomorrow.'

Pel's gloom deepened. He'd rather hoped Brisard might have been detained – nothing serious, just something slightly terminal – and a replacement brought in from another county or Madame Castéou called back from wherever she was holidaying. 'I'm delighted.' He sounded far from it.

The Chief slapped a file on to the desk making Pel jump. 'That's the report Darcy and Aimedieu prepared, together with Bardolle's on Martin's behaviour once he'd been arrested. Brisard is bravely preparing his own. Find out more about Martin's background, if there's a history of violence we've got him. Brisard wants him charged.'

As the Chief left, Pel crushed out his Gauloise and squinted at the blurred file, hoping Brisard might have a relapse. The phone rang.

'The gun shoots the right size cartridge,' Leguyder told him gleefully, 'and judging by the rust corrosion round the hammer and the insect deposits in the barrel, it was last used months ago, the end of March corresponds. Such a shame to leave such a beautiful piece uncleaned.'

135

'Oh, what is it?'

'It's a Robuste Idéale, a collector's piece, manufactured by Armes et Cycles de Saint-Etienne between 1920 and 1940.'

Without realising it Pel had reached out, tipped another cigarette on to the desk and placed it in his mouth. 'Worth a lot, is it?' His mind was working on overdrive as he lit up.

'A great deal – anything up to 40,000 francs.'

'Very interesting,' Pel said, trying to catch his brain up and slow it down with the help of a good dose of nicotine.

'Do I go on with the others?'

'What others?'

'The other guns, your chap brought me three others.'

'Er, no. We've got what we wanted.'

'Be charging the owner, will you?' Leguyder asked pleasantly.

'Mind your own business,' Pel growled and banged the phone down.

'Good morning, *patron*.' Darcy marched past his open door.

'No, it's not. It's bad, very bad,' then, raising his voice, 'Any news from de Troq'?'

The answer was in the negative and, trying to push Martin to one side, he dialled Pathology to speak to Boudet – maybe he'd heard something from Spain.

'Sorry, no news,' Boudet replied gaily, 'I'll let you know as soon as there is. Must rush, I'm inside an old dear who died in her bed last night. Good grief, she seems to have swallowed a fly, must have fallen asleep with her mouth open.'

Pel crashed the receiver down. Boudet was repulsive. Pel had never enjoyed Cham's post-mortem reports but since he'd been joined by the bounding Boudet, contact with the path lab had become as full of dread as knocking at the door of Dr Franken-stein's castle. Once he'd been convinced he'd heard a chain saw buzzing in the background, it'd made his mind boggle.

He walked towards the morning meeting, feeling his way along the passage, hoping the stroll might help settle his stomach. A number of heads were bent over paperwork as he entered the sergeants' room but he couldn't make out who they belonged to. Someone put a small package in his hand. 'Your mended specs, *patron*.' It was Annie's voice. Pel tore open the envelope and placed his glasses lovingly on his nose. 'Right, you lot! Now I can see you all,' he shouted, 'let's have your progress reports.'

As the meeting broke up, Pel realised the man with his brain in neutral had been hiding at the back of the room. 'Misset!' Misset shuffled in his seat. 'What's the matter, man? Haemorrhoids bothering you again?'

Misset stood and ambled over to Pel, followed by a large and very hairy dog.

'What's that?' Pel bellowed.

'It's Bobby, a stray I found tied to a dustbin. I untied him and he's been following me ever since.'

'Even in the car?'

'He tried.'

'So you stopped and let him jump in?'

'Yes, *patron*, he's a nice dog, honest.'

'He's ugly enough to have been crossed with an ape. Where have you been for the last week?'

'Watching the Sunshine Sect, like you said.'

'I said nothing of the sort,' Pel snapped. 'What are you doing wasting your time watching time-wasters?'

'Well, Darcy told me . . . I thought . . .'

'*Nom de Dieu*, Misset, you actually managed to think? For crying out loud, get on with it, go on, stun me with your eloquence, what have you seen?'

'They're reroofing the stables,' he said brightly.

'Alle-bloody-luja. So?'

'So it's a big job, *patron*,' Misset battled on. 'At the moment it's easy, just ripping tiles and rotten wood off, but the problems start with the rebuilding work, that's not easy.'

'The problems with you, Misset, are permanent.

Pel rang Spain. De Troq' wasn't to be found. He spoke briefly to Cham who was still waiting for permission to cross the border with his box of goodies. De Troq', he said, had gone to see his cousin who happened to be married to the niece of a high court judge, should be back soon.

When de Troq' arrived at the Huesca police headquarters that afternoon, he found the attitude there completely changed. Jourdain and Cham, who'd been keeping guard on the samples locked in a refrigerator, taking it in turns through the night, had been moved from a scruffy back office to a more comfortable waiting-room and were sitting patiently drinking coffee. A lot of bowing and scraping went on in front of de Troq', Señor Don Baron, as they were shown into the Head Man's office for the first time.

'I must apologise for my inspector's inefficiency,' Jefe Garcia waved them courteously into seats, 'a good man but inexperienced with the science of pathology. He feared a reprimand if he allowed you to leave with what he considered to be vital evidence – it is after all a Spanish death. However, I'm sure we can come to some arrangement, we can surely share your findings, *convenido*?'

'A copy of the report will be faxed to you as soon as it's completed,' de Troq' replied crisply.

'In that case, we are all in agreement.' The sycophantic smile proved it. '*Maravilloso!*'

They signed the receipts, packed the samples carefully into cold boxes, stuffed the necessary customs documents, the Scientific Samples Release Forms, and the permit from the Guardia Civile into an attaché case and headed for the airport as fast as they could, before the authorities on that side of the border changed their minds.

Pel was depressed. He wanted to talk to Martin at the local nick. However, he couldn't just pop in for a chat, the man had been arrested and already charged with wilfully attacking a magistrate while in the custody of the police. From now on any contact with the prisoner had to be backed up with properly signed papers. He knew damn well Brisard wouldn't give it, so he went directly to the *procureur* himself. Then he had to track down Martin's legal aid lawyer to avoid accusations of police misconduct, thereby endangering the chances of bringing Martin successfully to trial. The lawyer was in court and couldn't be reached. Pel left a message and lit a cigarette.

Much to his surprise, the call came back almost immediately and, having listened to Pel's explanation, the lawyer agreed to the visit. Now all he had to do was get some sense out of Martin.

'Found it, didn't I?' Martin said.

'You can't have just found it, tell me where you bloody got it.'

'Don't you swear at me, mate, or I'll thump you too, I've got nothing to lose now.'

'You silly clot,' Pel told him, 'you've got everything to lose, something like twenty years of your life. Don't you realise I'm trying to help you? Where did you get the damn thing?'

'Found it under an 'edge.'

He went on trying for well over his allotted fifteen minutes but Martin dug his heels in and wouldn't say anything more constructive.

Pel gave up. If Martin was going to be obstinate as well as dim there was little more he could do. Muttering, 'All that for nothing,' he went back to the office to consider and calculate.

Darcy and Bardolle came in half an hour later. They'd been out to Fontaine les Lacs as instructed and had found a winding footpath that led from Martin's farm to the scene of the crime. 'It's well hidden by trees,' Darcy told him, 'goes through the copse, beyond the *pigeonnier*, and runs along the edge of the stream directly behind the surgery.'

'From the flattened grass,' Bardolle boomed, 'it's clear it's been recently used, although it could easily have been the friendly neighbourhood youngsters.'

'Or Martin,' Pel added.

'We also went to see Madame Martin,' Darcy continued, 'with her original statement about their whereabouts on the morning of the murder. She was dead stroppy but eventually changed her story; her husband, instead of being at the house that morning, had in fact gone fishing, alone.'

'She said,' and Bardolle read from his notebook, ' "My sister turned up for the day and he scarpered, it's not that they don't get on, see, just that, well, he says she goes on a bit, if you know what I mean, he said he'd rather have some peace and quiet, you know, fishing is ever so peaceful, isn't it? Completely slipped my mind in all the excitement." '

At five o'clock, Nosjean turned up a *huissier* who'd received a handful of pellets in his backside when he'd gone to repossess Martin's second-hand car for non-payment of the HP. It had been a long time ago but added another nail to the peasant's coffin.

With Brisard breathing down his neck wanting to know when, Pel had no choice; he gathered the charge sheets together and took them to Rigal and his typewriter. Then he carried them to the magistrate's office and watched sadly as the magistrate signed it all, in triplicate, with a flourish, handing them back with a satisfied smile.

Just before seven that evening, Pel drove once again to 72 rue Auxonne where, in the presence of a second police officer, a prison warden and the young legal aid lawyer, he charged Jacques Klébert Martin with the wilful and premeditated murder of Hugo Christophe Aynard and Adrianne Rosette Fabres.

When he returned from the prison, the Chief nodded his approval as he accompanied Monsieur le Procureur towards the exit. Pel went to sulk in his office.

Rigal insinuated himself round his door; he was clutching reams of newly typed lists. 'Do we stop the search for the artist, *patron*?' he asked hopefully. They'd reached the thousandth sighting, saturation point.

It was a logical request but Pel hesitated. 'No, not yet, I'd still like to find him, if only for the kids' sakes.' It wasn't much of an excuse but it was the only one he could think of. Rigal sighed silently and retreated to consider selling washing machines for a living. He wasn't at all sure he'd made the right decision joining the police force.

As darkness began to fall, a plane touched down on the outskirts of Paris, at the Charles de Gaulle airport. Twenty-three minutes later a smaller plane took off and headed for Dijon. When they arrived, de Troq' and Jourdain accompanied Cham to his laboratory to see the samples safely stowed away. Dr Boudet was waiting for them. 'Don't you have a home to go to?' Cham called as he carefully bolted the cold room door.

'Wife and kids at the beach,' Boudet shrugged. 'Thought you might like some help.'

While most of the city was relaxing after supper in front of the television, and a few erudite members of the community were reading, Cham clipped the X-ray of Mariana Gomez's body on to a light box to study it. 'It was taken before the first autopsy,' he said as Boudet pointed immediately to the hyoid bone. 'That's the first thing I noticed too,' he agreed. 'Let's have a look at the photos.'

'She must have been a pretty little thing, poor kid,' Boudet said. 'What's this bruising on her neck? There are a lot of pressure points, but . . .' He hesitated. 'It doesn't look like manual strangulation – is that the mark of a ligature? If the hyoid – '

'Don't jump to conclusions,' Cham warned. 'Study what you see carefully and make notes. Here's one taken from behind, look at that.' He pointed at the fine line across the back of the neck. 'It's not a knife wound, it's a burn.'

They worked meticulously, recording every minuscule detail, and as the cathedral of St Benigne chimed midnight they'd finished their verbal report. Cham switched off the tape and rewound it. 'I'll have it typed up tomorrow morning. We'll go through it and make our conclusions afterwards, when our minds are rested. By then we should know what Leguyder's got from the swabs – he's busy DNAing everything he can lay his hands on. It is a fascinating subject.'

Boudet stretched. 'If the researchers manage to do what they hope to do, Pel'll be practically out of a job. Leguyder'll be able to tell him virtually who an attacker is, colour of hair, eyes, skin, height, age . . .'

'Pel's job is safe for a while,' Cham yawned. 'They've still got a long way to go. So far all they can do is match a sample of nucleated cells found at the scene of a crime with the perpetrator.'

'Even so, it's a great step forward. They say a fingerprint will be enough eventually – no more mucking about with semen and saliva et cetera. It would make life easier.'

Cham was yawning, stretched out in a chair by the window, when Pel saw him the next day. He'd dictated their conclusions on Gomez's body and had waited while his secretary typed the report. Now he was anxious to hand it over and go home for a snooze. 'I was just about to give up and leave,' he said amicably.

141

'Things to do,' Pel growled, slamming the door to his office. 'Have you seen Darcy?'

'Only Rigal bashing away at his keyboard.'

'Incredible how they can all vanish into thin air when I need them. Never mind, tell me about Gomez and leave out the gore, I've just had lunch.'

'Okay,' Cham said, opening his file. 'Bluish lips and ears, discoloration of nails, tongue forward in mouth, hands clenched. Death from asphyxia, it was correctly diagnosed. Her left hand held a number of hairs. She may have pulled them from her own head, they are certainly the same colour. Leguyder is checking.'

'What does that signify?'

'I've seen it before when someone's strangled. Tearing at the hair is suggested to be a spontaneous attempt to relieve the pressure to the throat.'

Pel raised his eyebrows. 'Strangled?'

'Hold on!' Cham warned. 'They could belong to the biter. It was quite a deep wound and must have hurt – she may have grabbed his head to try and pull his mouth off her neck. However, the hyoid, a floating bone, *was* broken. It can be damaged by an autopsy but I checked the X-ray of the body before the first one commenced. It was already broken, so yes, pressure was applied to her throat, breaking the hyoid and effectively shutting off the respiratory passages, hence asphyxia.'

'Murdered,' Pel muttered.

'I thought at first it had been done with a length of thin wire, there was a curious mark on the back of her neck, but it was only a tiny burn with minor abrasions – could have been produced when a fine chain, the sort often carrying a crucifix, was yanked off.'

'Didn't Patti, the girl at the Roman remains, have the same scar?'

'Mm, yes, I believe she did, but she had her skull fractured and died of hypothermia. The Gomez girl had a lot of bruising to the body, not the head. It was consistent with her rolling unconscious down the hill to the position where she was found, about fifteen metres from where the vomiting occurred, but,'

Cham looked up, 'some of the bruises were not made by the boulders she bounced over.'

'Go on.'

'The bruising to her throat baffled me. It wasn't something I'd seen before, it wasn't consistent with a hand or hands.'

'Thick rope, a leather belt?'

Cham shook his head. 'An unshod foot.' Pel again raised his eyebrows.

'I went to where the body was discovered and, as de Troq' will tell you, we walked back up to where evidence had been found of vomiting. Had she been standing at the time, it is possible she stumbled and fell. However – sorry about this, Pel – from the amount of vomit in her mouth, throat, smeared across her face and in her hair, quite clear on the official photographs, she must have been lying on her back, in which case she couldn't have rolled down the hill unaided.'

'Pushed?'

'It's likely.'

'What about rape?'

'No. Although she wasn't wearing underclothes when she was found, just a long skirt and shirt, she was intact and there wasn't any bruising on the inner thighs or genitalia. If you're looking for similarities, Patti's vaginal membrane was also unbroken.' He paused while Pel wrote. 'However, back to Mariana Gomez; she was, as the Spanish told us, quite drunk, the alcohol content of her blood, 1.14 grams, proves it. I would suggest she and an unknown person had gone off alone into the scrubby undergrowth, possibly to relieve her of her virginity, but having drunk too much, and not being used to it, the pressure of her would-be lover on her abdomen and stomach caused her to vomit. I would suggest her killer stood on her throat with his bare foot to stop the flow. Murderers can be strangely squeamish, can't they?'

'So can I.'

'Then, realising he'd killed her, he panicked and pushed her body, again with his foot, down the hill and bolted. Had he bothered, he could have hidden her in the prickly scrub away from the footpath, where she wouldn't have been found so soon. She died on 12th June, early evening. She was found two days later.'

'What were they doing there anyway, apart from the obvious? The site is a good fifteen kilometres from the village.'

'De Troq' asked the same question. The answer is they don't know, probably just wandering about hand in hand, there isn't another village for miles, only a few isolated farms.'

'What about the bite?'

'I couldn't compare it with the prints we took from Patti's neck. As I feared, it had been tampered with – that part of her would have been exposed in the coffin before burial and had therefore been made up. The pressure on the wound had distorted part of the print, plus of course the beginnings of decomposition had started softening the edges.'

'After your rudeness,' Leguyder complained, 'I'm not sure I should have bothered delivering this in person.'

'If I apologise and grovel,' Pel suggested, 'will that help?'

'Not in the least. It's only because I respect professionalism that I decided to do my duty and inform you of my findings. I am not prepared to be accused of being negligent. Negligence is a word – '

'Sit down.' Pel was already exasperated, he was going to have to find a way to cut Leguyder's lecture. 'Your diligence is a credit to you. Without you the police would be up shit creek without a paddle.' Perhaps it would work.

'I'm not sure I appreciate the expression,' Leguyder said huffily, drawing out his discontentment for as long as possible, 'but I do appreciate your appreciation.'

Pel smiled to himself; he'd won the first round.

'The three hairs Doc Cham brought back from Spain that were clasped in Gomez's hand,' Leguyder said importantly. 'I've finished the analysis and I can say without question that they belong to the same person that bit the girl Patti, the DNA was identical to the saliva in the abrasion on her throat.'

Pel sat up. 'You're sure?'

'DNA cannot lie,' Leguyder told him. 'It may interest you to know . . .'

Pel lit up and settled down for the inevitable sermon on molecular genetics. He didn't listen to a word, he didn't need

144

to, it was enough to know that the experts understood what they were doing and would go on giving him the results he needed to catch criminals. What he was actually thinking was how to tackle the next step in their enquiry. He'd got exactly what he had hoped for, a positive connection between the two dead girls, both bitten on the neck. Gomez had definitely been murdered and now they had evidence that it was the same man who had bashed Patti's head in. They were both virgins – had they led the man on and resisted, one way or another, at the last minute? And in his frustration he'd killed them? Whatever the reason, he was still out there and likely to be considering a third attempt at sexual satisfaction. His first victim had been in January, at Alesia in Burgundy; the second in June, in Spain; the third? Pel stirred the air with a pencil, deep in thought. Had he disappeared over the border? In that case, as a member of the Police Judiciaire de la République de France it was out of his jurisdiction, the Spanish would have to find him. Or had he travelled from France to Spain and then come back? All he could do for the moment was to alert the police throughout the two countries in case he bit some other poor unsuspecting girl. They'd already been through all the likely perverts and weirdos during the first few weeks after Patti was found. He lost his grip on the pencil and it shot across the room, narrowly missing Leguyder's nose.

'. . . have you understood a word I've said?'

'Fascinating, Leguyder, fascinating, now sod off, will you – I've got things to do.'

'I will not sod off,' Leguyder exploded. 'The intricacies of this new science are most important.' Pel sighed and switched off his ears again. Inside his head bits of information were jiggling back and forth, gradually slotting into place. When he was satisfied with his mental filing, he focused on Leguyder who was looking smug. 'So perhaps now you will understand . . .' He was still droning on. Pel made a couple of notes while he finished. '. . . with DNA there is no area of doubt.'

'DNA,' Pel mumbled, 'D and bloody A.'

'Not D and A,' Leguyder sighed, 'it's, D, N, A and stands for – '

'Yes, I know, some half-baked, unpronounceable formula.'

145

Pel grinned a hideous grin. 'Now will you sod off?' he asked sweetly.

When Misset came in that evening he looked ruffled and tired. 'Hangover?' Nosjean asked cheerfully.

'You can talk,' he replied aggressively, pushing Bobby the hairy hound under his desk where he continued to whine. The last thing Misset wanted was someone having a go. Had it been Pel he'd have shut up and taken it, but Nosjean was his junior. 'No wonder your wife's gone. With a face like yours I'd have left you years ago.' Annie and Jourdain stopped leafing through reports and held their breath.

Pel heard the scuffle from his office and, putting a Gauloise between his lips, he stopped briefly by the door to light it then wandered down the corridor to see what was up.

Nosjean had the much larger Misset pinned to a filing cabinet. 'Say that again,' he growled.

Pel leaned in the doorway to watch.

'Evening, *patron*,' Misset gurgled over Nosjean's clenched fist 'Enjoying yourselves?' Pel puffed gently on his cigarette.

'If you would excuse me, *patron*,' Nosjean panted, 'I'm going to do something someone should have done a long time ago, break this twerp's head.'

'Carry on, but keep the noise down. You're upsetting Rigal's typing,' Pel said calmly and turned to go.

He met de Troq' and Cheriff in the corridor. 'I wouldn't go in there,' he said casually. 'War's been declared, looks like Nosjean's operational again at long last.'

Annie and Jourdain decided it was time to call a halt, and peeled Nosjean off the perspiring Misset.

As Misset straightened his tie, he looked viciously at Nosjean. 'Disarmed by a couple of little girls,' he sneered.

Before Annie could stop her, Jourdain stepped smartly up and socked him one squarely on the jaw. He went reeling back, crashing into the filing cabinet again. De Troq' and Cheriff were through the door in a flash to find Misset in a crumpled heap on the floor and Jourdain examining her fist. 'God,' she said, 'his jaw's as flabby as the rest of him. Oh, well, I won't hit him so hard next time.'

146

'Jourdain!' Pel bellowed. 'In my office, double quick!'

Misset rubbed his chin and smiled as the Huguenot followed Pel into the corridor. He smiled again as he heard a door crash shut and Pel's raised voice, then he picked himself up and bolted for the washroom.

Jourdain stood to attention in front of Pel's desk, not daring to look into his blazing eyes. He took a last drag from his cigarette and extinguished it viciously. 'Young woman,' he began, 'this is a Hôtel de Police, not a boxing ring! If you can't behave correctly your career here will not last for long! I will not have fighting among my men!' He suddenly smiled. 'In the meantime, congratulations.'

'Sir?'

'You've just accomplished something we've all been wanting to do for years. Now get out!'

'Yes, sir. Thank you, sir,' she said, relaxing.

'And for the love of God, stop calling me sir!'

As she turned to leave, Jourdain noticed a photograph that Pel had been looking at. It was of a broken necklace and medallion bearing a circle with a dot in the centre.

'Sir? Er, *patron*?'

He sighed, '*Qu'est ce qu'il y a maintenant?*'

'This,' she said, looking more closely.

'It was found months ago up at Alesia, Leguyder did his ABCing on it and proved it was once round Patti's neck. It had particles of skin embedded in the chain link.'

'That's odd, Bobby's wearing the same, I think.'

'Who the devil's Bobby?'

15

Misset had slipped back into the sergeants' room to gloat over the Punk's ticking off. He'd spent half the day traipsing round the market behind two Sunshine people, and the other half lying under a thorny hedge spying on the house before he'd been seen by Michel Moiré the minion, and invited to join them for tea; nonetheless his legs were aching and his clothes dirty.

Now he'd suffered the indignity of being thumped by a slip of a girl and his chin was puffy and raw. He hoped her ears were being scorched by Pel's choicest words. Bobby was fidgeting at his feet. He pushed the dog away and fell into the chair with relief, wondering what the hell he could do for the rest of the evening to avoid going home to the hordes of overgrown children and his militant mother-in-law. Within seconds he'd been frog-marched into Pel's office. His four-legged friend looked round guiltily and set off at a trot behind him.

Annie glanced up from her stack of papers then went on reading. She stopped, wrinkling her nose, and stared at the page in her hand. 'Cheriff! Look!'

'This is Bobby?' Pel asked accusingly.

'Well, sort of,' Misset admitted, frantically trying to work out how he could evade the responsibility.

'Where did this come from?' Pel pointed to the collar from which a small gold disc dangled bearing the name 'Bobby'.

'I was given it,' Misset frowned, 'but it's not real gold, so I had it engraved for him in case he got lost. Adds a touch of class, don't you think?'

'Nothing would add a touch of class to such a repulsive animal,' Pel replied.

There was a crashing in the corridor and Annie tripped through the door followed by Cheriff, who succeeded in catching her before she collided with the conference in progress.

'Yes?' Pel enquired patiently.

'That dog crapped under my desk! Sorry, *patron*, but it's stinking the place out, permission to shoot it or Misset.'

Pel held his hand up. 'Shut up, Annie,' then, turning to Misset, 'Where exactly did you get this disc?'

'*Patron!*' the redhead cried again. 'That's what I've been searching for! I've just found a photo of it in Patti's file.'

'Annie, I repeat, shut up. Answer me, man,' he said to Misset.

'The Sunshine Sect I've been watching. They know I'm keeping an eye on them and occasionally invite me in, they've all got one. You should see Viguier's, it's much bigger and the real thing, must be worth a bit.'

Cheriff bent over and took a look at the piece of metal. On

the front was the dog's name, on the back in the centre of a large circle was a single dot. 'Patron,' he said calmly, 'Annie and I saw one just like this in the jeweller's on the Place Dupuy. It had been brought in to be repaired.'

'Go and claim it. Whatever you do don't let the jeweller start work on it, he's bound to clean it and remove anything work ABCing,' Pel snapped. 'Take it to Leguyder, and you, Misset, will remove that from your baboon's collar and hand it over also for analysis, then you will go downstairs and collect a bucket and spade, a floor cloth and a bottle of disinfectant, and deal with your dog's dumpings in the sergeants' room. I may not fire you after all.'

While waiting for news on the medallions found at the Roman dig, at the jeweller's in the city and on Bobby's collar, Pel chewed pencils and studied reports, those in the Aynard/ Fabres file in particular. The question mark plugging a hole in the double shooting kept bobbing to the surface. It didn't fit, whatever Brisard said.

The pompous magistrate was crowing with pleasure: not only had he had Martin successfully charged but he'd also spent a great deal of time digging personally into the prisoner's past. He'd swept into Pel's office and announced he had irrefutable evidence that Martin was an habitually violent man, and swept out again. Pel leafed through the neatly printed pages; Brisard's findings amounted to a number of irrational fights during his teenage years and early twenties. Although the statements were over two decades old, it was clear and precise. Martin had never been in prison before but he'd certainly been hauled up in front of a judge and fined a few times. Pel sighed. Where there was trouble, Martin made it worse. But was he capable of planning and carrying out a cold-blooded murder? To Pel, Martin was more the sort of man who'd have one too many drinks, lose his temper and lash out. Had he been peacefully fishing, perhaps with a bottle at his side, seen Aynard arrive at the surgery and decided in a flash of vindictiveness to blast his head off? But why had he taken a valuable gun along with his rods? And if it was his gun, why hadn't he sold it before to avoid the bailiffs repossessing his car? Where had he got it? He couldn't have bought it, he and his wife obviously worked hard to gain every centime they had.

Although the Chief would advise against another visit to 72 rue Auxonne, and knowing that Brisard would probably forbid it if informed, Pel pocketed the *procureur*'s permission, hoping no one would notice the date, rang the lawyer and discreetly left the Hôtel de Police.

Martin was deflated, not the turbulent, noisy peasant he'd seen a few days earlier. He sat miserably at the small desk in the cubicle provided, and looked with loathing at the prison guard, always necessarily present.

'Monsieur,' Pel began, 'let's start at the beginning. Correct me if I'm wrong.' The dispirited farmer showed no enthusiasm for the exercise. 'You went to Aynard for a bout of toothache,' Pel said. 'It was a Sunday and he refused to treat you immediately.'

'Snotty bugger.'

'Was it the first time you met him?'

'And the last.'

'Adrianne Fabres,' Pel carried on, 'the nurse, you met her when she came to treat your mother . . .'

'Sexy bit of skirt that.'

'Is that when you first met her?'

'Yes.'

'You made comments that upset her and she handed the treatment of the old lady over to her colleague, Crystal Combes?'

'Only said Aynard was a shyster, a slippery bit of shit.'

Pel's eyebrows twitched. 'Well,' Martin went on, warming to the subject, 'you know, she was all right, it would have suited me fine if she'd kept coming to the house for my old Ma, but me wife took against her, she had quite a wiggle to her bum – the nurse, not the wife.' He grinned, showing a row of blackened teeth.

Pel persevered. 'What made your wife take against her?'

'How should I know? You know what women are like, strange creatures, they are. She turned away some tourists once, said they didn't look clean, couple of young girls in tight shorts. I said their money was as good as anyone else's but she wouldn't have them in. Same with the nurse, she didn't have tight shorts of course but you know, she had a nice pair of knockers, my boys made sure they was sitting at the table when she bent over to give the injection to my old Ma.'

'So was it your wife who prevented her from continuing the treatment to your mother?'

'Nah, she just didn't come back one day. Crystal turned up instead. Nice woman but no tits.'

'Let's go back to Aynard,' Pel suggested wearily. 'Did you resent him for not caring about your toothache?'

'I did that Sunday, it was flippin' agony, had been all week.'

'Enough to shoot him?'

''Ere, shouldn't I 'ave my lawyer here?'

'He knows I've come to see you and this is off the record.'

Martin shrugged. 'Didn't give a shit about the sod really.'

'*Bien*, what about the gun found in your pigsty?'

'I told you that already! Flippin' 'eck, how many more times? I found it under a bleedin' 'edge, didn't I? All covered in muck it was.'

'When?'

'Coupla weeks ago.'

'When exactly?'

'Dunno, a coupla weeks ago.'

'Not in March, for instance?'

'No, not in flaming March.'

'Suppose I told you I believe you,' Pel said, 'will you tell me which hedge?'

Leguyder was delighted, he'd finished his analysis of the three golden medallions and had a surprise for Pel. They were identical in size and manufacture, all gold plated on to nickel, not worth more than 200 francs, the cost of a good meal with wine. One had belonged to poor little Patti with her head bashed in. Another had been given to Misset by Moiré, who'd attached it to his dog's collar; Leguyder confirmed that after his investigation, intense and exact, Bobby was the only living thing that had worn it. However, the one Cheriff and Annie had found was a real bonus. He'd taken a DNA print from a tiny particle of skin embedded in its broken chain and started comparing it with everyone he had on record. He'd matched it almost immediately. It had belonged to the Spanish girl, Mariana Gomez.

Cheriff and Annie shot off to the jeweller's to find out who'd brought it in and came back to make their announcement to Pel. 'Viguier,' Cheriff said. 'That's the name that was given, although,' he went on doubtfully, 'the jeweller said he was a small muscley chap; Viguier's as tall as I am.'

'Perhaps he wears high heels?' Pel suggested.

'Flat sandals,' Cheriff remembered.

'Easy to kick off?' Pel was thinking about the bare footprint across Gomez's throat.

'Very easy, he could simply walk out of them,' Cheriff agreed, frowning. 'I was talking to Debray earlier, in his spare time he's still checking into the history of the Peuple de Soleil. There is apparently an offshoot that's establishing itself near Ledàna. He'd got the ordnance survey references for the property, it's a tiny place not marked on the Michelin map but we managed to pin-point it in the end. Their land is seventeen kilometres from the girl's village and only six from where she was found up in the hills. They're not registered yet in Spain, he uncovered it while going through information sent via Interpol on European religious sects. A handful of members from each of the Sunshine properties, including our lot here, were invited over the Spanish border to celebrate the coming of summer, the season of sun. Their working festival lasted on and off for a fortnight, most of them left on 14th June, the day before Gomez's body was found and brought down for burial. Viguier was in Huesca, less than an hour away, we've got a hotel reservation for him.'

'Who else went from here?'

'That's the trouble, it was a bit of a free-for-all, and most of them stayed at the farm to help with the building work. The Spanish police have been unable to put much of a list together. All they've come up with is a confirmation that Viguier did stay at the hotel, they remembered him, he wanted an air-conditioned room and a comfortable bed – which, incidentally, the manager said, he shared with a tall Scandinavian blonde. He arrived later than the others, on the 10th, and stayed only three nights.'

'It's long enough.'

'And we've found out what the circle and the dot mean,' Cheriff said. 'It's an astrological sign for the sun.'

'That's no surprise,' Pel sighed, 'but worth knowing. One of those necklaces belonged to Mariana Gomez, it must have been wrenched from her as she died. Her killer's probably been waiting to make sure the coast is clear and, finally feeling confident, took it to be mended for the next victim. We can for the moment assume the man is here in France and believes he's safe.' Pel paused thoughtfully. 'Bring the guru in for questioning, he has all the necessary credentials, and get the jeweller here at the same time to identify him.'

That evening Viguier walked into the Hôtel de Police with an amused smile on his face. He liked being the centre of attention at all times and had agreed willingly to answer their questions at headquarters. He was shown into the interview room that contained a small two-way mirror; behind it stood Maître Brisard, Pel, Cheriff and the jeweller who'd agreed to mend the broken necklace. As Viguier paced casually round the bare room, coming to a halt behind the hard chair, pulling it out and sitting in it, Pel looked at the jeweller. 'Well?' he asked.

'Well what? I thought you wanted me to identify this Viguier chappie.'

Pel nodded.

'Well, get on with it, will you?' the jeweller said. 'I've got an election meeting to go to – I'm a local councillor, you know.'

'So you don't recognise this man?' Pel asked, indicating Viguier who was nonchalantly lighting a cigarette.

'Never seen him before in my life.'

Cheriff took the jeweller to see Debray, who would put together a computer portrait of the man he'd seen, and Pel went with Brisard to talk to Viguier. 'This is all very interesting,' the guru told him. 'I've never been in a police station before.'

It was probably true. Viguier had no official record, only the whispering of immoral conduct when he'd been a teacher; nothing had ever come to court, no parent had complained outside the school walls. He was enjoying his role of star guest and happily agreed he'd been in Spain but disagreed he'd met anyone called Mariana Gomez. As Cheriff came into the room and quietly closed the door, Viguier smiled confidently. 'I didn't stay at the farm,' he said. 'It was a shabby affair, not much more than four walls and a roof, actually quite squalid. I like a bit of comfort. You ought to see my place, it's clean and tidy, well run, isn't it Monsieur Kamel?' Although he would have liked to, Cheriff couldn't deny it.

Pel doggedly insisted with his questions, gradually breaking through Viguier's barrier of self-assurance, slowly reducing him to their own level of ordinary humans.

'Look, what's all the fuss about?' he cried at last. 'I've done nothing wrong.'

Pel enlightened him on past suspicions of seducing his students. Brisard opened his mouth to object but Pel held up his hand and he shut it again as Viguier started speaking.

'That's years ago! I was much younger, I don't need to go asking girls to pay attention to me any more, they flock to my house begging to be taken in, they fall at my feet demanding I love them!'

'Aren't you the lucky one,' Pel said sarcastically. 'How does killing girls appeal to you?' Again Brisard tired to intervene; once again he was shouted down by Viguier.

'No! Never!'

'It has been known,' Pel pointed out, 'for gurus like you to abuse their position for their own gains. Only recently a man called Einhorn was taken into custody near Bordeaux. He's suspected of killing his girlfriend and keeping her in a trunk in her bedroom for weeks. He was a guru of sorts, and the murder was committed sixteen years ago in America. In the seventies he won a fellowship at Harvard where it was known for him to provide joints, strip naked and dance in the classrooms.'

'Not me! Not me!'

'We already have an idea of what you got up to while you were teaching, then you disappeared to Holland. Since you've been back in France we've been told of naked dancing in the field behind your farm. Go on,' Pel urged, 'tell us about it.'

They weren't expecting Viguier to burst into tears. 'I've done nothing wrong!' he wept. Pel and Cheriff looked at one another in expectation. 'Okay,' he went on, 'I took advantage of the girls I taught, but they asked for it, they flaunted themselves. They found me attractive, couldn't resist me, I can't help that!'

'And after that?'

'I had to leave, after that no one wanted me in their school, the bastards had been informed, so I went to Holland to join a group of hippies. What else could I do? No job, no parents to fall back on, only an ageing uncle who thought of nothing but his bloody farm. He offered me work but I wasn't born to be a peasant so I pissed off.' He sniffed and wiped the back of his hand across tearful eyes. 'Then the old sod went and died and left me the thing. Well, I didn't want to spend the rest of my life mucking out cows and driving a tractor. At first I thought I'd sell it, but the market was bad and the house was in a hell of a state. Then I had a brainwave, I'd open up my own commune. It was brilliant! The Sunshine Sect even helped me, within a couple of months I had a team renovating the building and working the land. I was the boss, everything was going like clockwork and not a wage to pay – better than that, sometimes my disciples would offer financial help. I didn't ask for it, I swear it! All I had to do was sit tight and let them labour and harvest. They'd have parties sometimes – you know, barbecues in the meadow behind. It's got a river running through it, some of them swam, even in the spring, they were hot after working and dancing. I didn't ask them to undress, I promise! In fact I got rather uptight about it – when things were getting out of hand, I'd stroll across the field and give them a speech about the power of the sun and so on, to calm them down. It worked too, sitting listening to me they got chilly and started pulling on their clothes again.' He sniffed, looking pleadingly at the policemen. 'I slept with one or two of them, of course I did, but they are over age, I made sure, it's not illegal!'

Either he was a very good actor or he was telling the truth. Pel and Cheriff were disappointed and disgusted. He was a pathetic specimen.

'Who went with you to Spain?'

'I'm not sure. I flew down, they went in the van, half a dozen of them. Ask Moiré, he'll know, I only stayed a couple of hours then I went to a hotel.'

'With a tall Scandinavian blonde.'

155

'She's twenty-three!'

'What's her name?'

Viguier was looking worried, his forehead rippled with anxiety. 'Kari or something,' he replied slowly. 'We didn't spend a lot of time talking.'

'I bet you didn't. Kari what?'

'I don't know! I called her Kari, she called me Master.' The room raised its eyebrows. 'She was rather overwhelmed, you see,' Viguier stumbled on, 'to meet someone as important as me. Well, important to the Sunshine movement.'

'Where is she now?'

'I don't know, I don't know! I think she was going back to see her parents, in Norway, or was it Sweden? I can't remember!'

It was no good, even though they pointed out she was his alibi, Viguier couldn't help them identify the tall, blonde Scandinavian. After another five minutes Brisard stopped the questioning; it was his right to do so. They'd have to do it the hard way. It might take months, if they ever found her at all.

Pel swallowed his frustration and asked Viguier if he'd be willing to allow them to take a sample for DNA analysis. He refused. 'If you are not involved, the DNA profile will prove it,' Pel insisted but Viguier wouldn't be persuaded.

'But I don't want to,' he whined, 'I hate needles.'

'A swab could be taken from inside your mouth.'

Viguier pulled a face. 'It's revolting.' His upper lip curled in distaste.

'Or a hair root?'

'No!'

'Pel,' Brisard interrupted again, 'you have requested and been refused. It is perfectly clear that there is not enough evidence to hold this man any longer. He is not under arrest, merely helping us with our enquiries. Therefore you cannot force Monsieur Viguier to participate in the experiment.'

'I can beg,' Pel muttered.

While Cheriff showed Viguier out of the building, the *juge d'instruction* had some advice to give Pel. 'You'd better tighten up your act,' he said menacingly. 'It's quite obvious that you brought the wrong man in. I shall go personally to see Moiré about their other participants in the Spanish trip, I'm sure he'll

156

co-operate, if asked correctly. If you go you'll probably terrify him.'

'You do that!' Pel was fuming. 'And while you're there, why don't you join the club and leave me in peace to proceed without poking your nose in.'

'Pel, I think we've forgotten something, haven't we?' Brisard was at his pompous worst. 'Promotions, Pel, think promotions.' He reached the door just in time, leaving the policeman turning purple with rage.

To calm his nerves Pel went for a walk, a walk that took him in the direction of the forensic lab. Although under normal circumstances he'd avoid Leguyder like the plague, he tapped on the door and asked for an audience. The scientist begrudgingly allowed him in. He disliked Pel, but they needed each other and for a brief five minutes peace was declared while they discussed the disappointment over Viguier refusing to play ball.

'One of these days,' Leguyder told him encouragingly, 'every baby will be DNA fingerprinted at birth. Eventually we'll have the whole population on record, then when something like this happens, all I've got to do is match what we found on the girls' bodies to the library of profiles, and you'll know immediately who to arrest.'

'Doesn't sound like much fun,' Pel grumbled.

'But think of the time saved.'

'Criminals'll think of something to confuse the issue, they always do. When you consider the energy, imagination and ingenuity they employ to get away with a bit of law-breaking, it makes you realise that had it all been channelled into something else they could have been brilliant mathematicians, doctors, biologists, anthropologists.'

'Indeed,' Leguyder agreed, 'teachers, psychiatrists, even politicians perhaps.'

'They're criminals already.' They sighed and without thinking Pel lit up. 'Our murderer's got to be there somewhere, everything points to the sodding sect.'

Leguyder was waving his arms. 'You can't smoke in here, you imbecile!' Grabbing Pel by the arm, he tipped him into the corridor. As Pel walked away, Leguyder called after him, 'DNA the lot of them then.'

As Leguyder settled back into his spotless office, readying himself for the next series of analytical tests, a cloud of smoke seeped round the slowly opening door.

'Out!' he shrieked. 'This is a smokeless zone!' He followed Pel into the corridor again.

'Say that again,' Pel asked.

'I said, this is a smokeless – '

'Not that you dope.'

'I'm not a dope!'

'No, of course not,' Pel agreed. He was puffing heavily on the last of his Gauloise. 'Tell me again what you said about DNAing the lot of them.'

Leguyder took a deep irritable breath, coughed noisily and waved his arms again. 'Put that cancerous thing out!'

Pel dropped his cigarette on to the clean lino and ground it out. Leguyder was speechless. Pel didn't notice the scientist's state of alarm. 'Say what you said again.'

'If,' Leguyder began, 'you are certain of the location of a murderer, but cannot prove which one among many is guilty, you could swab the lot and I'll give you your culprit. That way no one person is being singled out, no one can complain it's unfair, and if everyone else agrees, the likelihood is that Viguier will too. Surely he'll see that if he's the only one to protest, your suspicions will become stronger. It'll take time, of course, and I'm very busy, but it's surely quicker than chasing round in circles asking questions to which anyone and everyone can lie when answering. DNA does not lie.'

'Could we?'

'It's been done a couple of times before. The general public don't like the idea very much, but after a clear explanation people do consent simply to clear their name.'

Pel wandered off, his frown developing into a deep scowl.

'Never mind the thank yous!' Leguyder shouted after him, then opened his assistant's door. 'A mucky little bugger just left a deposit in the corridor. Get it cleared up, will you?' The assistant collected a shovel and some newspaper, and was extremely relieved to find only a well-chewed cigarette end.

16

'No!' Brisard was adamant. 'It's an invasion of civil liberties. I cannot authorise a team of policemen upsetting so many perfectly innocent and peaceful young people. You will not analyse the spittle of the Sunshine Sect.'

'All over the age of eighteen, is that it?' Pel asked.

'What's that got to do with it?' Brisard said, knowing damn well.

'Registered voters,' Pel replied. 'I bet if it was a school of five-year-olds, you'd be persuaded.'

Brisard snorted; there was no reply to the truth.

'Local politics,' Pel sniffed disgustedly, 'what a load of tripe.' He took off his specs and wiped them slowly on his shirt front, considering an idea that was forming. It was worth a try. 'By the way,' he went on quietly, 'how's the wife? Our late President's widow tolerated her husband's mistress, but I wonder if a local magistrate's would be so understanding, and the press would have a field day at election time.'

'Look, you detestable little man, your insinuations are going to cost you dearly.' Pel shrugged at Brisard's threat. 'Keep my personal life out of it and you are to stop harassing the Sunshine People. Moiré told me when I was there that you have been watching them for weeks and he's getting sick of it.'

'Did you find out who went to Spain or just sip cocktails?'

'Moiré was most helpful, a charming little chap. You can cross him off your list of suspects for a start, he wouldn't hurt a fly. Leave him alone, do you hear?'

Pel decided that Moiré must have promised to campaign for Brisard in the commune, but unfortunately he knew damn well Monsieur le Juge could make life extremely difficult for him, even remove him from the investigation if he felt it was necessary. He glared eloquently and accepted the order. 'What about the others that went then?' he asked meekly.

'Oesch, Cournac, Alayrac, Delrieux and Sirven.' Brisard read the names from his notes. 'They are all delightful. Only

Delrieux made me hesitate, he's a *bûcheron* and very strong – I suggest you find out more about him.'

'Don't worry, I will,' Pel agreed and turned to leave. 'Give my regards to your wife and the widow in Beaune,' he added maliciously.

'You'll be hearing more about this!' Brisard retorted, slamming the door.

'They all refused,' Darcy said.

Pel had been expecting it. He'd instructed Cheriff, as he knew the set-up, to go with Annie, as she was female and could possibly soften the request with a stunning smile, very politely into the Sunshine Sect and ask extremely nicely if the members who'd travelled to Spain would accept, at their convenience, of course, to have a swab of saliva taken to help them with their enquiries, please.

'Bloody Brisard tipped them off,' Pel stormed, 'told them not to co-operate.'

'He wouldn't be that foolish,' Darcy pointed out. 'It was Viguier who dissuaded them, or Moiré. However, the pair of them did seem to know the law, apparently they said if there was no court order they didn't have to.'

'Brisard pointed that out loudly when Viguier was in for questioning.'

'They also let slip that a suggestion had been made about council grants for religious communes. Brisard may have gone to ask questions as an examining magistrate but he spent some of the time campaigning.'

'What about Delrieux,' Pel asked, 'the woodman with muscles?'

'He came back from Spain early. His sister was in a car crash and he caught a train home the day after he arrived. He wasn't there when Mariana was murdered. Cheriff checked his journey right to his parents' front door. It's true.'

Pel was furious. Brisard had won a battle, but not the war. He marched through the Hôtel de Police to Debray's computer room, slapped the entire list of the sect's members on his desk and demanded complete dossiers on every one. Misset's lazy research showed nothing of interest. Turning from the lighted

160

screen in front of him, Debray replied by handing his senior officer a slim folder.

'What's this?'

'You asked for information on vampires, *patron*, that's it.'

Pel opened the file. There was precious little inside. 'All this time and only six pages!'

'Vampires don't exist,' Debray said apologetically. 'They are a fictional invention based on the exploits of Vlad Tepes, the Impaler, a Wallachian prince born in Transylvania in 1431. If you want to know more about him, I'll give you the relevant volume of Rumanian history. However,' he went on, 'vampire-like creatures first appeared in Greek mythology as far back as AD 125, and I might add that even Shakespeare makes reference to them in *The Tempest*.' Pel looked bored; Debray decided to cut the lecture short. 'The vampire we are familiar with is, of course, Count Dracula, his name being taken from Vlad the Impaler's father. The Count from the famous stories was one of the undead and fed on the blood of humans, virgin girls' being the most tasty. The victim either died afterwards or became another vampire, it depends on the author. They recoil from sunlight, hiding in their coffins in a cellar or graveyard, and only come out at night. They can transform themselves into bats and they don't have reflections in mirrors. To protect possible victims a crucifix is worn, garlic rubbed round the entrances to their rooms – '

Pel sniffed. 'And Dracula always finishes up with a stake through his horrible heart,' he said. 'Yes, I saw the films when I was a kid.'

'The most up-to-date source of information about vampires I found was on the Internet, an American site. It confirms a vampire's need to drink blood but refutes the belief that the donor must die. It points out they prefer sex to food, and are not successful in long-term relationships, one-night stands being their limit.'

'It's easy to see why.'

Debray chuckled in agreement. 'One of the writers,' he continued, 'who calls himself Corelous, makes it quite clear that he does not believe in their existence but is fascinated by their legend. He does however get mail from those who are truly convinced they are vampires.'

'So indirectly they do exist.'

Debray hesitated. 'In a way, I suppose so.'

'Look,' Pel said heavily, 'daft as it may sound, cross-check this information with the stuff you've collated on our sunbeams. You never know, one of them may be living out some vile childish fantasy.'

'It's a bit of a paradox though, isn't it? If someone believes himself to be a vampire, I wouldn't have thought he'd join a group who'd chosen the sun as their symbol.'

'Don't analyse the workings of a madman, leave that to the psychiatrists – they'll be champing at the bit once we've got him. You just dig, that's your job.'

As he was coming back, Pel was met by the Chief at the end of the corridor. 'Ah, so that's where you are,' he said. 'Follow me.'

Pel pushed his hands into his pockets, found a packet of Gauloises and whipped his hands out again, he shouldn't smoke so early, today he'd crack it, today he really would make an effort.

Sitting in a comfortable chair in the Chief's office was Monsieur le Procureur, their boss, and in Pel's opinion a pain in the backside. He didn't look a happy man and while the Chief arranged his heavy frame into a reinforced chair, Pel's hand wandered again to his pocket. In shocked silence he removed it and clamped it behind his back, holding it tight with the other one.

'Sit down, Pel,' the Chief ordered. Pel sat on the one remaining uncomfortable upright. 'We have had a complaint of harassment,' he announced, looking at the Chief Prosecutor. 'Maître Brisard tells us you have been behaving in a threatening manner to achieve authorisation for action that in his opinion is entirely unnecessary.'

'Brisard's an old fool,' Pel said, 'with hips like a washerwoman.'

'What have his hips got to do with it?'

'Everything.'

'Pel!' The Chief breathed in. 'Stop being obtuse. Everyone is being careful at the moment – '

'Bloody elections.' Pel gave up and allowed himself to finger the packet in his pocket.

'Precisely,' the *procureur* agreed. 'We, as public servants, are very much under scrutiny at times like these. Brisard is only being correctly careful.'

'Bugger Brisard.' He shook out a cigarette and placed it in his mouth.

'Pel!'

'You made a request to an examining magistrate that was refused,' the *procureur* continued. 'Even so, you sent two of your team to make your demands to the people concerned. We are not pleased. Your enquiries must be carried out on more traditional lines.'

'Look,' Pel puffed luxuriously, what the hell, he'd make an effort tomorrow, 'this case of Patti at the Roman dig has been dragging on since February. Since then another girl has lost her life, in Spain. We have a number of leads all pointing to the Sunshine Sect and there it stops. The brilliance of science,' Leguyder would be pleased with that, he thought, 'would enable us to wheedle out the guilty party so simply. We only need swabs from their dear little gobs. All I want to do is get on with my job and close the ruddy file before some other poor kid or kids end up dead.'

'I think you're over-reacting. I hope you've said none of this to the press.'

'Now there's an idea.'

'Pel, you are forbidden to make such statements to the newspapers, it could cause panic,' the *procureur* told him. 'It's not the time for that sort of thing.'

Pel finally lost his temper. 'It's never the time for a kid to be killed!' he bellowed. 'What does it take, for God's sake? I'll tell you what, I'll see the press and ask them to alert the criminals of our fair city to the importance of the sodding elections and the fact that they have no right to continue their practices until it's over and all the stupid buffoons have been re-elected. Jesus Christ! I've got a murderer wandering about out there – for the love of God let me go and catch him!'

Monsieur le Procureur rose from his chair and went towards the door. 'Pel, you're becoming a nuisance. Fortunately for you, you're a good policeman or you'd have been out on your ear long ago,' he warned, 'but don't think you can play fast and loose with authority. It is that authority which allows you to work at all. Put a foot wrong this time and you may find yourself stuck at chief inspector for the rest of your career.'

'Monsieur le Procureur,' Pel said respectfully, 'I really don't give a damn.'

The Chief sighed, let their superior out and closed the door. 'Pel,' he said seriously, 'you're playing with fire.'

'Then I might get singed, but when will the stuffed shirt brigade understand that I'm not actually playing at all! This is real life and, tragically, real death. If I'm passed over for promotion, so be it, at least I won't die pushing useless paper about in a posh office, but for crying out loud, let me catch criminals!' He stormed towards the door. 'And you can tell Brisard his private life stinks. Sooner or later someone's going to get a whiff of it.'

The morning meeting was short and explosive: it consisted of a massive list of orders. Pel's team listened silently, sensibly saying very little. The complete inventory of Sunshine and Light members was going to have to be checked, from birth to date, discreetly. Debray could only turn up facts listed in the national data records: Mairies' knowledge of births, deaths and marriages, the Préfectures' records of car ownership, the Chamber of Commerce's register of businesses opening and closing, hospitals' entries, and the police computer showing proposals for prison sentences, of course. They all gave names and dates, but the really personal details, which were what they wanted, would have to be discovered by long hours of patient enquiry.

Which one of them had known Patti and Gomez? Who, extraordinarily enough, hadn't been members, or so it appeared, although they'd worn the gold disc with the circle and the dot. They knew it was the astrological sign for the sun, which explained why Viguier and his followers all had one and which was one of the reasons why Pel was convinced someone there had something to do with the deaths. But then, Misset's smelly dog had been wearing one too.

And more complicated contact with the Spanish police about their movements over the border would be needed. Were they actually interested in getting to the bottom of Gomez's murder?

Or were they sitting in the shade sipping sangria, letting him do all the work? To be fair, they had been helpful, and like Pel probably had a million and one cases on their hands, particularly now tourism was doubling the population of their homeland.

And then there was Martin quietly rotting in jail awaiting trial. If only the bloody artist would turn up. Although why a complete stranger would have shot Aynard and his nurse was a mystery, he'd like to have the chance of asking him. And Alain Fabres had been seen dining with Madame de Maupou, the wealthy widow. He couldn't arrest him for that, Pel himself had married one and was very pleased about it. Perhaps Cousin Roger would keep his promise, he always had in the past.

'I haven't had much time,' the accountant apologised into the phone, 'my partner's on holiday, double the workload and all that. However, so far what I've got is this: the Fabres' house belonged to her, the nurse. She bought it with a small endowment left to her by her parents when they died eleven years ago. It was bought for 100,000 francs. It was a good investment, the walls were sound and it stood in half a hectare of land, which, while it had been wildly neglected, did contain a number of magnificent trees. She bought it outright, no mortgage. At the time she was living in Paris married to a doctor. As soon as she inherited the money, she left him and moved south to work as a temporary replacement wherever there was a slot. Her place in the nursing practice was paid for by her divorce settlement, a year later, a matter of another 200,000 francs. From her earnings each month she paid a building firm for the conversion work on the house. In 1996 they added a swimming pool.'

'And her next of kin is a brother in Canada who'll inherit it.'

'He did,' Cousin Roger agreed.

'But Fabres's still living there.'

'Ah, yes. He bought it. He recently arranged a loan through his business, it's standing as collateral, and paid the brother off. I have it on good authority that he wrote to him making an offer for the property, enclosing a copy of the original purchase contract showing the price paid. He pointed out that certain work had been carried out and asked whether double would be acceptable.'

'What's it really worth?'

'At least ten times the original price, so I'm told.'

'And Fabres will know exactly, he's an estate agent.'

'The brother was ready to sign and Fabres went to a solicitor to have the contracts drawn up. The solicitor's bookkeeper, my informant, says his employer refused, quite correctly requiring the revaluation of the house by a neutral party. Fabres at that point produced the correspondence that had already been exchanged, saying it was quite unnecessary. The solicitor, showing a surprising amount of integrity, insisted on inviting the brother to come and inspect what he was selling before putting his signature to the legally binding contract. Fabres agreed.'

'He wasn't risking much,' Pel put in. 'He didn't bother to show at the poor cow's funeral.'

'The brother replied saying he didn't have time and expected the exchange of contracts to take place without delay. He thanked them in advance for their attention and Fabres for his generosity. The deal was done and the house is his.'

'Crafty sod.'

'I'm afraid that's as far as I've got.'

'And although I don't like the way he did it,' Pel concluded, 'it was the brother's fault Fabres got away with it.'

At the end of the day, the team came wearily back to the office and began the tiresome task of typing everything into readable reports. Pel was sitting hunched over three files, Aynard/ Fabres's, Patti Fauré's, and Mariana Gomez's. He'd read every scrap of paper they contained a dozen times and he'd smoked a million cigarettes, making his mouth feel like the bottom of a birdcage. He crushed out the last one viciously and wandered along to the sergeants' room to watch the bent heads at work over their reports.

'If we draw a blank,' Annie was suggesting to Jourdain, 'how about you and I enrolling as little sunbeams. I'm sure they'd accept.'

'Out of the question,' Pel said to their backs, making them turn. 'For a start they know you, Annie, and secondly, more importantly, if the murderer is among them, I want none of my men poking about incognito.'

'*Patron,*' Jourdain pointed out, 'that's just the point, we're women.'

'Same difference,' Pel replied, 'and twice as dangerous.'

As the heat seeped out of an exhausting day, striping the sky with orange and finally pink, Pel heard the offices go quiet. It was well after nine, and picking up the three files, he wearily plodded down the stairs to his car.

The evening was heartbreakingly beautiful as he drove out of the city into the countryside. Glorious Burgundy, the only place to live, filled with fools all fighting a potty little election. Sometimes he wondered at human intelligence. He drove thoughtfully home, parked his car crookedly in his drive and staggered to the front door. Madame Routy was waiting for him. 'Your wife's out,' she announced. 'She'll be back late, gone to Paris on business to see next winter's collections, phoned at seven to say she'd been delayed and you weren't to wait up for her.'

It was the perfect bloody ending to a perfect bloody day.

17

Pel stared again at the computer portrait Debray had put together with the jeweller who hadn't identified Viguier. His team also stared at their crumpled copies. They'd been searching for days. No one recognised the man: dark glasses, badly shaven and hair all over the place. 'Looks like anyone and no one,' someone commented. 'He could have shaved and had a haircut since then,' someone else offered. 'And the trouble is,' Pel bellowed, 'that the jeweller wasn't sure about any of it except for the beard and the hair, that's all he really noticed, thought he was about to be robbed.'

'When was the necklace due to be collected?' Darcy asked.

'The end of this week,' Cheriff said. 'The jeweller has instructions to waffle about misplacing it. He'll ring here, direct into this office, and ask if we've got it upstairs, implying he's speaking to a workshop above the shop.' They'd have to cross their fingers and hope a suspect would turn up.

'What's the news from Spain?'

'Not very encouraging,' de Troq' explained. 'They said it could be any one of many men. They are trying to establish who went in and out of the village enough to have met Mariana but are having difficulties. It's a very mobile commune, people coming and going all the time, no one tells anyone where or why, no records are kept.'

Pel sighed. 'When are the elections over?'

'The second and final round is in ten days,' Darcy told him.

'We'll have to wait till then. Once Brisard's job is safe for another century he might consent to the DNA experiment. In the meantime we've still got the robbery at Les Chartreux, a mugging in the park, a bar brawl with a knifing in the rue de la Liberté, not to mention the other couple of thousand cases still on the books.' He sighed again. 'And of course there is, as always, Aynard and Fabres.'

'You asked me to see Alain Fabres when he came to work this morning,' Annie offered, 'to speak to him about his dealings with his wife's brother in Canada.'

'What did he say?'

'He said he couldn't bear the thought of losing his home, the memory of his wife was indelibly absorbed in its rooms. It soothes his grief, it was all he had left of the woman he loved.'

'And cheap at the price,' Pel muttered. 'Any news on the artist?'

'Still following up all the calls, a hundred or so to go.'

Pel felt weary and it was only eight twenty-five, by the sergeants' room clock. 'Any hints, clues, ideas?'

Again there were none. 'Congratulations!' he shouted. 'Plug your brains in, all of you, and go ferreting.'

'But, *patron*,' Misset said, 'you arrested Martin for the shooting, where's the problem?'

'Go back to worshipping the sun, Misset, the rest of you remember this, Martin is innocent until proved guilty. That means we don't just sit back and relax because he's in custody. There's still the elusive artist at large – he scarpered straight after the shooting.'

168

Another morning meeting dispersed and Pel went to think in his office. He sat back in his chair, shocked to discover a lighted cigarette in his mouth, and tried to relax. Maybe Martin had done it. Maybe the artist had nothing to do with it at all.

'*Patron?*'

Pel scowled. He disliked being interrupted, but his stomach rumbled reminding him it was well past lunchtime, and seeing it was de Troq', he waved him in, prepared to listen.

'What's Jourdain on?'

'Ask Darcy.'

'I have. There's nothing specific noted on today's duty roster; filing in the office, free to accompany a senior officer if needed.'

'Does Annie know?'

'No.'

Pel pulled off his glasses and straightened up. 'What are you trying to tell me?'

'Officer Jourdain hasn't been seen since yesterday when she left at midday to eat. She's not at her flat and the landlady says she didn't come home last night. I've done the usual rounds of hospitals et cetera, and telephoned her parents in case she was ill, then her brother who lives in Mâcon. None of them know where she is.'

Misset shuffled through the door, holding a sheaf of papers limply in his hand. 'My feet ache,' he mumbled.

'Get out!' The door banged closed, but before de Troq' and Pel had gone much further in their discussion about the missing Punk, Darcy burst in, dragging Misset back behind him.

'Repeat!' he shouted at Misset.

'I only asked if I could stop watching the sect now that girl's there. I'm running out of places to hide.'

'What girl?'

'You know, the punk one. I said hello yesterday when she brought the cow in, I'd found my way into the barn,' to doze, but he left that out, 'and she told me to fuck off, so I thought she'd taken over the surveillance.'

'Lock him up! Put sticking plaster over his mouth. Misset is not to talk to anyone until Jourdain comes in.'

It was the worst piece of news they could have had: a young inexperienced copper infiltrating a commune very probably housing a murderer, and Misset had said hello! The sunbeams knew exactly what Misset was and what he was doing there. No wonder she hadn't wanted to chat, no one was supposed to know her, stupid child. Thank God she'd only been accompanied by the cow.

'We've got to get her out,' Pel said urgently. 'If she's discovered by our killer to be a member of the police . . .' He left the sentence unfinished. Darcy and de Troq' knew what he meant. 'Go down to Debray and his magic box,' he said, looking at his watch. 'Get him to print her photo from the personnel files, then go hell for leather for the Sunshine farm and pull her out, under suspicion of . . .' He thought for a moment. '. . . pill-pushing, attacking old age pensioners, cruelty to animals, use your imagination, but get her out!'

Darcy and de Troq' followed his instructions, speeding out of the city twenty minutes later. They returned as most of the offices were emptying for the night. Pel, however, was still sitting behind his desk, his thinning hair in a tangle and his thousandth cigarette smouldering in the ashtray. 'Well?' he snapped, seeing the two officers enter.

'It was a waste of time,' Darcy told him. 'We had to wait to see Viguier, he was giving spiritual guidance to a newly arrived wet who was searching sanctuary from the wicked world. Moiré wouldn't let us move from the entrance hall. When we did get to see him, they wanted to ring Brisard to find out if we had permission to be there. We managed to persuade them not to and showed them the picture. Viguier recognised her and after a lot of diplomatic reassurance, he resentfully gave us permission to go and look for her. By the way, I told him she was a missing person and her father was very worried – it seemed prudent in view of things. I couldn't risk implying they were sheltering a pill-pusher or Brisard would certainly have been told. Moiré showed us round, then we hung about until everyone came in at five but she wasn't there. We apologised and left.'

'Thank God for that,' Pel replied. 'When she turns up for work tomorrow morning I want to see her immediately. An official reprimand is going on her file – she deliberately ignored an order.'

That evening Pel unwound in front of a glass of whisky. The *météo* had warned of electric storms with deluging rain for the end of the week and he hoped they'd hurry up, it was still suffocatingly hot outside. He stretched and sipped, feeling entitled to the few soothing hours of rest he was allowed. He could hear his wife chatting to Madame Routy while they made final preparations for the evening meal in the kitchen. He could smell garlic-laced green beans; it made his mouth water. A cork was popped out of a bottle of wine. It was good to come home.

The phone rang, and because it was sitting on the table beside him, he idly reached out and picked it up. 'Evariste Clovis Désiré?' Pel stared at the phone in horror, no one ever called him by his Christian names! Whoever it was, was not a friend.

'Well, yes?' he said doubtfully.

'Watching telly, are you? If not, you should be, try Channel 5,' and the whirring buzz in his ear told the puzzled policeman that his caller had disconnected. Pel replaced the phone and picked up the *télécommande*, thinking how wonderful modern technology was when you understood it – very soon men would lose the use of their legs, everything would be done for them by pressing buttons, except policemen of course, they'd still have to gallop about like idiots. The screen flickered; he played hopscotch with his fingers to find the appropriate channel and settled to listen to the suggested report. Quite interesting, he admitted, although kidnapping didn't concern him often. He sat forward abruptly: he had a nasty feeling it might suddenly be of the greatest importance.

Madame Routy crashed crockery on to their dining-room table, his wife called gently to him to come and eat, but Pel remained in his chair studying the names of the journalists who'd made the programme.

The phone rang again. He snatched it up. 'See it, did you? I've got your daughter, Monsieur Désiré. Listen.' Pel would have told him he didn't have a daughter, but his mouth snapped shut when he heard a female voice he vaguely recognised.

'Papa, it's your little girl, I'm sorry, truly I am.'

Pel's frown deepened; he waved away his wife, who was standing at his side, and concentrated on the original man's voice. 'I'll tell you what I want later. Don't talk to anyone, specially the police – if you try and find me the girl dies.'

'They're beautiful little boys,' Darcy said, putting his arm round Kate as they stood by the twins' cots, 'and so are you.' He kissed her tenderly. 'Clever, clever lady.'

'I love them,' she murmured, leaning against him.

'And I love you,' Darcy whispered, 'and the other two terrors snoring in their beds. You've got five of us chaps now.'

The phone rang in their bedroom next door. Darcy went to answer, listened, waved to Kate and left. 'Four most of the time,' she sighed as the front door banged shut. The old Range Rover roared into life and skidded away down the forest track.

At midnight the lights in Pel's house were still burning. 'I've been racking my brains, wondering why the hell someone would give my number to a kidnapper and claim I was her father,' he said to Darcy, 'and the only person tricky enough to do that would be our Huguenot, Jourdain. She wasn't at Sunshine farm because she'd been bloody whipped. So, when the phone rings, don't touch it. If this man's under the delusion that he's holding my daughter, let him continue – for any other communication we use the mobiles. Annie's on her way. If Jourdain's allowed to talk, she might want to talk to another woman. In the meantime, go in the kitchen and make sure my wife's managed to gag the housekeeper and,' he added wistfully, 'bring me back a sandwich, I haven't eaten yet.'

Darcy turned towards the kitchen and stopped. 'Does that mean that her own father knows nothing about it?'

'It does,' Pel agreed thoughtfully, 'and although Jourdain deliberately didn't contact him, I think we must, after all . . .' His voice trailed off as he considered the situation.

'Wait a while?' Darcy suggested and Pel nodded, unconvinced.

172

Annie arrived and parked her car outside the Pasquiers' house as arranged. Yves let her in and showed her through to the hole in the hedge that led to Pel's back garden. It was perhaps an unnecessary precaution but they didn't know for sure they weren't being watched – from what he'd seen on the television programme they were going to have to be very careful. He briefed Annie, her eyes widening rapidly, while Darcy plugged in the phone she'd brought, one that showed the number of any caller, and connected the recording machine, activated by the human voice.

They tested the new piece of machinery by phoning from next door; as promised, Yves's number appeared on the slim screen as the bell was ringing. The hours passed slowly. They smoked, paced impatiently, ate a sketchy meal, drank cup after cup of coffee, sat stiffly to browse blindly through Madame's latest fashion catalogues, and opened yet another packet of cigarettes.

Shortly before dawn Darcy climbed out of an armchair where he'd dozed off, ran his fingers through his hair and stood up; he looked well groomed and as bright as a newly polished button. Pel, his eyes full of grit, his clothes in knots and his remaining hair standing on end, decided it wasn't the moment to loathe him.

'I ought to get in touch with Nosjean, *patron*. He'll need to know what to tell the team when they start arriving at the office, our joint absence won't go unnoticed.'

'When Misset turns up, he'll order an about turn and send him off to investigate wild flowers on the motorway. Instinct tells me, as always, we've got to keep him out of the way. When you've finished I'll speak to the Chief.'

'What on earth made you send her in alone?' he demanded.

Pel rubbed his unshaven chin. 'I didn't.'

'Then why in God's name did she go?'

'Ask her when we get her back.' The connected phone rang, stopping all conversation on the mobile. Pel glanced quickly round his sitting-room, from Darcy to Annie, both alert and tense. 'I'll ring you back,' he said to the Chief, cutting him off in mid-sentence, then he reached out and picked up the receiver. 'Yes,' he said, turning up the volume so the man's voice came loud and clear into the room.

'Listen to your little girl, she's got something to tell you,' it said and after a brief interval they heard Jourdain. 'Papa, I have been told that if you don't co-operate with this man, he will kill me. I believe him. This morning's headlines in *La Dépêche* read: "Transport strike likely as negotiations break down," that's so you know I really am still alive today,' and the line went dead.

Darcy nodded. 'Well, we've got the number he was calling from.'

When the phone rang again two minutes later Pel counted to ten and snatched it up. 'So far, so good. I want thirty million francs in folding notes, unmarked. Try and find me and I'll beat her to a pulp then slit her throat slowly. Keep the *flics* out of it!'

Again Darcy nodded. 'Same number.' He frowned. 'Odd prefix, not regional.'

The Chief's voice when Pel spoke to him again was worried. 'Jourdain was taken from the Sunshine Sect,' he said. 'Someone may have seen something, I'll send a team out there. I'll call in every man on the force if necessary, and bugger Brisard,' he added belligerently. 'We've got to find her.'

'I'm not sure that would be sensible,' Pel replied, remembering the viciousness with which the kidnappers on Channel 5 had disposed of their victim before fleeing as the police unwisely closed in. 'He said quite clearly that if we tried to find him he'd kill her.'

'If he killed her he wouldn't get the ransom he's asking for.'

'He could always take someone else after getting rid of her body,' Pel pointed out. 'He's obviously got no idea he's holding a member of the police force or that he's dealing directly with it. It's something he mustn't find out, the consequences are horribly obvious.'

'But, my God!' the Chief protested. 'We've got to do something!'

'I'm calling in Sarrazin.'

'The newspaperman! You must be mad!'

*

The recorded conversations were copied, in the hope that they might be able to make a voice match once an arrest was made. France Télécom confirmed what Darcy had feared: the kidnapper also had a mobile, very difficult to trace, they said, specially if it was on the move which it could well be.

'Seems likely,' Pel agreed. 'Hence the stop start routine, to change background noises, not that I heard any. At least he wasn't tearing round the countryside in a car with Jourdain locked in the boot, there was no engine running.'

'He could have switched it off,' Darcy pointed out dully. 'I'll get it taken to the experts. They might be able to tell us something – they'll identiy any echoes we couldn't hear, voices sound different in different locations.'

'Can France Télécom tell us who the subscriber to this number is?'

'Eventually. There are rather a lot of companies dealing in mobile phones now, all trying to protect their clients' privacy.'

Sarrazin turned up in a borrowed car, one without 'Press' emblazoned on the windscreen, and greeted Yves Pasquier next door as if he were his favourite nephew. They parted company at the hole in the hedge.

'So what's all this cloak and dagger lark?' Sarrazin demanded cheerfully as he came in through the french windows.

'Listen to this,' Pel told him, rewinding the tape cassette.

Sarrazin sat down slowly, his eyes fixed on the small machine delivering its deadly message.

When it had finished, Pel looked earnestly at the newspaperman. 'You were one of the journalists that put together the programme on Channel 5 last night,' he said. 'I didn't know you were so talented. From what I understood, the psychology of kidnapping is complicated. 'Tell me about it again.'

'First things first,' Sarrazin said quietly. 'Believe him when he says he'll kill her.'

18

'Second,' the journalist went on, 'the ransom is negotiable, always is. He's demanded one hell of a lot, does he think that Jourdain's father is wealthy? Is that why he picked her? Clever kid that, to get him to ring here. Where was she taken from, do you know? Does her real father know yet?'

As the questions tumbled out, Pel registered and stored them in his mind, knowing the answers might help his young punk policeman. That's how he thought of her, a policeman for whom he was directly responsible. 'She was lifted from Le Peuple de Soleil et Lumière,' he said. 'They have a farm out at Pont le Vieux, we were interested in them in connection with the teenager found at the Roman dig in February.' There was no need any longer to keep it from Sarrazin, he had to have all the facts. 'She decided to do a spot of undercover work there. We tried to get her out claiming she was a missing person. By the time we got there, she was.'

'I said her father was very worried,' Darcy added.

The newspaperman frowned. 'Giving the impression he was loaded?'

'Not deliberately.'

'He was being careful,' Pel said. 'He could hardly say he was acting on behalf of her superior officer.'

Sarrazin agreed. 'Okay. So why her?'

'I've been wondering myself,' Pel admitted. 'There are plenty of other girls in the sect.'

'Probably because she'd just arrived,' Darcy suggested. 'No one would miss her, she hadn't had time to make friends. Plus she looks younger than her age and she's pretty.'

'It's very likely,' Pel said. 'Jourdain was chosen for the same reason Patti and Gomez were chosen, to ease his twisted frustration. However, the police turning up, ostensibly at her father's request, may have made her abductor think again, giving him the idea of a hefty pay-off, it would make rape seem very sweet. And if,' he continued, 'he mentioned Darcy, bragging about his craftiness, teasing her with her father's anxiety, as he might well do, it probably gave her the idea of giving him my number. She knew her real father wouldn't have asked the police to find her, he didn't know she'd been lifted.'

'Sounds logical,' Sarrazin nodded. 'Who did you talk to, anyone in particular?' he asked Darcy.

'Everyone. I made an announcement at teatime, they were all sitting at the table with drinks and biscuits.'

'Sounds like a kids' tea party.'

Pel couldn't allow the conversation to degenerate. 'Which means all the members knew.'

'That she was a valuable commodity,' Sarrazin agreed, 'and we haven't a clue who we're dealing with.'

'And to answer your final question,' Pel went on, 'I decided her family must know. De Troq's with them, her mother and father are in a state of shock but swear they'll do as we ask.'

'Which is?'

'Nothing for the moment, I'm still playing Papa.'

The jounalist rubbed a hand over his face; he glanced at the waiting faces, feeling the weight of a responsibility he didn't enjoy. For him, the one and the only thing worth worrying about was a young girl's life. For a policeman, he knew it wasn't so simple. A crime had been committed, a crime that carried a heavy prison sentence. Trapping the criminal would be the priority, stopping his revolting practice for as long as possible. 'Which is more important to you, Pel?' he asked. 'Getting the kidnapper or freeing the kidnapped?'

'As an officer of the law, catching the kidnapper, of course. However . . .' Pel hesitated. 'As a human being, freeing the girl. We can always nab him afterwards.'

It wasn't the reply expected from most detectives investigating a kidnapping. Sarrazin let out a sigh of relief, it made things easier. 'Good,' he said. 'At least we all agree her life is more important than losing the ransom, or the bastard who collects it. How much can you raise?'

'I don't honestly know. The Chief must decide, who'll have to ask the *procureur*, who – '

'And so on and so forth,' Sarrazin interrupted. 'That's a hell of a lot of people in the know. Leaks happen, as you are well

177

aware – it's dangerous, and in the end I suspect you'll probably end up with precious little.' He shrugged almost apologetically. 'It's election time, men in high places won't want to be seen to be giving in to criminals.'

'How much do you need?' A softly spoken question made them all turn. Pel's wife stood nervously in the doorway of her sitting-room. 'Don't worry,' she said to her husband, 'Madame Routy's spring-cleaning the attic.'

Pel smiled at her. 'Why do you want to know?'

'Because I've got quite a bit gathering dust at the bank,' she said. 'An airing would do it good.'

Sarrazin was delighted. 'Great, that saves a lot of arsing about. When he rings again,' he told Pel, 'make him an offer, less than what you've got, and increase it if he gets stroppy. Tell him you don't have the full amount, that you'd have to sell things which would take time. Make him an offer, emphasising that delivery would be immediate.'

'The kidnapper's mobile's been traced,' Darcy said. 'It's Viguier's.'

'Him again!'

Sarrazin looked up. 'Is he a suspect?'

'He was, we've had him in the interview room once already. He knows we're watching him. I don't understand it – surely he wouldn't be daft enough to do this so soon afterwards, and use his own phone. It's crazy, he's not short of money either,' Pel added.

'He might want more.'

The phone rang. Everyone stopped breathing as Pel reached out. It was Cousin Roger. 'Thought you might be skulking at home,' he said enthusiastically. 'Hot, isn't it?'

'Roger, not now.'

'But I've some more information.'

'Not now! I'll call you back.'

Madame Routy was fetched down to cook lunch and for a brief half-hour Pel wandered into the garden to suck fresh air into

178

his lungs. Yves caught sight of him through the hole in the hedge. 'How's it going?' he called.

'What?' Pel replied absently.

'Whatever it is.'

'Ask me when it's over. Is our right of way still open?'

'Mum says to help yourself.'

Pel thoughtfully ran a hand over his thinning hair. What I've got to do is help Jourdain. Papa indeed! She's got a nerve! Just wait till I get her back to the office . . . if I get her back to the office.

The day wore on, long and boring. They discussed the case round and round in circles, and always came to the same conclusion: they couldn't move in any direction until the next lot of phoned instructions came through and the haggling over money was completed satisfactorily. So they tried playing cards. No one won; they gave up when the first hand was lost. Nosjean reported at six that a reasonably peaceful day had been spent at the Hôtel de Police. At seven, Madame Routy started crashing around in the kitchen again in preparation for supper and Pel suggested beers all round. He was just lifting his bottle to quench a stinging thirst when the telephone trilled. He carefully placed the beer on the table and went to answer. It stopped. He relaxed. Then, seeing his wife waving frantically, he lifted the receiver and understood her panic; the fire-eating housekeeper had answered. She was talking to the kidnapper.

'. . . don't you touch a hair on that girl's head!' she threatened. 'You're a filthy bully, people like you should be castrated and have their balls minced into bolognaise sau – ' There was a clattering then a click as Madame Pel replaced the phone in the kitchen and frog-marched the housekeeper up to her bedroom.

'This is Monsieur Désiré speaking,' Pel said calmly. 'I'm sorry about that, emotion is running high here.'

'As long as it wasn't a policeman,' the voice said, clearly shaken.

'Let's get down to business, shall we? You've asked for too much, I don't have that sort of money readily available. To raise it will take time – I'll have to sell things. I have 30,000 francs in cash. I could bring you that today.'

'It's not enough, I'll accept three million.'

'But it'll take a week to raise,' Pel insisted, 'and even then – '

179

'Listen.'

The listeners' blood ran cold as they heard a piercing scream then, 'That was her little finger.'

Jourdain gasped, 'Papa ... still alive ... I'm sorry.' And the line went dead.

'Play it back!' Sarrazin was on his feet.

Darcy obliged and again they heard her agony.

'It's a recording,' the journalist said. 'It's punctuated with faint clicks, and what she said, it was made up out of the other messages.'

'But the gasping!'

'If someone put their hand over your face and stopped you breathing, you'd gasp when it was taken away.'

'So what?'

'So he's not actually with her, that was prepared in adance, the scream could have been her little finger but it could also have been the result of a couple of slaps.'

'My men,' Pel replied, 'do not scream as the result of a couple of slaps. However, I sincerely hope you're right, that he's trying to terrify her family.' He rubbed his forehead, as if trying to rub away the pain he'd heard. 'It's very effective. Thank God her parents aren't here.'

When Madame Pel returned the following morning, having delivered the housekeeper to her sister's, she carried a black attaché case. Putting it down on the dining-room table in front of her husband, she opened it. '300,000 francs,' she said brightly. 'There go the winter collections.' She put a hand gently over Pel's. 'Will you still love me when I go bankrupt?'

He kissed her cheek and closed the case. 'You possess another sort of richness,' he replied. 'Let's hope this will be enough.'

Yves stepped through the french windows. 'Pel, you've got visitors, Messieurs de Troquereau and Jourdain.'

De Troq' stepped over the threshold followed by a distinguished grey-haired businessman whose face was creased with anguish. He extended his hand to be shaken. 'I had to come,' he explained. 'The waiting was appalling. I won't get in the

180

way, but please let me stay, it's intolerable not knowing what's going on.'

'Jourdain's mother is under sedation at home,' de Troq' said. 'Their older son's arrived, he's looking after her.'

Pel briefly went through the events that had occurred while Monsieur Jourdain nodded sadly. 'Shouldn't that be my money waiting to be handed over?'

'We'll sort out who owes who what later. If he accepts our offer, we won't need more; if he holds out for a larger sum then we may need to have yours. How much can you raise?'

'In cash, today, probably not more than 100,000. Given a while to organise it, ten times that amount, our home must be worth at least that.'

'We don't want to wait,' Sarrazin interrupted, 'we must persuade him to accept what's there. The longer it takes, the more dangerous it becomes for your daughter. Kidnappers suffer from a great deal of nervous tension, the negotiations must be concluded quickly to keep him calm.' He smiled sympathetically at Monsieur Jourdain. 'We want your daughter back as much as you do.'

'I doubt that very much,' Jourdain said and sat heavily in a chair, his head in his hands. 'We wanted her to have a sensible job. We told her joining the police was foolish, we told her she would have to take risks but,' his intelligent eyes were full of tears, 'we didn't think anything like this could happen. Oh God, why did we let her join up?'

When the next contact came, Pel, encouraged by Sarrazin, tried to sound more emotional. 'Look at the state her real father is in,' he urged. 'He's going to start wondering at your coolnesss.'

Pel found it difficult. At the best of times he lacked the ability to show his feelings; however, once the sum of money had been finally agreed, he made an effort. 'When?' he pleaded. 'When do you want it delivered? Please let it be soon.'

'Tonight, on the Sentier de la Madeleine, it's a lane that runs from Chaumercy to Chaussun village. Six kilometres outside Chaumercy there's a crossroads, T-junction actually, just before a bend. There's a ruined shepherd's house. The door's still standing – put the money out of sight just behind the door. Put it there at midnight. I'll be watching so no funny business. You will come by car and park on the bend, then you'll walk back and leave the money. Walk away without looking round. Get back in your car and continue to Chaussun, then go home. Do as you're told and you'll get your daughter back. Cock it up and I'll have to spoil her a bit more.' Jourdain's father let out a high-pitched wail.

'Who's there with you?' The sharp ears of the caller missed nothing.

'My wife, of course. This is a nightmare for her.'

'Is she the bitch I spoke to the other day?'

'No, that was our housekeeper, we've sent her away.'

'She needs roasting on a spit.' Although Pel was of the same opinion, he said nothing. 'Tell your missus she should have a word with your daughter, she doesn't enjoy sex. Still, I've taught her a thing or two – mind you, I had to tie her up first.' He was enjoying himself.

They held their breath as the line disconnected, every one of them looking strained and shocked. Was it nearly at an end? Pel thought not. He replaced the receiver and went to the drinks cupboard to pour a double measure of brandy into a glass. Crossing the room, he handed it to the man slumped on the sofa, his fist in his mouth plugging the scream trying to escape.

'He's confident and a novice,' Sarrazin said as Pel turned towards him. 'I expected at least a few stops at phone boxes to check you weren't being followed. He's accepted you are acting alone and will do as he says. He thinks you're frightened, thanks to your hysterical housekeeper who convinced him of the family's concern. He remembers her well.'

'Who will take the money?' Jourdain's father asked weakly.

'I would be honoured,' de Troq' suggested.

'No way,' Sarrazin said. 'It's the father that's expected, no one's mentioned a brother or a boyfriend. It's got to be someone who looks the right age, and I don't think Monsieur is up to it. It's got to be Pel.'

Pel had to agree. They spread a large-scale map over the dining-room table and found the spot where he was to go.

'Not much cover for my men,' Pel said, running his finger along the thin black line of the road. 'Perhaps a ditch or two, or a tree, no buildings for miles, nothing that will make hiding easy. I'll send someone out to take a look. They'll have to be in position well before midnight in case our man is snooping about before time.'

'Forget it,' Sarrazin said sadly. 'You're delivering the money, not receiving the girl. Start your investigations after you've got her back. If he sees anyone but the one person he's waiting for he won't make the collection. Negotiations after that will be considerably more difficult, and for his victim disastrous – you heard him. He could be lying about what he's done and intends to do, but don't tempt him to make it the truth. If he does collect and is chased, either you'll catch him and he'll refuse to tell you where she's hidden. You might never find her. Or he'll get away and she'll pay, possibly with her life. I know it's a hard decision to take, Pel, but play it straight until she's home.'

Jourdain's father beseeched them to follow these instructions. Pel said nothing. He went on staring at the criss-cross of country lanes and rivers, winding in and out of villages, still laid out in front of him, trying to work it out in his own mind; a policeman's mind, a policeman whose job it was to put criminals behind bars, not watch them disappearing over the horizon with a lot of money at their disposal. That money could buy him a ticket to anywhere in the world, to freedom and possibly another kidnapping or worse. He couldn't let that happen. But could he take the risk that they may never find Jourdain alive because his detecting instinct was so strong? Would the arrest be worth it? What if it went wrong and Jourdain never came back? Would he rather lose the kidnapper or the kidnapped? If the kidnapper went free they might get a second chance when he started spending the money. If Jourdain died because of his decision, there would be no second chances for her, she'd be nailed into a wooden box ready to rot in a graveyard.

It's not good being sentimental, he told himself, that's not part of my job. He pushed his specs up on to his balding head, profoundly troubled by the contradictory thoughts he was having.

He had to come to a decision fast. Reaching out for the packet of cigarettes, he sighed deeply, knowing what had to be done, whatever the consequences.

19

It took until nearly eleven o'clock to list all the numbers of the banknotes. Shortly afterwards Pel picked up the attaché case and went to the door.

His wife closed it quietly behind him and went back to join the others. Darcy, de Troq' and Annie were studying the map, still unfolded on the table; Sarrazin was trying to reassure Monsieur Jourdain. He'd aged ten years since he'd arrived and although he appeared relatively in control, accepting they were doing the best they reasonably could, he was now visibly trembling.

Madame Pel made hot toddies and brought a plate of smoked salmon, cheese and small pieces of buttered bread. They nibbled distractedly, leaving most of it uneaten. The minutes ticked by.

As the clocks of the city and surrounding villages were striking one hour into a new day, the exhausted inhabitants of Pel's sitting-room saw bright headlights swing into the drive and extinguish.

Pel pushed open the front door and closed it behind him. His eyes were dull, his footsteps heavy. 'I did exactly as I was told,' he said. 'There was no sign of anyone or anything, just the moon lighting flat, empty fields.' Looking tiredly at Sarrazin, he asked, 'When will he release his hostage?' He accepted the brandy his wife offered him as the journalist opened both hands. He had no idea, he said, not long, usually. They waited. It wasn't easy.

The following day was hell. There was still no news and, as darkness covered the countryside once again, Pel's nerves were in tatters. Monsieur Jourdain's were hidden under Pel's best scotch; he was on his second bottle, but not a drop was regretted, he'd remained as calm as could be expected and certainly hadn't hindered them. Pel wondered when he would crack up completely.

Sarrazin was doing his best to keep their spirits up with stories of successful exchanges, suggesting reasons for the delay – surely today the girl would be released – but even he eventually fell quiet.

Nosjean again made his report of comings and goings at the Hôtel de Police and told them the Chief was impatient for action, complaining of pressure from a great height. Pel shrugged it all off as if he didn't care.

When the phone rang at last, he snatched it up aggressively. But it was only Cheriff.

'*Patron*, it's the pig-killing peasant, Roux, who alerted us to the Sunshine Sect.'

It was on the other side of the city, fifty kilometres from the ransom drop where they hoped to find Jourdain. 'For Christ's sake, deal with it yourself!' Pel's irritability was sharp.

'*Patron*, I'm going over there,' Cheriff insisted. 'He's found a body. The body of a young girl.'

When Pel arrived outside the house just behind Cheriff, a solitary light shone through half-open shutters. He and de Troq' climbed out of the car. Roux came frowning from his front door. 'Follow me,' he said, turning quickly away and following the puddle of light from his torch, jerking in a zigzag across the concrete yard as he limped on mismatching feet. 'Hope I did right to call you this late. She's way over there in the thicket. I didn't touch her.'

They came to a lop-sided gate. It scraped over the ground, caught on a stone and stuck, and they squeezed through the opening impatiently. Roux hurried off across the field, the policemen a short step behind. 'What were you doing out this late?' Pel asked conversationally.

'Now that's something you *flics* shouldn't ask a peasant like me.'

'Poaching?'

'Now would I ever?'

185

'If I know you, regularly.'

On the other side of the pasture, going into a small wood, they fought their way through thick undergrowth. It was hard work forcing a path through the brambles laced between the trees, catching their clothes and tripping over fallen branches; the crescent moon had been snuffed out by the canopy of leaves, and their only light came from hand-held flash lamps.

Roux stopped abruptly, examined the bark of a tree, found his mark and set off to the right. 'Over there,' he said, 'it's easier from the other side but this was quicker.'

For another fifty metres or so they struggled through waist-high obstacles, then suddenly they burst out on to a rough path. The trees were thinner here, the ground springy under-foot; they were moving more quickly now.

As Pel was hoping it wasn't much further, the peasant came to a halt. At his feet lay the crumpled body of what looked like a sixteen-year-old girl, her young skin pale in the darkness. Her legs were folded at the knee, her ankles bound together, her shoulders hunched, thrust forward by arms that were tied tightly behind her back. An old patched jacket covered her nakedness. 'I put me coat over her,' Roux said in explanation. 'She was . . . well, it didn't seem decent to leave her like that.'

Pel nodded, understanding, and bent over the body taking in the bruised face, the swollen split lips, the puffy purple eyes, closed now, the livid smudge of violence on her cheekbone, the savage bite on her neck; she'd taken a brutal beating before dying.

It made him want to weep.

Beside him de Troq' reached out and touched the lifeless face, gently removing a twig from her short blonde hair, no longer spiky but flatly encrusted with blood, dark brown in the torchlight. 'Jesus Christ, Jourdain,' he whispered, 'who did this to you?'

'Don't touch!' Pel said, surprised de Troq' had. 'You know damn well the lab boys and Boudet need her exactly as she is.' Anger was emerging through his sadness.

De Troq' ignored the order, and extended his fingertips to her neck. His eyes widened; he looked up slowly at the ghostly faces in disbelief. There'd been a flutter of pulse. 'She's still alive!' But his whispering voice was full of doubt.

'Only just.' Boudet shrugged miserably. 'Poor kid, she's in a bad way, the only saving grace is she'd been heavily doped.' He removed a pill from the foil he was fiddling with and put it under his tongue. 'Nerves,' he said. 'Don't like seeing thugs' work.'

Dr Boudet, efficient and unmoved by his work in the path lab, had been touched by Jourdain's torture. The paradox always surprised Pel.

The doctor had arrived in the farmyard expecting a girl's corpse, to be met by Roux who'd panted out the words, '*Elle est en vie!*' They'd hurried across the field and charged into the thicket. In the silence of night, Pel had heard their noisy approach, Boudet crashing his way through the brambles and branches, shouting orders over his shoulder to the ambulance men trying to keep up. He'd arrived in a rush, clothes torn, hands badly scratched, and glancing at Jourdain, he'd knelt beside her and opened his case. After that, it had seemed to those watching that he'd switched to remote control, mechanically examining and dealing with the wounds, silently binding and supporting fractured bones, adding a padded collar to hold neck and head. Pel had noticed the latex gloves he wore made his hands seem inhuman, glowing white, like a futuristic robot's, he thought, but they moved precisely and firmly, without hesitation.

While Boudet worked, de Troq' and Cheriff continued beating a path through the woodland, smashing the thorny walls back between the trees, leaving a passage wide enough for a laden stretcher. The doctor had gone back with her, beside her all the way, occasionally checking her pulse, always weak, quietly telling the men carrying her to take care, not to stumble, not to jolt her. Reaching the ambulance at last, he'd stood to one side as they'd eased her gently into place, then, saying, 'Take it smoothly,' to the driver, he'd climbed inside for the journey to the hospital.

Now his part in the emergency was over, he looked worn out, his large body stooping in the antiseptic-smelling corridor

187

leading from *Urgences*. 'She may not survive the anaesthetic,' he said, 'and she's drowning, one of her lungs is full of blood, punctured by a broken rib, among other things.'

Pel was looking depressed. They'd got Jourdain 'back, but in what state? For her parents the nightmare wasn't over yet. Sarrazin had brought her father to the hospital, and he'd seen his daughter briefly before collapsing on to a chair in the waiting-room to cry.

De Troq' was on duty outside the operating theatre, uncharacteristically pacing to and fro.

And the kidnapper had got away.

Darcy and Cheriff were overseeing the lab boys as they hunted under powerful spotlights in the woods, hoping against hope they might pick up some tiny piece of evidence to point them in the right direction. What was making Pel crosser than anything though, was the waste of an intelligent, if perhaps headstrong, young woman. Jourdain hadn't been with them long but she'd brightened the place up with her startling hairstyle, she'd been so full of life and ambition. Now she was silently dying on the operating table. Sometimes he hated being a policeman.

'Did you see her hands?' he asked as Boudet accompanied him towards the exit.

'Yes,' the doctor frowned. 'Why?'

'How many fingers did she have?'

'Four on each hand, plus a thumb apiece,' came the puzzled reply.

'That's all right then,' Pel said, knowing that it made little difference in the circumstances, and they continued walking, both deep in thought. As they stopped to shake hands and separate, Boudet sighed. 'She'll be in theatre for hours', he said. 'If you don't hear anything consider it good news. The only thing that'll change today will be if her heart stops. In the event of cardiac arrest it'll be impossible to save her.'

Pel turned away across the parking area. He put the key into the door of his car and turned it, thinking gloomy thoughts about young women in the police force.

'Hey! Pel!'

Sarrazin was cantering towards him. 'I'm sorry,' he said, studying his feet. 'I'm sorry it didn't turn out better.'

'Not your fault.' Pel folded himself into the car, fumbling with the ignition. 'We played it to the rules. There is only one man responsible. I'll get him, if it takes me the rest of my life.'

'Er, I don't like asking this,' the newspaperman was embarrassed, 'but can I print the story?'

'Print the truth, no trimmings, for the sake of her family,' Pel agreed, 'and don't mention she was a police officer, we'll keep that to ourselves for the moment.' He removed his glasses and momentarily massaged his eyeballs. 'Between you and me, and this is not for publication, I believe all this could have been avoided if we'd been given permission to DNA a certain group of people. It's the same man that killed Patti and Gomez.'

'How do you know for sure?'

Sarrazin hadn't seen the bite and Pel didn't tell him. 'When I've made an arrest, I'll give you the scoop,' he said in gratitude for his help.

'Okay, I accept that, but tell me why you weren't allowed to DNA your certain group of people?'

An evil gleam came into Pel's eye. 'How about asking Brisard where he goes in the evening?'

The peasant Roux poured Pel some coffee. 'Will she live?' he asked.

Pel shook his head. 'Your guess is as good as mine,' he replied. 'Her chances are slim but better thanks to you. If she'd stayed out all night, she'd already be dead.'

'So you won't be prosecuting me for poaching then?'

'Who, you?' He smiled sadly. 'Have you seen any more of the Sunshine and Light lot recently?'

'Not really, I think they've been warned off. They keep themselves to themselves nowadays, not that I've been looking, of course.'

'Of course.'

'Came across a couple of them this morning though, wandering along the road in their pyjamas.'

'What did they look like, apart from their pyjamas?'

'Wet, thin and limp, real yoghurt weavers. You don't think it was one of them, do you? They couldn't organise a piss-up in a brewery.'

189

'I'm convinced one of them is involved.'

'Nah, the only one with any muscles is the chap doing the stable roof.'

Pel's eyes flashed. 'Are they rebuilding already?'

'Certainly are.'

'What's he called?'

'Haven't a clue, only saw him back view. Looks a wimp until he takes that tunic thing off. Strong little bugger wearing a big straw hat. But I could hardly engage him in friendly conversation, he was up on the woodwork chucking beams about, and I wasn't supposed to be where I was, was I?'

'Could this be him?' Pel pulled out a now very dog-eared picture of the jeweller's customer.

Roux took it and studied the portrait. 'So much hair,' he said. 'They all look alike to me.'

As daylight faded, Pel's men came in. The searches and questioning had been thorough, but not enlightening.

The track on which Roux had found the body widened to a clearing, crossed an almost dry stream and continued to meet a small road that wound its way round the other side of the woods; this was the route by which Jourdain's kidnapper had carried or dragged her. The scientists had spent most of the night and the following day examining every inch of it, meticulously lifting and bagging their hundreds of samples. Now it was only a question of time before knowing what they'd found, if anything.

Surrounding the pick-up point, no one had seen a thing, which wasn't surprising as it had been a lonely junction on a small country lane, not a house in sight. Pel was half regretting having followed Sarrazin's advice in not keeping watch as the money was collected, but although he knew he would be severely reprimanded for letting the man get away, he also knew he'd had no choice. At least they weren't hunting for a dead body, they had found her. It was small consolation.

Pel read the reports, his anger growing stronger. 'You do realise,' he said to Darcy, 'that if we don't find him rapidly he's likely to do it again? Sarrazin tells me there are those who virtually earn their living by removing children and demanding money for their return. This may be his first kidnapping but it's not his first killing.'

'It had crossed my mind, yes,' Darcy agreed. 'It also crossed my mind that Jourdain got herself clobbered because we were closing in on our vampire and she looked like his ticket to freedom.'

'Everything points to the Sunshine Sect but we can't just go in and arrest twenty-seven people hoping one of them will confess. Unfortunately it's against the law.'

'What about this chap on the roof?'

'Where are the personal reports on the sodding members?'

Debray had provided the basics from his computer searches. In between all the other cases, anyone with a spare half-hour, usually unpaid overtime, had been obstinately digging for the more private details of the Sunshine People's lives, following every unusual incident to its conclusion. Now everyone was at it. They'd spent the day out asking questions and it looked like they'd spend most of the coming night putting it on paper. Objections were non-existent. The team worked willingly and thoroughly.

They weren't finished but Darcy went round all the desks collecting what had been written so far and carried the bundle of papers into Pel's office. Together they started reading.

'Viguier's playing the innocent, he says his personal phone was removed over a week ago,' Darcy commented. 'He didn't report it because he thought it would turn up in the end. Personally, I think he's scared silly and doesn't want any further contact with the police, in fact he's being so careful it's infuriating. He's accompanied by at least two people wherever he goes, even to bed.'

'I wonder if he is behind it after all. Could he be the brains telling someone else what to do?'

'Why kill Patti, and Mariana Gomez?'

'Maybe he didn't. Maybe he discovered who had and decided to use the man for his own gains; a hefty ransom to help him disappear again. The last time there was trouble in his life, he fled to Holland to be a hippie, perhaps he was planning a repeat performance. It was his name used at the

191

jeweller's, it was his phone that was used. Suppose he's not just a clever devil but greedy too, and now, as you say, running scared.'

'Or suppose,' Darcy suggested, 'our vampire is jealous of his position as head of the sect and is deliberately trying to get him into trouble, hence removed?'

'Are all these little sunbeams still there?' Pel's eyes skimmed professionally over Debray's pages.

'Annie and Cheriff spent two hours this morning confirming just that and apparently they were all present and correct – mind you, they had to tramp through the fields to find them all. Since then Misset has been lurking in the bushes with Bobby in case someone makes a move. Cheriff discovered something though: Moiré's name wasn't on any of the lists.'

'Understandable,' Pel pointed out. 'He wrote them.'

'Anyway, it is now. Debray's been flashing through the records trying to fill him in.'

'This is ridiculous!' Pel banged his fist on the desk. 'One of them killed Gomez and Patti. One of them took Jourdain and smashed her to a pulp. All three girls were bitten. Someone must have been behaving oddly. I'll turn the whole bloody commune upside down and sod the consequences, we've got to find him!' Pel fell silent. 'I say, look at this.'

Darcy took the computer sheets. '"Father a defrocked priest,"' he read out loud.

'Does it say why he was defrocked?' Pel began rifling through more hurriedly scrawled notes.

'Hang on, Debray's scribbled something in the margin, see Appendix 1, paragraph 13.' Darcy's finger flipped through the pages. 'Appendix 1, paragraph 13, here it is! It says here he liked choirboys. Custody of son given to mother.'

Pel was still deciphering a tangle of pencilled words. 'Mother hated church for wrecking marriage. Refused to allow son confirmation classes. Secretive child, could be aggressive. Ran away from home aged sixteen. Apprentice carpenter, employed by a roofing firm in Normandy. Joined Peuple de Soleil, St Dizier, up north.'

'Social security have him arriving here last November,' Darcy said. 'There's another note, Appendix 3, paragraph 8A. It's a good thing Debray cross-referenced all this, otherwise we'd be

192

here for days. Got it! He was arrested in February at Le Vigneron.'

'Which wine-maker?'

'No, it's a bistro in Langres. Refused to pay for meal. Gendarmes called out. Complained food was poisoned. Took him away to cool off. Wasn't charged. See Rigal notes. You've got them, they're the only ones that are typed.'

'Le Vigneron, can't find it. Hang on, perhaps this is it. Sergeant Laignel, Langres Gendarmerie, spoken to: remembers small man, immensely strong, took three of them to get him into cell. The sergeant said, "A right weirdo, spent the night reciting strange poetry, told him to put a sock in it. For breakfast he asked for fresh parsley. When asked why, he said it was to erase the evil within.'

'Parsley?' Darcy looked baffled.

Pel didn't. 'It stops your breath smelling after eating garlic. Garlic! In the films it was rubbed round doors to stop vampires coming through them, they hate it.' He lit a cigarette and spoke very quietly. 'I think we've got him.'

'He's still at Sunshine farm, he opened the door to Annie this afternoon.'

'I don't want her near him. Who else has met him, would recognise him in a crowd?'

'I met him but Misset spent weeks watching the place. Cheriff would know him pretty well.'

'Ask Cheriff to come and see me – and Darcy,' Pel said slowly, 'cancel all leave, don't let anyone go home yet. I'll be in the sergeants' room in an hour. We're going to have to be quick. Catch him while he's still gloating, before he realises Brisard can no longer protect him.'

'What about Brisard? Won't we need a search warrant?'

'The Chief said recently, and I quote, "Bugger Brisard."'

20

Crouched behind a hedge, Misset shivered. Dawn raids were all very well but it was raining, *comme une vache qui pisse*. The day before had been bad enough, hot and sultry and spent behind another boring hedge. That night, however, the weather had finally broken, lighting the sky with brilliant flashes of electricity, filling the countryside with the deafening rumble of thunder. Now it was pelting down. He'd told Pel it would but the *patron* had ignored the information saying, 'So we'll get wet.'

Misset was getting very wet. Bobby whimpered by his side. 'It's rotten, isn't it, old lad.' He put a hand down to the soggy dog. 'Won't be for long this time, I hope.'

He and two other men, together with Darcy who was responsible for the exterior activity, were strategically placed in the garden as look-outs, in case the plan of flushing the murderer out flushed him further than the four solid walls of the house and sent him running. Each of the four men was well concealed, their eyes fixed on windows and doors.

Edging closer to the building, the rest of Pel's men pulled up their collars and fingered their guns as they waited for the signal.

Pel watched the shadows merge and disappear. He looked at his watch: any minute now. Raids of this kind were prohibited between 2100 and 0600, and although the warrant authorising forced entry sitting in his pocket wasn't strictly valid, lacking as it did Brisard's signature, he didn't want to break more rules than necessary. If they got their murderer, the paperwork would be sorted out later. If they didn't ... well, he'd be for it.

It was 0558.

They knew the lay-out of the ground floor from information put together by those who'd been in there. They'd enter through the three doors, which had been expertly picked with a set of housebreaker's tools, fan out into the corridors and rooms then take the two staircases, one front, one back, to the dormitories and bedrooms.

0559. Patience was something Pel didn't possess much of, particularly with Jourdain's life still seeping away. He wanted the bastard, he wanted him badly.

Dawn would be later than expected, he thought vaguely, glancing up at the black clouds overhead blotting out the light, chucking millions of gallons of water on to the thirsty ground. Puddles were forming rapidly, running together into small lakes, the foliage round the house swayed hysterically, caught in the storm, branches whipped by the wind were lashing at the sky. Another crack of lightning turned the faces of the waiting men white, like ghosts emerging from the stone walls, making the scene eerie, perfect for catching a vampire. Pel counted out the seconds then flashed his headlights and climbed out of his car into the rain.

Because of the storm, the occupants of the house didn't hear them coming. Within five minutes the upper floor had been efficiently emptied and the entire contents were standing huddled in the large entrance hall wondering what the hell had hit them.

'Okay, Cheriff,' Pel said pleasantly, 'you know what to do.'

The tall, black-haired detective walked slowly round the group looking carefully at faces. Behind him, Big Bardolle kept one hand on his gun, the other free for swinging when things turned nasty.

Pel was temporarily at a disadvantage. He didn't know what the suspect looked like, apart from small and hairy, and staring at the men and women standing shivering in the hall, he remembered what the peasant Roux had said, 'They all look alike to me.' He'd been right, it was hard to tell the men from the girls.

Cheriff finished his tour, he'd made a complete circle, and stopped beside his boss, putting his mouth to his ear. 'He's not there.'

'He's got to be,' Pel hissed back in desperation.

Misset stood up. He'd had enough. He was drenched and cold. And it was typical that he'd been put in the worst place, on the

195

edge of a field at the top of a valley. The wind was tearing up the hillside, boxing his ears and soaking his clothes. Perhaps Pel had forgotten him – just like Pel, probably deliberate. He'd go and find out. He was opposite the scullery door, which was standing open. To his left Aimedieu was hidden behind a barn wall. To the right, Pujol was in the shrubbery, his brown bobble hat barely visible. Darcy was squatting in the undergrowth by the main gate, out of sight. If he looked slippy, he could take cover without being stopped.

'Viguier!' Pel shouted.

His disciples opened a passage for the Main Ray to come forward. He was making no attempt at hiding his boredom. 'Chief Inspector,' he yawned, 'how charming to meet you again.' He put his hand out to be shaken, or kissed. Pel ignored it.

'Where's Moiré?'

'How should I know?'

'Where's his room?'

Viguier yawned again. 'Does Monsieur le Juge know you're here?'

'Where's Moiré's room!'

The guru took a step back. 'I say, keep your hat on, rudeness never got anyone anywhere.' He turned and took a girl by the hand. 'Marie, *ma chère*, show them where Moiré sleeps, would you? At the top of the steps on the landing balcony.'

Marie trudged off with Cheriff and Bardolle in her wake.

'I'd like to make a phone call,' Viguier said.

'No phone calls!'

Viguier looked worried: although he was considerably taller than Pel, he was feeling diminished. Pel glared at him, then at the crowd in front of him and the policemen round the edge of the room, wondering at what point in this investigation he'd finally be sacked for his unorthodox procedures.

Misset, followed by bedraggled Bobby, pushed his way through the tempest, found the gate and wrenched it open. It banged shut behind him. He didn't bother to lock it, turning into the

196

wind would mean another full-blast soaking. He screwed up his face and plodded towards the house. The dog stopped abruptly and barked, head held high, body quivering.

'Oh, come on, Bobby, now is not the moment to be after rabbits.'

Moiré wasn't in his room.

Pel received the frustrating news with a blink. 'Was he here for the evening meal?' he shouted. Various heads nodded.

Misset grabbed the dog's collar but he wouldn't budge. He was growling now, a deep rumble at the back of his throat.

A figure on the roof, crouched against the bombarding squall, unaware of being watched by canine eyes, balancing carefully, arms outstretched, stood up and started along the new beam. Bobby barked again; the wind whipped his voice away. Misset gave up and decided to leave him there, glancing up as he did so. Bloody dog, nothing but trouble, what the hell had set him off?

The figure moved slowly, silhouetted black against the hesitant dawn. Misset rubbed his eyes, already filled with stinging rain – was that a man up there? He looked back at Bobby, still rigid and shouting, then again at the roof. A flash of lightning ignited the heavens, thunder crashed too close for comfort. It was a ruddy man!

'Holy Mother of God! Someone's got to know where he is!' Pel bellowed. 'Moiré, Michel! The little chap with all the muscles. Come on, you lot, wake up!'

A door crashed open, letting in a blast of cold air that ruffled the gathering of flimsy night-clothes.

'Moiré, Michel!' Pel repeated, trying to ignore the apparition of Misset looking half drowned.

'*Patron!*' he gasped.

'Get back to your post!'

'But, *patron!*'

'Good grief! What is it?'

197

'On the roof.' Misset squelched across the floor. 'There's a man on the roof!'

Bobby was still barking. The shadow had stopped and was looking down at the group of policemen, trying to focus through the driving rain. Powerful torchlight shone upward, framing a flapping tunic plastered to bulging pectoral muscles. He brushed the long hair from his wet face, his biceps round and hard, pausing on the working platform and wondering which way to turn. He'd been so confident. He hadn't heard them come while he lay in his attic room, but he'd heard the shrieks of surprise as the lights had gone on. He'd listened to the grumbling as the members of the household were marched down the main staircase. Then, climbing through his window as he often did, he'd made his way across the tiles, knowing immediately how to get away; over to the open beams, across them into the oak and down into the lane. But he'd been seen.

At his feet were lengths of wood intended for continuing the work on the new roof. He bent and curled his hands round one of them, lifting its five metres into the air, over his head. It was no effort, he was used to carrying heavier loads.

The beam came hurtling down, a battering ram of lethal wood, as deadly as a sledge-hammer. The policemen scattered, seeing it fall, losing track of it in the fuzzy light, knowing it would hurt. It hit the ground with an almighty crash and bounced, catching Bardolle on the small of the back, whacking the breath from his lungs, felling him like a tree. As he went down, his arms flung out, he caught Misset round the ankles and flattened him into the mud, spluttering and cursing.

Pel, when he turned back, could see Darcy, Nosjean and de Troq' scrambling precariously up the scaffolding towards the roof; instead of running away they'd run forward, towards the house. Below them, Cheriff and Aimedieu, understanding where they were headed, clattered on to the planking and disappeared from view. Splashing along behind them was Pujol.

As Darcy reached the top of the second ladder, another beam came ricocheting down into the yard, cracking Bardolle's head and knocking him unconscious, missing Misset by inches.

Cheriff's large form rose at the other end of the construction followed by the frailer but unmistakable Aimedieu, scrambling up beside him. They separated to the corners of the newly built skeleton. Darcy was now up near the main framework, sheltered slightly from the wind by the slope of the main house's roof, his leather shoes slipping over the undulating tiles. De Troq' was behind him, edging out to the right, Nosjean crawling to the left, surrounding the madman.

Moiré was lifting another beam over his head when he became aware of the approaching forms. For a moment he was bewildered, not expecting to be challenged up there, then he swung round and heaved the wood towards Darcy.

He ducked instinctively, wavered dangerously. He lost his footing and plummeted five metres into the open attic.

De Troq' was swept from the roof spread-eagled, crashing through the branches of an oak tree. He landed with an unpleasant thud in the yard, a twisted motionless body. Pel pulled the phone from his pocket.

Moiré turned, saw Cheriff, and set off along a cross-beam at a run. He tottered, righted himself and continued.

Aimedieu was on that side. Pujol came into view, shakily climbing from the scaffolding to the wooden frame. Underneath them, Darcy was on his feet again, but only just, biting his lip, in pain, slithering and stumbling over the piles of tiles and heaps of wood.

From where Pel was standing it looked like a fiasco.

Moiré was running out of ideas and ammunition. He came to the place he'd been working that day and grabbed a hammer, swinging his arm.

Cheriff fell from his perch, the gash on his forehead opening wide. Spitting the blood that was pouring into his mouth from the wound, he swung in mid-air, his shoulder hooked over a beam, his feet and his free hand waving, trying to steady himself.

A clay tile hit Nosjean, and for a moment it looked as if he too would fall. He swayed precariously, dropped to his knees. Touching his nose, he winced and crawled forward a little further, not daring to look down.

Moiré was surrounded; on all four sides of the roof was a dripping, wounded, but alert policeman. All routes blocked.

He swivelled round urgently, frantic to find another means of escape. He was screaming, howling with the wind, grabbing at anything that he could tear free and hurling it at the crouching figures, always creeping closer.

Darcy was limping, his left arm was agony, he'd almost passed out securing it with his belt to his body, but it no longer flapped with every step he took. He scowled towards the sky into the needles of rain. Moiré was up there somewhere. Ten more careful steps and he saw him. Judging the distance too far, the wind too strong, he hobbled on.

Pel's eyes were glued to what little he could see. He was shouting instructions to the ambulances speeding out of the city. He took his waterlogged glasses off and peered again. That was worse, just silhouettes attached to the roof's framework, like birds in a cage.

There was a searing white flash. Not lightning. Gunshot. Pel snapped his specs back on his nose.

Moiré's arms flew up as if calling for help from heaven; he was momentarily stationary against the grey sky. Then slowly, incredibly slowly, he toppled over and dropped on to the attic floor.

While Darcy was having his fractured humerus set in a plaster cast, Pel finished visiting the row of cubicles occupied mostly by his men. Outside the rain was still slanting viciously from the sky, making the morning dull and gloomy. The mood, however, in *Urgences* was almost one of hilarity, every one of them grateful to be alive.

'De Troq' s okay,' he said, coming through the curtains to see Darcy, obviously relieved. 'Various breaks and rather shredded by the branches that saved his life but he's being his usual infuriating aristocratic self and saying it's nothing. Nosjean's nose was bent half-way round his face but it'll have to stay like that because they can't put it right until the swelling's gone down and they're sure there's no infection. He's complaining about having to take antibiotics, he doesn't like them, silly ass.' Pel couldn't help a gargoyle's grin. 'However, there's a very pretty nurse persuading him to co-operate. He says she looks like Naomi Campbell, whoever she is.'

200

Darcy smiled and accepted the offered cigarette. 'Cheriff's forehead has eleven stitches in it,' Pel went on cheerfully, 'he'll have a premature wrinkle, and his shoulder is badly wrenched, nothing worse. Bardolle's still laid out with a nasty bump on his head but threatening to flatten anyone who laughs at the bandage. I'm told his kidneys took a thumping but he'll heal. And Misset,' Pel sighed, 'is making the most of a sprained ankle and asking anyone to hand if they'd like to adopt Bobby, his dear little dog, who is, by the way, exuding a disgusting odour under his bed. Why does that animal stink?'

Darcy laughed and regretted it, flinching as he was reminded he'd cracked a couple of ribs into the bargain. 'It was thanks to that putrid hound that the old fool saw Moiré on the roof.'

'I'll buy him a bone and a deodorant.'

'What about our vampire?' Darcy asked.

'They're working on a voice match and he's been thoroughly ABCed. He'll stand trial, a bullet in the knee, not a stake through the heart.'

'*Bien*, I don't like killing people. And Jourdain, what about her?'

'No change, although they say if she was going to die she'd have done it by now, so keep your fingers crossed.'

It had been an exhausting few days. Pel calculated the hours of sleep he'd managed since Jourdain's disappearance; they weren't many. Damn it, the Hôtel de Police would survive without him. He headed home.

After three short hours, he woke to see Yves Pasquier standing in the french windows of the sitting-room. His young neighbour was staring at him with an amused grin on his face. 'Not like you to snooze after lunch,' he said, 'but by the look of it, maybe you needed it.'

'Wife's at work, Dragon Routy still at her sister's.' Pel yawned, rubbing his chin, the only place on his head hair seemed to want to grow. 'Didn't make it up the stairs, too tired.'

'Don't fancy joining me for a jog then?' Yves teased.

'Not on your life! Only clots jog.'

'I jog.'

'Then you're a clot.' He stretched uncomfortably, easing his feet to the floor. 'Why, for crying out loud?'

'Keeps me healthy and attractive for all the girls at university. They go to the trouble of making themselves desirable for me. It's a reciprocal arrangement, you see, they expect it.'

'All that puffing and panting to attract a girl, potty, completely potty. In my day, young men used their charm and intelligence.'

Yves laughed out loud at him and left for his run. But Pel considered what he'd said on and off throughout the day. While he was receiving a dressing down from the *procureur* for launching a campaign without the correct authority, he was thinking about it. In fact, he was concentrating so hard on trying to dredge something up from his memory that he didn't hear the congratulations that followed. When he came home that evening he served his wife a drink and asked her if it was true.

'Yes,' she replied, 'If a woman takes a lot of care over the way she looks, she'll want her man to too. You rarely see a well-groomed woman with a scruff.'

Pel looked down at his crumpled trousers and worn shoes. 'Oh, I don't know.'

'There are of course the exceptions,' Madame chuckled. 'I'm talking about women in general. Most women think they can improve their man and expect him to make an effort.' She kissed his cheek happily. 'I knew there was no point trying.'

'I wonder if that's why he went on jogging when she stopped. I wonder if his haircut was her idea ...' Madame waited patiently as her husband's brain whirred gently through its self-interrogation. 'I wonder if your cousin Roger would mind me ringing him at home?'

He was delighted, it always surprised Pel. 'Sorry about last time,' he said, 'obviously the wrong moment. Was it the kidnapping I read about?'

Pel nodded, realised it was no good on the phone and grunted agreement.

'Congratulations on the arrest, it sounded exciting. Sarrazin writes a good story, doesn't he? Talking about stories, I've got one for you.'

Pel listened carefully; from the city accountants, Roger had uncovered the metamorphosis of a farm labourer's lad, an inheritance bequeathed to irritate, and surprising wealth in tomato soup and scrambled egg.

21

When he arrived at the Hôtel de Police the following morning most of his team were back; only de Troq' had remained in hospital. Darcy had his arm in a sling and, although he was still limping, he looked smart and handsome. Pel scowled and made his way to his own desk, signalling for his second-in-command to follow.

He pulled a thick file towards him. 'Today is a day for paperwork and reading,' Pel said, pushing his sliding glasses further up his nose. 'You can write up the report on Moiré's arrest, can't you?' He reached out without guilt for one of the many packets of cigarettes scattered across his desk. 'Ever been jogging?'

'Once or twice,' Darcy admitted. 'I was going out with a health freak at the time, lovely body but her brains were like All Bran.'

Pel frowned. All Bran? Irrelevant. 'Did you wear gloves?'

'Only in the winter when it was cold.'

'What sort, woolly ones?' hoping not.

'I did, she had ski mitts.' Pel was disappointed. 'It was so bloody freezing once,' Darcy went on, 'that I put on the rubber gloves she used for washing up under mine.'

'Ha! Take the morning meeting, I haven't come in yet.'

He lifted the phone and dialled Crystal Combes' number. The idea hadn't occurred to him when he'd been watching Boudet's strange robotic hands dealing with Jourdain's wounds and breakages; it had been much later, when he'd woken to see Yves Pasquier grinning at him – funnily enough that's when he'd started wondering.

'Crystal Combes, rural nurse, good morning!'

Pel cleared his throat, apologised and asked what was probably a very silly question, but he had to be sure. Satisfied with her answer, he sat back to think about it.

The Chief exploded into Pel's office. 'What the hell happened in the sergeants' room?' He'd gone to congratulate them and found a disaster area. The previous day when he'd put his head round the door, he'd accepted their absence as perfectly normal; tying up the loose ends of the Moiré case, what else?

'They had a night out on the tiles.'

'Pel!'

'Moiré didn't come quietly,' Pel replied. 'Brisard said he wouldn't hurt a fly – I shall take great pleasure informing him he was wrong. Moiré, the charming little chap, the one rebuilding the roof single-handed, who murdered Patti and Gomez and very nearly managed to do the same to Jourdain. And that pompous fool of a magistrate has the audacity to complain about my methods!'

'By the look of your team, maybe he's got a point.'

'Yes, well, there were one or two casualties. It's not easy chasing criminals across open beams half a mile high in a thunderstorm. Even I accept it was rather hazardous.'

'Pel, I think you'd better come into my office and explain to Monsieur le Procureur. Yesterday he was prepared to overlook certain irregularities and congratulated you on another successful statistic, but today he's received conflicting reports from the SAMU ambulance men about rescuing werewolves or vampires or some such creature from roofs and finding policemen scattered like broken dolls in puddles of mud.'

'Can't, I'm busy.'

'Doing what?'

'A social call, a keep-fit class, and a lesson in arithmetic.'

Misset hobbled along the corridor with the help of a stick, exaggerating his sprained ankle; Bobby shuffled in his wake. Pel held his nose and followed them into the sergeants' room, leaving the Chief scratching his head.

'Morning, *patron*,' Bardolle boomed from beneath his bandages.

'No brain damage?'

'Only Misset.'

'He's got no brain to damage,' Annie grinned from her corner.

Nosjean was sporting two beautiful black eyes and a very crooked, lumpy-looking nose, but he was smiling, he had an appointment at the hospital the following week and the nurse that looked like Naomi Campbell had promised to be on duty. And Pujol's cheek was bruised. Pel raised an eyebrow, he couldn't remember him being injured. 'Slipped coming down the ladder,' Pujol explained, looking bashful.

Only Rigal, Annie and Aimedieu were unscathed.

'*Nom de Dieu*! A bit of action and you're all flippling cripples, and me in need of an athlete. However,' he unfolded the notes he'd made while talking to Cousin Roger, 'there's a bit of telephone work to do. Nosjean, ring round the antique dealers, you're looking for valuable guns, a collection of six, once in the possession of a chap known locally as Rara, he died in the St Vincent old people's home a year and a half ago. And Cheriff, do your Arab prince act on Madame de Maupou's solicitor, it's the Cammas practice – find out what the terms of her husband's will were. The rest of you, carry on!'

Satisfied with his instructions, Pel left them to it, collected his jacket and set off into the city.

At about ten o'clock, Alain Fabres's secretary showed him into the estate agent's private office. While Pel registered what he was wearing, from head to toe, not missing the gold signet ring, they shook hands in a friendly way. 'Just passing,' the policeman said. 'Noticed your name on the sign outside and thought I'd look in, see how you were coping.'

Fabres smiled at his concern and waved him to a seat. 'Slowly but surely,' he replied. 'It's not easy but I find my work helps to keep my mind off my wife's demise.'

'I've just seen your ex-employer. He says you were a good employee and isn't surprised by the success of your business. You were well liked by your clients.'

'It was kind of him to say so. Would you like a coffee?'

'Except the rich ones,' Pel added, watching for a reaction. 'No thanks, no coffee.'

Fabres unexpectedly laughed. 'I must confess I was probably an embarrassment the way I looked in those days. I've learnt Armani suits and Gucci shoes are a good uniform for snobs.'

'Did your wife persuade you?'

Fabres looked tragically down at his hands. 'Yes, she did, she had excellent taste.'

'It must cost a lot, though.' Pel knew exactly how much, thanks to Cousin Roger.

'Of course, but it's worth it, I have counts and countesses eating out of my hand.'

'Like Madame de Maupou?'

'Indeed! A valued client, a charming woman, she's filled a few of my lonely hours. But it's no good, we shall remain friends, nothing more. I don't think I'll ever be able to replace Adrianne, I miss her terribly.'

'I'm sure you do, it must be very distressing, worse than losing your father.'

'That old rogue, he left me nothing but debts to pay!'

'I see, yes, not a very pleasant legacy.' It hadn't been that much, just a couple of week's rent. 'He was in a home, wasn't he?'

'Extremely expensive for what it was. I had his roomful of rubbish cleared by a firm of professionals, I couldn't face it.'

Pel lifted himself out of the chair and made for the door. 'Well, I must be going.' He stopped and turned back. 'Who cleared his room? My wife's aunt is about to make her final journey, we might as well be prepared – if you were satisfied, of course.'

Fabres opened the door and accompanied Pel past the secretary. 'They were efficient. I can't recall the name, just stuck a pin in the Yellow Pages.'

They shook hands again and Pel left for his rendezvous in Fontaine les Lacs.

Standing on top of the *pigeonnier* with Rigal nervously taking notes, Pel waited for Annie and Aimedieu, carrying an unloaded shotgun, to arrive. They set off from the indicated garden gate at eleven twenty at a fast trot and headed along the footpath. Coming into sight twelve minutes later, jumping across the stream, Aimedieu easily, Annie just, they made their way to the front of the nurses' surgery, opened the door and entered. Rigal read the time off Pel's stop-watch. They waited thirty seconds before setting off again, jumping back across the stream and running full tilt round the edge of the field and disappearing into the copse. On the far side, they stopped briefly while Aimedieu hurled the gun as hard as he could towards a high hedge. Hearing it hit the ground, they set off again and reappeared shortly afterwards on the other side of the field, going back towards where they'd come from. Pel nodded, satisfied so far with the experiment.

They were walking slowly towards the village when Pel picked them up. 'On my reckoning it took you approximately forty-five minutes to do the circuit.'

'Just over forty-seven,' Annie puffed, 'and we're out of practice.'

'What do joggers do immediately after a run?'

'Have a shower, I should think, then a drink, or the other way round.'

'You both look a bit red in the face, how long will it take to wear off?'

'Depends,' Aimedieu said. 'If the shower is cool, not long. If it's hot, well, you could always say it was the water that did it, couldn't you?'

Pel frowned. 'Yes,' he agreed, 'you could. Let's see where your gun landed.'

Pel banged the telephone directory on to Bardolle's desk, rapped out an order and strolled down the corridor to settle himself comfortably back into his office chair just before two. He'd had a successful time, delightfully successful, and Cousin Roger had bought him a good lunch and filled in the holes, it was incredible what he'd found out. They'd been so busy looking for a *crime passionnel* because of what the nurse and her patient had been doing in the surgery, it had confused the enquiry. Martin's arrest, the artist's existence and disappearance had confused it further. He now in fact believed no one was aware of the nurse's sexual liaison with her patient, except the painter in the *pigeonnier*.

Sifting through all the information he had, trying to get it in order, he came across a note he'd made. His wife had said women think they can change their men; Adrianne Fabres told

Crystal Combes that she was proud of her man. Her man, or what she'd made him into? His wife had also said women who seek love affairs are often bored with their own lives; the nurse had become bored with her life in Paris being housewife to a doctor, bored enough to spend vast sums of his money on rearranging her body. The moment she was financially independent, she'd left him and set up home with Alain Fabres. It had been a challenge starting all over again, an exciting time. He looked down at the figures he'd been given for her expenditure. To begin with and until quite recently it had been the house, the heating, the air-conditioning, the jacuzzi and the swimming pool. She'd stopped jogging, preferring to laze in the sun, Fabres had said so. Her man was tamed, she had no children, never would have. Was she growing bored again? Lately, she'd enjoyed buying more new clothes than a woman could possibly need, and modern art. It was staggering what scrambled egg in tomato soup canvases were worth. Cousin Roger had seen the insurance policy – it had made the accountant whistle.

Alain Fabres and she weren't married, they were simply born with the same name – it could have been the original attraction. He definitely wasn't her next of kin, another bit of clever confusion. Although he'd said they'd been married eight years. A slip of the tongue perhaps?

And he'd made it clear they didn't mix business with their private lives, Crystal Combes had confirmed it. But since Adrianne's death, Nosjean had seen him dining with the wealthy widow, Madame de Maupou, 'a valued client'. He'd admitted spending lonely hours with her. Although apparently the affair had come to nothing.

He added up a column of figures for 'Him': restaurants, haute couture, haute coiffure, holidays, oddly never out of France, but always five star hotels in Cannes, Nice, Ste Maxime, St Tropez. Electricity, water, food, cleaning woman. Then he added up the second column: secretary, stationery, telephone, petrol. Rent?

He flipped through his notes to the page marked 'Her': she was the owner of Fabres's office, albeit with a mortgage, and, comparing the payments, Pel frowned; she paid less for the mortgage than he paid her in rent. As was agreed in the contract, he had an option to replace her at any time she was unable to continue the reimbursements.

Being dead would qualify.

The total earned and spent by the two of them was staggering, but the difference in where they spent their money in the last six months was marked. He paid the essentials for the household, plus holidays, restaurants and so on. She bought only for herself. But as Cousin Roger had pointed out, she was the one who'd made the initial investments, in a home and its renovation, a place in a nursing practice and an office in the city for her man, it was only fair that she should earn interest in some way. However, she had expensive tastes and it left Fabres with nothing at the end of the month; twice he'd been unable to pay the rent and he'd had to argue with his bank manager to allow him to be overdrawn. She'd insisted it should be paid in full. His recent financial instability had been one of the reasons why borrowing money to send to her brother in Canada to buy his own home had been difficult. In the end it had come from a private lending house connected with his business, the business standing as collateral.

Extraordinary that an estate agent should learn about investing in property from his common-law wife, but that's the way it looked. It was a good investment too; the contract of sale had stated 'house and contents', and the brother had kindly thrown in the car. From the invoices and insurance documents Roger had seen, the contents tripled the value of the house and he'd bought it all for a song. A house that 'he couldn't bear the thought of losing'. What else had he told Annie? 'The memory of his wife was indelibly absorbed into its rooms.' Pel sighed. It certainly was in the shape of enormously valuable oil paintings.

Adrianne hadn't left him a thing in her will, she'd not written one. They'd been fooled by that, because now he'd got the lot, even the office would become his if he paid the mortgage to its conclusion. The farm labourer's son who was sick of eating rabbit stew, who disliked his father's hunting habits and his humble background, who didn't bother to go to his funeral. But he'd been named in that will; 'to my only child, Alain, I bequeath my collection of antiques.' Apparently Rara had laughed when he'd instructed the solicitor; it was a big joke

209

that the only thing he possessed of any value was the one thing his son despised: guns. So where had they gone?

Bardolle knocked and came in. 'No luck, *patron*,' he said. 'I've been through the Yellow Pages and finally found the firm who cleared the old boy's room. They said it was just the usual rubbish: clothes, a bit of tatty furniture, magazines and a television. No guns.'

'Interesting,' Pel said. 'Fabres seemed satisfied with the firm and I'm sure he wouldn't have been if they'd whipped something so valuable. Perhaps he sold them.'

Nosjean joined them. 'They haven't turned up in the antique trade either, although I came across one man who knew what I was on about. He'd been to see Rara to value them for insurance purposes. He made an offer there and then, they were rare. He wouldn't sell, said he wanted to leave a surprise for his wimp of a son.'

Cheriff added to the gathering crowd. 'Madame de Maupou, *patron*, isn't worth a penny. She has the right to remain in the Count's house and live off the income from his tenants, she's pretty well off, but on her death, everything, absolutely everything will be sold, and the proceeds divided between his favourite charities. Do you want to know which ones?'

'Unimportant, she's been discarded, now we know why.'

Pel shook his head and waved them all away. He lifted the phone and dialled Roger's number. Side-stepping the friendly greeting, he asked him if he could find out who was paid to install the insulated doors of the surgery.

'Easy,' came the reply. 'Is it urgent?'

When he phoned back ten minutes later, Pel thanked him and invited him and his family to lunch. It was a rash invitation as Roger had rather a lot of boisterous children but it would please his wife, and would be a wonderful welcome home to Madame Routy, all that extra work! He could just imagine her face when he announced Chaos Corner was coming for lunch. He didn't have time to enjoy the thought; the door firm answered his call.

Pel lit a cigarette. So he'd been there when they'd discussed it; he'd known that it was soundproof as well as weatherproof all along. And they'd worked out how he'd got to the surgery

210

and away again, only coming into view for a matter of seconds. If only the bloody artist would turn up, the case could be closed.

'They've found Jourdain's prison,' the Chief bustled in. 'It's a room off a condemned cellar, no one ever went down there. They nearly missed it behind all the clobber, it looked as if it'd been boarded up years ago, but the boards opened with the door. It's a small damp cell, probably used for storing wine once. Inside was a home-made coffin with a hinged lid. That's where he kept Jourdain – thank God he fed her sleeping pills.' They looked at each other, wondering at Moiré's cruelty. 'They also found,' the Chief went on more cheerfully, 'an attaché case stuffed full of money. I'm told it belongs to your wife.'

Pel agreed. 'No doubt it'll take until next year to get it back.'

'It's evidence.'

'When the hell is Castéou coming back?'

The Chief held up his hand. 'She already has, and it's her dealing with this one – in fact she tells me that as the ransome was not officially logged because you were running your own private side-show, the existence of the attaché case is doubtful . . .'

'What!'

'Therefore you can go and collect it from her as soon as you like.'

'A wonderful woman, a delight to work with. If only Brisard would break a leg occasionally it would be a pleasure to do business.'

'About Brisard,' the Chief said, 'he's supposed to be suffering from flu, personally I think he's gone into hiding. A group of reporters collared him yesterday evening having dinner. He refused to answer their questions earlier in the day so they discreetly followed him when he left the office. There was a scuffle and the local gendarmerie got involved.'

'I bet they didn't manage to arrest him.' Pel was smiling.

'Not on your life, he was chucking his weight about, pulling rank. Unfortunately, the chap in charge made the mistake of apologising to the woman he was dining with and called her Madame Brisard. She told him very curtly that she wasn't. A bit of a mess, if you ask me. Anyway, the journalists obviously thought it was wonderful and were scribbling happily. Brisard had to buy their silence by answering questions on, would you believe, DNA sampling as a modern detective.'

Pel lit a cigarette. 'I'd believe it,' he said, then changed the subject quickly. 'I think I've just cracked the Aynard/Fabres murders.'

'Someone put those newspapermen up to it, Pel, we've definitely got a leak in this building. You have? *Accouche!*'

Pel didn't. He got as far as opening his mouth and there was a knock at the door. Darcy hobbled over the threshold. 'Shooting, *patron*, at Fontaine les Lacs. Alain Fabres is dead and it sounds very similar to the surgery murders. Blood and brains all over the place.'

'Bugger, that's torn it.'

22

'Oh, it's dreadful, simply dreadful!' The Fabres' housekeeper dabbed her reddened eyes and wept.

'When did you find him, madame?' Pel asked.

'When I came back from lunch, I always go and have lunch with my daughter.'

'Did he often come home to eat at midday?'

'No. He usually stayed in town, but he wasn't well today, you see. Had a cold coming on.' She sniffed in sympathy. 'He came home from work about eleven, didn't look well at all. Well, I made him a hot drink and told him he should be in bed and up he went. But he didn't go to bed, oh no, he was padding about, I heard him go into the bathroom, for a glass of water or something, and after that, well!' Her eyes widened to show her shock. 'After that, he must have had an awful temperature, delirious, I'd say.'

'Delirious?'

'He was sweating, running from room to room, talking to himself. I wanted to ring for the doctor. Told him I was going to. But he said no, called me a stupid woman, said to go away and leave him alone. Well, I couldn't, could I? Not with him in a state like that!'

'What was he talking to himself about?'

'Can't rightly say, it all seemed so confused, you know, something about a girl with her head on fire, that's right! Delirious, like I told you. He said he'd recognise her anywhere and then all sorts of rude words! He paced up and down, slammed doors – oh, it was awful! He went back in the bathroom and locked the door – well, you do sometimes, don't you? When he came out, I was getting ready to leave, it was nearly midday, he was worse than ever. Went up to the attic he did, he was rummaging about up there, it sounded like he was taking the floorboards up, very strange. Well, I went up and asked if I could help and he just screamed at me to go away. Actually,' she lowered her voice to a whisper, 'he told me to eff off.'

She gasped at her employer's treatment of her. 'Well, it was after twelve by then,' she went on, 'so I thought, well, bugger you, oh forgive me, but I did, bugger you I thought, and off I went to my daughter's.'

'What time did you come back?'

'Just now! I couldn't find him anywhere. I nearly didn't come back at all, I thought, well, the way he'd spoken to me it would serve him right if I just up and left for ever, but poor Monsieur, he's been so brave after his wife died, and well, I couldn't, so I came back. I searched high and low, and then, well, then I found him. Oh, it was dreadful! Simply dreadful!'

Pel left the housekeeper in the arms of a comforting police-woman and went upstairs with Aimedieu behind him. The bedroom was out of bounds while the pathology and forensic departments completed their tasks. The bloody remains of Alain Fabres could be seen through the open door. An ambulance man was leaning against the wall just outside, a body bag in his hand. Madame le Juge appeared as they approached. 'I've been, I've seen, we'll meet later if you've anything to add, let me know how it goes.' She smiled her charming smile. 'And don't forget your left luggage in my office safe.'

Pel watched the attractive female magistrate leave. 'That's what I call a *juge d'instruction*,' he said to Aimedieu. 'Nice to have her back.' He crossed the landing into a luxurious bath-room, thickly carpeted and decorated with more mirrors than he liked; his reflection glared back at him from all four walls. 'Good God!' he said. 'It's like something out of a horror film.'

There was a circular bath, big enough for a rugger team, an outsize shower with two shower heads, and a double wash-basin. 'His and hers,' Aimedieu commented, still chuckling.

'The only thing that's missing is a second lavatory so they can shit holding hands.'

'That's taking togetherness a bit too far, *patron*,' Aimedieu grinned as Pel went to the single piece of porcelain under a small window and startled him by standing directly in front of it with his legs apart. If he hadn't known better, he would have sworn his superior officer was about to use the thing.

'Your turn,' Pel said. 'Take a look outside as you stand there.'

They changed places and Aimedieu stood as instructed, looking down on to the neatly mown lawn towards the care-fully clipped hedge and a small white-painted gate. 'The garden gate,' he said quietly, 'that's where Annie and I set off from this morning. *Merde*! Her red hair, she looks as if her head's on fire.'

'*C'est exacte*. We'll take a look in the attic now.'

Among the usual jumble of unwanted furniture and racks of plastic-covered clothes, they found a number of old suitcases, and two trunks. All empty.

'Look for broken boards above and below,' Pel suggested. 'The housekeeper said it sounded as if he was tearing the floor up.'

Aimedieu didn't find a broken board, but he did find a couple of loose ones in the corner. The nails that had held them were twisted in their holes; a claw hammer lay at his feet on a pile of stained material. Between them they lifted the wooden boards off the beam. Instead of finding insulating material in the cavity, they found two long parcels of oiled rags.

'The third and fourth in his father's collection of guns. Rara had six,' Pel told the surprised Aimedieu. 'Bring them down with you if you like, they're part of his inheritance. Martin found the first chucked under his hedge, the housekeeper downstairs found the second, not long after Fabres put the barrel in his mouth and pulled the trigger. Inconsiderate sod,' he added, 'it'll take her months to get over it.'

Going out into the garden, Pel glanced round at the attractive property. 'What a waste,' he sighed. 'All that killing because he wanted to be boss.'

Pel rang Brisard's door bell and stepped back to wait. Madame Brisard opened it and stared at the police identification. 'Need to speak to your husband,' Pel said.

'He's a bit poorly, Chief Inspector, could it wait?'

'No.'

The magistrate wasn't ill, although he clasped a handkerchief and sniffed occasionally. The perspiration on his forehead had nothing to do with the need for medication; it was Pel's presence that was upsetting him.

'You're expected at the office this afternoon, to sign the release of Monsieur Martin.'

'He's guilty of shooting the nurse and her patient,' Brisard said obstinately.

'Are you judge and jury? Here in the République of France, a man is innocent until proven guilty – by an elected court of law,' he added, 'not a piffling little examining magistrate. I have evidence, rock solid evidence, that it was another man who did the shooting. Alain Fabres committed suicide realising he'd been found out and would spend the rest of his life in prison mixing with common criminals. He was the one who shot his common-law wife. He'd grown accustomed to living in luxury and resented her power over him, he had it all but ownership. Paying over the odds for his office was what probably tipped the balance, when he found out. He must have hated her for that, perhaps thought she was simply using him for her own amusement. For all I know, she might have been. The fact that she was larking about with her patient had nothing to do with it, he didn't know until he opened the surgery door. Having successfully removed her from his path of greed, he was planning the addition of another rich woman to his life to help things along, la Vicomtesse de Maupou. Unfortunately she wasn't quite what he hoped. It was Nosjean who suggested he might be a fortune hunter; it started me thinking about how he'd supposedly got nothing after the nurse's death and I became interested in his financial affairs. We turned up a lot of surprises. He'd worked out how to pocket the lot and he might just have got away with it if Martin hadn't been such a bloody-minded little bugger. I wasn't ever convinced he was our murderer. However, he must be released, and apologised to. You signed the charge sheets. You signed him in, therefore you must sign him out. It should be done today. And if I were you, I'd withdraw the case of assault too. Our diligent journalists may just misconstrue his being wrongly charged for murder as an act of revenge by a *juge d'instruction* who got bopped on the nose. Not good for your reputation, *n'est ce pas?*'

'Tell me, Pel,' Brisard said weakly, 'why did you never believe it was Martin?'

'Because, as I said, he was a bloody-minded little bugger, he never changed his story. He insisted he'd found the gun under a hedge. He wouldn't have made that up, it was too absurd. And while his wife was meticulous, he was a mucky bloke, he always had mud on his boots, even when it hadn't rained for weeks. The entrance to the surgery was spotless, it just didn't fit, plus the fact that when he took a pot shot at my men, they said he raised the gun to his shoulder. An automatic reflex, you see. The nurse was shot from the waist, unusual for a hunting peasant, don't you think? So it had to be someone else. Fabres had been remodelled by Adrianne, he works hard at keeping up the image, and he goes jogging. It made getting to and from the surgery after his wife left home and before their cleaning lady arrived perfectly plausible. He must've been wearing a pair of latex gloves, all medical personnel use them, they have to, and they have to change them between patients. Crystal Combes confirmed it, she and Adrianne had boxes of the things at the surgery and in their homes. Fabres was wearing a pair, therefore no fingerprints, and on his feet soft-soled running shoes. It was carefully thought out. He waited for the right day, when the ground was bone dry. It didn't rain for weeks at the end of March, if you remember. He took the footpath, no more than a well-compacted dusty track from his garden gate. He went on running afterwards and chucked the gun into the undergrowth a long way from the scene of the crime. Unfortunately for Martin, his wife was nagging about cleaning the farm up for Easter visitors and he found the damn thing, just as he said.'

'But he hid it in the pigsty,' Brisard whined.

'Probably didn't want his wife giving him a lecture on what he should do with it. You can ask him when you apologise.'

Pel couldn't help grinning to himself as he drove away. Brisard would be back in harness but nicely blinkered. And Martin would go free. He was pleased – funnily enough, he liked the silly fool.

When he arrived in his office, Leguyder was waiting for him. 'What have you done to your men?' he asked. 'They're falling to pieces.'

'They'll mend.'

'What a pleasure it must be working for a man like you. If you don't have your lungs filled with toxic smoke in the office,' he went on, watching the inevitable cigarette being lit, 'you're sent out to break a leg. And don't tell me to sod off this time, I do not appreciate it!'

Pel sighed, inhaled deeply and coughed until he was purple in the face. 'I appreciate your lack of appreciation,' he gasped, 'but while your non-appreciation is noted, I would appreciate your co-operation.' He coughed again, choking on his eloquence. By the time he reached retirement he might be able to out-talk the scientist.

'You'll die young if you continue smoking.'

'Too late,' Pel retorted smugly, 'I'm already ancient. Look, Leguyder, let's bury the hatchets, I'm an elderly idiot who enjoys a cigarette occasionally.'

'Occasionally!'

'All right, I chain smoke, I can't help it, call it weakness of character, call it lack of intelligence, call it what you like.'

'I call it dangerous for you and all those working in the same building, if not the same city.'

'Leguyder! Please.' Pel was hanging on to his patience by the skin of his teeth. He stubbed out his cigarette savagely. 'There,' he said. 'I've stopped.' He picked up a pencil and started chewing the end of it. 'Please, Leguyder, just tell me why you've come.'

'It's about Moiré.'

'What about him?' Pel chewed some more.

'You asked for a DNA analysis and comparison with previous data.'

'Yes?' Pel asked, still chewing.

'The DNA matches are positive on the sample of saliva taken from Patti, the hair clutched in Gomez's hand, and the semen removed from Jourdain's vaginal cavity. He is your biter.'

'And?'

'Isn't it enough? It is conclusive evidence that you've caught your vampire.'

Pel knew that already, a phone call would have been enough. 'Sod off!' He began spitting splinters of wood and lead. As Leguyder stormed out, he reached for his cigarettes and lit one rebelliously, flapping at the cloud of blue smoke. 'That'll teach the bugger!'

While the Spanish police were unable to identify Moiré, one of the Sunshine Sect over the border remembered him well. She'd been impressed by his agility while mending a hole in the roof and disappointed by his lack of attention. 'She was lucky,' Pel commented to Darcy as they finished the paperwork. And now they had a recognisable picture to show around, the owner of a small bar came forward and agreed he'd seen Moiré with Mariana Gomez at least twice. The connection with Patti was still vague, but it didn't really matter. Thanks to Leguyder, although Pel would never say so to his face, they had the proof needed to take the case to trial and expect a conviction.

'He tried giving a prison warder one of those necklaces,' Darcy said. 'He refused, believing it could be misconstrued as a bribe.'

'Which of course it was. He handed out his silly bits of sunshine hoping he'd get something from the girls, mainly their virginity.'

'And two of them resisted. In his fury he ripped them off again, sending them into darkness. Poor Jourdain was so heavily drugged she couldn't fight him off.'

'Let's hope she doesn't remember a thing about it.'

'Let's hope so, for her sake. And ours,' Darcy added. 'She'll be a very good police officer one day.'

'If she stays.'

'Give de Troq' time, he's already working on it.' Darcy helped himself to Pel's packet of Gauloises, shook out a cigarette and lit up. 'But you know,' he said, oblivious of Pel's beady eye counting what was left in the packet, 'he also gave one of his wretched necklaces to Misset, knowing he was a policeman watching the sect. He probably thought it might come in handy for a favour later. For once he behaved with acceptable intelligence and pinned it on grotty Bobby, not one of the undead, but definitely one of the unclean.'

'But why did he bite them?' Pel was still puzzled.

'Because he was unbalanced?' Darcy suggested simply. 'They found a lot of strange literature in his room, comics and articles all about vampires. I suppose in a way he carried it off very well, under his flowing tunic and pyjama bottoms no one would ever have guessed a monster was lurking. While his records show him as a weakling at school, perpetually teased, they didn't show his muscles developing as he grew from a perturbed adolescent into a perverted man, or the obsession he had with his changing body. We got the pathetic childhood, the defrocked father, his mother hating the church; he found an alternative religion with Le Peuple de Soleil then he met Viguier. It could have been him that pushed him one step further into his fantasy, he does look incredibly like that chap that played Count Dracula in the old films.'

'Christoper Lee,' Pel said.

'No doubt the psychiatrists will tell everyone he's the victim of a broken home and should be helped.'

'If they lock him up good and tight they can say what the hell they like. Victim!' Pel had no sympathy for the unacceptable conclusions of psychiatrists. 'Do you know, Darcy,' he said in disgust, 'I heard a joke on the radio coming into work this morning. Two psychiatrists are walking along the road when they come across a man lying in the gutter badly beaten. Both the psychiatrists look sadly at the man, step over him and continue on their way. "My God," says one psychiatrist to the other, "the poor devil who did that needs our help."'

Darcy didn't laugh.

'And the worst of it was,' Pel went on, 'the audience thought it was hilarious.'

'Obviously not policemen,' Darcy sighed. 'Anyway, the two sticky cases are cracked, congratulations.' Pel grunted at the compliment. 'But there is one thing I don't understand,' Darcy continued. 'Why did Fabres throw the gun under Martin's hedge? Why not simply trot home and hide it again? After all, our searches didn't turn the others up initially.'

'God knows.'

Darcy finally grinned. 'I'll ask him.'

'Probably,' Pel said, thinking aloud, 'because, although he'd worked out how to murder his wife and her patient, he must've known there'd be one with her, I'm sure he didn't expect to see them doing what they were doing. Having shot the pair of them, he cantered away in the wrong direction, either through confusion or to run off the shock. Finding he was further from home than anticipated, he could have looked at his watch and realised it would be a close shave to be home in time for his cleaning lady to believe he was just getting up when she arrived. Panic set in and he chucked it away. You know, a gun can fly like a javelin and it may have gone further than he expected. He set off again at full speed, sprinted through the garden gate and belted up to the bathroom to switch the shower on.'

Darcy nodded. 'And the tracksuit, it must have been splattered with blood?'

Pel sniffed. 'Mud and blood look very much the same absorbed into a coloured material.'

'But there was no mud,' Darcy objected, 'the tracks were dry.'

'He'd leapt across the stream to get back into the field, he could have splashed himself deliberately.'

'So where is it?'

'What, for crying out loud?'

'The tracksuit.'

'You're worse than the Spanish Inquisition! So he washed it or destroyed it, go and ask the cleaning lady, she'll be the one in charge of the linen and dustbins.'

'It wasn't found when the house was searched.'

'We weren't particularly looking for it, were we? We were looking for the gun. And he may have taken it with him in the car when he left for work, before the murder was discovered, and chucked it in a communal dustbin on the edge of the city, from where it would have disappeared in a puff of smoke at the local dump.' Pel shrugged. 'It's not of great importance now. Any more questions?' he bellowed.

'Don't think so.'

'Good. Hold the fort for an hour, will you? I'm going to see Alex.'

'Alex?'

'Alexandra Roxanne Jourdain, our punk.'

'So that's what she's called! I spoke to de Troq' last night, he's still confined to a wheelchair but reckons he'll be out of hospital soon. He spends most of the time in her room, says she plays a mean game of backgammon.'

'Gammon,' Pel said absent-mindedly, collecting supplies of tobacco for his journey into town. 'I like mine grilled with a good mustard sauce, the sort that makes your eyes water.'

Chuckling, Darcy limped after his speeding superior. 'By the way, we're having the twins christened,' he called. 'How do you feel about being a double godfather?'

'Tomorrow perhaps, not now! For the moment I'm occupied with visiting hospitalised policemen.' Pel stopped, turned and stared at Darcy. 'Oh, I say! I'll think about it on the way.'

The day had other plans, however, and as Pel lifted his jacket from its peg on the door, Nosjean came in. '*Patron*,' he announced apologetically, seeing him prepare to leave, 'the elusive artist has given himself up.'

He was sitting in the interview room biting his nails. He must have been six foot tall but looked spineless. He had grey hair but no beard, and was peering through an enormous pair of red-framed glasses.

'Monsieur would like to make a statement,' Nosjean told Pel as they went in.

'I – I was frightened.'

Pel sighed, some statement. He sat down and stared at the dithering man. God give me patience, he thought. 'Start at the beginning,' he suggested, 'and tell us all about it.'

'I – I was too frightened to come to begin with. I ran away. I – I saw what happened. I shaved off my beard and changed

221

my glasses. I saw my picture in the paper. I thought I would be arrested. I had to hide my car at my mother's. I've been riding a bicycle ever since. But I was nothing to do with it!'

Pel and Nosjean looked at each other then back at their witness.

'I saw the man who did the shooting. He was wearing a black tracksuit with a hood. I was terrified he'd come after me if he realised there was someone in the *pigeonnier*. I – I saw everything!'

'With the help of your binoculars?' Pel asked.

'Yes! That's right. He just went in and shot them. I couldn't believe it. Then he came out and ran away, in the opposite direction, round the field. I caught sight of him again after a few minutes, coming out of the copse.'

'Ah, the copse,' Pel said innocently. 'Monsieur, you do realise how much time you could have saved us if you'd come forward immediately? It's taken us over four months to solve the case and the murderer will never come to trial now.'

'No – I mean, yes. Well, I read about it, you see, in the newspaper, knew it was safe to come out of hiding, that's why I'm here.'

'As you are here, monsieur,' Pel continued silkily, 'perhaps you'd tell me about the copse? And why you went to the *pigeonnier* so early every morning?'

'The sun coming up, the light was interesting.'

'The light in the surgery? Caught your eye, did it? And your binoculars, I'm interested to know why someone painting pictures should need a pair.'

'Well, I – I . . .'

'What a pathetic specimen of the human race,' Pel said to Nosjean, 'scared silly of helping the police solve a murder but perfectly capable of peeping where he shouldn't. I wouldn't be surprised if he'd sat up there day after day watching the nurse give her patient a bit of extra therapy.'

'It was disgusting!'

'So are you,' Pel said tiredly. 'Why have you come forward now? To be congratulated? To revel in telling us what you saw and give yourself another cheap thrill? No, monsieur, we don't want to listen. If you'd stayed and talked in the spring, we would have believed you'd seen it by chance, but we now

know you also spied on a couple of kids kissing behind a tree.'
He stood up and went to the door. 'Nosjean, take down his
details, I want them on our computer. We can't book him for
bird-watching, the best we can do is "Obstruction of the police
during their enquiries". He'll be fined. However, I want to keep
tabs on this one. He might turn out to be a future vampire.'

As Pel made his way across the steaming city, he listened to
the news. The elections were over, thank God. The country was
packing up for their August holidays. Incredible really, no
sooner were they re-elected than they disappeared to top up
their tans. He'd never understand politicians, or psychiatrists,
or computers, or peeping Toms, or people that went around
killing each other. He understood policemen, however – it was
something. His team was recovering, except Misset, he'd never
recover. Damn the man, once again he'd fallen over his own
feet and come up trumps, thank God Bobby had been doing
his job. Life wasn't too bad after all. Pleased with his conclusion, he lit up, swerved, narrowly missed a *mobilette*, and
shot straight past the hospital gates.

As he pulled over to turn round, he reached for the phone.
'Tell Misset it's his fault!' he bellowed and inhaled luxuriously,
smiling contentedly. 'That'll keep him from smirking.' He
allowed himself a short burst of laughter. The smoke caught in
his throat and, coughing himself purple, he engaged first gear
and kangaroo-hopped across the road to see Jourdain and de
Troq'.